A Gift for You

For Your Participation in the
United Synagogue Leadership
Delegation Trip

**Monday, February 27 -
Tuesday, February 28
2023**

**ORTHODOX
UNION**
תורה ומצוות

Kan Tzipor

Kan Tzipor

INSPIRING STORIES

on Seizing
"Magic Moments"
of Opportunity
to Do Chessed

STEPHEN J. SAVITSKY

DISTRIBUTED BY  FELDHEIM

ISBN 978-1-68025-571-3

Copyright © 2022
by Steve Savitsky

DISTRIBUTED BY:
Feldheim Publishers
POB 34549 / Jerusalem 9134402 Israel
208 Airport Executive Park
Nanuet, NY 10954
www.feldheim.com

DISTRIBUTED IN EUROPE BY:
Lehmanns
+44-0-191-430-0333
info@lehmanns.co.uk
www.lehmanns.co.uk

DISTRIBUTED IN AUSTRALIA BY:
Golds World of Judaica
+613 95278775
info@golds.com.au
www.golds.com.au

Printed in Israel

This book is dedicated *l'iluy nishmas*
my esteemed parents
Hilda and Jerry J. Savitsky *z"l*
who sacrificed beyond their means to give
me and my siblings a Torah education.
They merited to see generations of
Torah-observant children, grandchildren,
and great-grandchildren.

It is also dedicated *l'iluy nishmas*
my beloved in-laws
Amelia and Aaron Seif *z"l*
who were exemplary role models of
how to live a meaningful Jewish life;

and *l'iluy nishmas*
my wife's father
Irving Tennenbaum *z"l*
who passed away at a very young age,
but whose legacy lives on through
his children, grandchildren, and
great-grandchildren.

Contents

Acknowledgments

BEFORE THANKING THOSE WITHOUT whose involvement you would not be reading this book, it is with sincere humility that I express my most profound gratitude to HaKadosh Baruch Hu for granting me all of the blessings with which He has showered me throughout my life. I am especially thankful that I merited, in some small measure, to work for the benefit of *Klal Yisrael*, which to me has been a tremendous honor. This acknowledgment could be pages long and it still wouldn't adequately thank Hashem for opening my eyes and heart to the mitzvah of *shilu'ach ha-kan*, in which I discerned an interpretation that would make it applicable to all Jews — in all times and in everyday situations — thereby enriching countless lives with the blessings reserved for those who fulfill this special mitzvah.

My sincerest thanks to my *aishes chayil*, Genie, who has been my guide and source of encouragement in all of my endeavors, especially while I've developed my *kan tzipor* speeches and worked to bring this book to publication. Genie, I couldn't have done it without you!

Thanks are also due to our children and their families, who have constantly cheered me on and have inspired me by becoming alert to and acting upon their own fleeting moments of opportunity for *chessed* that Hashem presents them with.

To our daughter Julie and son-in-law Shabsi (Schreier), with their family: Ashie and daughter-in-law Elana, with children Aharon, Akiva, and Eitan; Elana and son-in-law Chezkie (Glatt), with children Tova, Ami, Chana, and Yosef; Yoel and daughter-in-law Lauren, with children Yehuda and Daniel; Atara and son-in-law Yoni (Warshaw), with daughter Mahlia; and Devorah.

To our son Avi and daughter-in-law Cheryl, with their family: Shimmy and daughter-in-law Eliana, Ari, Donny and daughter-in-law Ashira, and Yoni.

To our daughter Penina (whose *kan tzipor* moment is included in this book) and son-in-law Zvi (Wiener), with their family: Zahava and son-in-law Eli (Ginsberg), Josh and daughter-in-law Val, Naomi, Shira, Abby, and Amelia.

And to our daughter Estie and son-in-law Jud (Berman), with their children Ezra, Miri, and Nate.

Thanks are also due to a very special person whom I got to know while writing this book, Mrs. Sarah Birnhack, a very experienced published writer and editor, who was there for me from the moment I decided to pursue this opportunity. Every one of these stories are mine, but only through her amazing writing skills have they come alive on the pages you are about to read. She has been an absolute pleasure to work with, and I strongly encourage anyone who is thinking of writing a book to contact her at sarahbirnhack@gmail.com. This book could never have been published without her.

Kudos are also owed to the people at Feldheim Publishers: Rabbi David Kahn, General Editor, whose devoted shepherding of my manuscript into the wonderful volume you hold in your hands is much appreciated; Mrs. Tzipora Frankel, for her expert editing; Mrs. Eden Chachamtzedek, for her professional design and typesetting; and Mr. Michael Silverstein, for his beautiful cover. *Acharon, acharon chaviv*, my sincerest gratitude to Mr. Yitzchok Feldheim who, after reading my manuscript and finding in it an important message for the Torah world, encouraged me to embark on this wonderful journey.

Last, but certainly not least, I would like to thank everyone reading this book. If any of you would like to share your own, personal *kan tzipor* moments with me for possible inclusion in the next volume in this series, please feel free to contact me at savitsky@kantzipor.com.

With best wishes always,
Steve Savitsky
Woodmere, New York
Sivan/June 2022

Introduction

I BELIEVE ONE OF the most esoteric mitzvos in all of the Torah is
shilu'ach ha-kan, where we are instructed:

> Should a bird's nest appear before you on the way, on any tree
> or on the earth, chicks or eggs, and the mother is resting on
> the chicks or the eggs, you shall not take the mother with the
> offspring. You shall first send away the mother, and take the
> offspring for yourself, so that it will be good for you, and will
> prolong your days.[1]

At first glance, this appears to be a very strange mitzvah.
Firstly, compared to many other mitzvos in the Torah, there is
absolutely no preparation necessary before fulfilling this commandment. Pay attention to the language: "*Ki yikarei kan tzipor
lefanecha ba-derech* — Should a bird's nest appear before you on
the way." In other words, you have to "chance upon" this mitzvah; it must suddenly appear before you with none of the prior
planning or preparation necessary for other mitzvos such as observing Pesach, building a sukkah, or even laying tefillin. Rather,
it's a mitzvah that is totally unexpected.

Torah Jews do nothing by chance; everything we do requires
prior thought and preparation. We prepare the entire week for
Shabbos: *Yom Rishon b'Shabbos, Yom Sheini b'Shabbos*. We prepare
weeks before Pesach. And, indeed, a major tenet of *Yiddishkeit* is

---

1. *Devarim* 22:6–7.

that This World is simply a preparation for our entrance into the eternal World to Come.

Do you know a Torah Jew who does not prepare for a son's bar mitzvah by ordering tefillin? Who does not prepare for Purim by studying *Megillas Esther*, arranging for a lavish feast, assembling costumes, and creating *mishloach manos*? And even for Yom Kippur, we prepare by asking forgiveness from those we might have harmed! It seems that as soon as one holiday ends, we look ahead on our calendars for the next one, always making plans so that we will be able to fulfill our Torah obligations in the best way possible. Preparation is so much part of our DNA that many of us smile when we see hotel advertisements, touting their upcoming Pesach programs practically the week after Sukkos! That is why this mitzvah of *shilu'ach ha-kan*, which can only be fulfilled if one "happens upon a nest," raises questions in our minds that require introspection and answers.

The second reason this mitzvah is puzzling is that it is one of the few of the six hundred and thirteen Torah commandments whose promised reward is specified.

I was also perplexed by the fact that to fulfill *shilu'ach ha-kan*, a Jew doesn't have to spend even one red cent. How could it be that to earn such a great reward — "…so that it be good for you, and prolong your days" — one doesn't have to spend any money at all?

Finally, how could it be that a mitzvah that is described in Torah literature as a *mitzvah kalah*, a very simple mitzvah that takes but a few seconds, earns the person who fulfills it the very greatest of rewards: happy days and a long life?

But that wasn't the end of what baffled me about the mitzvah of *shilu'ach ha-kan*.

When we study Torah, it's important to remember that when G-d gave it to us, He informed us that there are four levels of understanding every verse. This is alluded to by the word *pardes*, meaning orchard, which is an acronym of four Hebrew words: *peshat, remez, drash,* and *sod.*

Peshat means "surface," or literal meaning.

Remez means "hint," or the deeper meaning beyond the simple, literal sense.

Drash means "inquiry," alluding to the comparative meaning as given through similar occurrences.

Sod means "secret," or the esoteric/mystical meaning.

Although on one level, the Torah appears to be talking about mother birds and nestlings, and about a Jew strolling along when he suddenly comes upon them and desires to take the chicks for himself, we have to understand that there is much, much more being taught beneath the surface.

Additionally, we have been taught that there are *shiv'im panim laTorah,* seventy facets to Torah. *Hafoch bah v'hafoch bah,* we can turn it over and over, *d'kulah bah,* because everything one needs in order to live a G-dly life, a righteous life, a happy life, is contained in it. We are required to dig deeply and try to understand the lesson being taught because every word of Torah, even every letter, contains a world of meaning.

I knew that there had to be much more to this so-called simple mitzvah of *kan tzipor*; I was convinced that it must contain an incredible lesson for each and every one of us. This is especially so because I am sure that if I polled a random sampling of a hundred Orthodox Jews, fewer than ten of them could honestly tell me that they had fulfilled this commandment by shooing away a mother bird.

Could G-d have been telling us, "Here is a mitzvah that needs no preparation, doesn't cost money, takes but a moment to fulfill, guarantees a happy and long life, but you'll most probably never get a chance to do it?" This question bothered me to such an extent that I delved into every *mefaresh*, every commentator I could find who spoke about the mitzvah of *shilu'ach ha-kan*, or as I call it, *kan tzipor*, but always came away feeling that there must be more to this mitzvah than I was understanding.

I have no doubt that the mitzvah, as stated, surely applies to the rare instances when a Jew actually chances upon a nest and wants to take the nestlings for himself. The Torah always must be, and is, first and foremost studied using the tool of *peshat*, the surface or literal meaning. But as time went on, I was convinced that there is a deeper, more profound lesson embedded in the mitzvah of *kan tzipor*, a lesson that can enrich the life of every Jew, in every generation, and I was determined to uncover it, even though that meant that I had to invest additional effort.

And that is how I came to the conclusion that by commanding us with the mitzvah of *kan tzipor*, the Torah was giving us a profound message.

There are moments in the life of every person that I have dubbed "*kan tzipor* moments." These are moments that happen when you least expect them, as in *ki yikarei*. Sometimes G-d calls out to you, He "taps you on the shoulder," offering you a unique opportunity. He might say, "Shmuel Yosef Savitsky, I have a spectacular opportunity I am about to offer you. If you take advantage of this moment, your reward will be *lema'an yitav lach*, you're going to feel exceptionally good about what you did, and the bonus will be *v'ha'arachta yamim*, your days will also be lengthened."

Finally, I felt that this was the interpretation that I had been seeking for so long. Although I had not seen this interpretation discussed by any of the commentators,[2] it felt so right that I

---

2. That doesn't mean that it doesn't exist, just that I couldn't find it.

couldn't get it out of my mind. *Such an explanation,* I thought, *is what could make kan tzipor a mitzvah that every person could fulfill, whether or not he or she ever saw a birds' nest. It could turn kan tzipor into a mitzvah that could be a life-changing experience, both for the person who fulfilled it and anyone who is affected by it.*

One need not chance upon a bird's nest to merit day upon day filled with good feelings, but one must certainly become an "Observant Jew." By that, I mean a Jew who constantly *observes those around him,* alert to someone who might need a helping hand, or who might benefit from a smile, a compliment, a hug. We need not be meandering in the woods where we might chance upon a nest. We could be in an airport, at a wedding, on line at the checkout counter, at a business conference, or simply at home with our families when suddenly we "hear G-d calling out" to us, presenting us with an opportunity to do something special for somebody.

To qualify as a *kan tzipor* moment, four criteria must be met:

1. The opportunity comes upon us in a totally unexpected way.
2. The opportunity presented to us is somewhat out of our comfort zone, or something very difficult for us to do.
3. We have no one with whom to consult before accepting or declining the challenge.
4. If we don't seize the opportunity, if "the mother bird" flies off on her own without being shooed away, the chance to do that mitzvah will have escaped us. It will be gone. Forever. G-d called out to us and we weren't listening, or we dithered so long that it was simply too late.

After much introspection, that became my own definition — one of the seventy possible interpretations — of the mitzvah of *kan tzipor.* And that's when I said to myself that this is a message that I would love to share, first with my family, and then with the many people whom I have the merit to address when I am invited to be a scholar-in-residence for Shabboses, in hotels during Pesach and Sukkos, at organizational dinners, and on kosher cruises. Living by this interpretation of the mitzvah of *kan tzipor*, I would not only enrich my own life, but I could hopefully do so for many others.

As you read this book, you'll meet many people from many walks of life who experienced such moments. While some of the stories happened to me, most of them were told to me by those to whom these moments happened, and I've even included a story that I read about people far removed from our Jewish world. What they all have in common, however, is that when they heard G-d calling out to them, *ki yikarei*, they heeded that call.

My greatest hope in writing this book is that you will not only enjoy reading these stories, but that you will then become alert to when you, yourself, "chance upon" an opportunity to hear G-d calling to you; to unshackle yourself from preconceptions of who you are and what is expected of you; and to soar ever higher by making someone else's life a bit happier, a bit easier, a bit more meaningful.

Kan tzipor moments happen at any time, at any place. The circumstances make no difference: day, night, hot, cold, a nice day, a terrible day, you're in top form, you're down in the dumps. All you have to be is an "Observant Jew," alert to G-d's call. Then you might be fortunate enough to experience your own *kan tzipor* moment, one that you might even want to share with me.

Winston Churchill famously said:

> To each there comes in their lifetime a special moment when they are figuratively tapped on the shoulder and offered the

chance to do a very special thing, unique to them and fitted to their talents. What a tragedy if that moment finds them un-prepared or unqualified for that which could have been their finest hour.

Flight Encounter

1

MY LIFE WAS TRULY blessed, not only by my devoted wife, Genie, and my precious children, but in my business as well. At that time, part of my responsibilities as the founder, chairman, and CEO of a publicly traded, national company providing home health care services was to raise money, sometimes for either a bond or stock offering, and often for both at once. I would often tell people that this aspect of my life reminded me of something that Rabbi Joseph Baumel, *zt"l*, my rabbi, had said back when I was a youngster growing up in the Crown Heights section of Brooklyn. "Listen, boys," he'd say. "People think that life is like a bowl of cherries, but to me life is more like a bowl of raisins: you're either raisin' kids or raisin' money!" And when I reached the point in my life at which I was blessed with being a CEO, it occurred to me that I was spending too many days on road trips to either meet with financial analysts or actually raise money.

The story I am about to share happened immediately after I returned to New York from one such multi-day trip, on which I had been accompanied by Gregg Petit, a financial public re-lations person who had travelled with me many times in the past. Gregg is a wonderful, non-Jewish fellow whose contacts and professionalism contributed greatly to our success, and through the years of our working together he got to eat in more kosher restaurants than do most Jews! We'd been away for a few days and when we landed at La Guardia Airport all I could think of was spending time with Genie and the kids. In fact, as I opened our front door and inhaled the aroma of the meal Genie had prepared for my homecoming, I thanked Hashem for everything good in my life.

But even before I had taken my first bite, my cell phone rang.

I was quite surprised to see that Gregg was calling me so soon after we had parted, and I was not too happy to hear what he said: "Steve, an important fund manager who lives in Columbus, Ohio, wants us to come out and make a presentation tomorrow at 1:00 p.m. I've been working on this for a while, so it's important that we show up."

"Gregg," I said, "I'm simply too tired! I've been on the road for what seems like forever. Can we discuss this another time?"

"No way, Steve! We'll get on a flight out of La Guardia at ten tomorrow morning, we'll get there at 11:15 or so, and we'll be back in New York by five o'clock. This guy can be the key to something really important, so let's not allow this opportunity to slip through our fingers."

While the happy sounds of our kids chatting around the dining room table encouraged me to turn him down, I told him I'd call him back as soon as I cleared it with Genie. Understanding my responsibility to keep our business growing, not only for the sake of our family, but for all those who worked for me, Genie stood by my side as I called Gregg to tell him to book the flight. Very early the next morning, I got into my car, which by then could almost have found La Guardia by itself, and Gregg and I headed toward the United Airlines counter where we checked in.

As we sat in the terminal waiting for our flight to board and Gregg was busy on his laptop, I noticed a woman carrying an overly long and heavy garment bag approach the ticket agent's counter. For some reason my curiosity was piqued. What in the world was she planning to carry on board? I continued observing her as she spoke to the woman behind the United Airlines desk, and although I couldn't hear their conversation, which appeared quite animated, when she walked away from that desk and headed to a corner of the waiting area, I realized that she was crying.

I swiveled around to see if anyone nearby had noticed what I had, and I realized that everyone else was busy chatting on the phone, reading a newspaper, or glued to a laptop. I turned my attention back to the woman, who by then was sobbing. In a flash, the words *Ki yikarei...ba-derech*[1] popped into my mind, and I remembered that often, out of the blue, Hashem sends us an opportunity to fulfill an important mitzvah — exactly like when I once came upon a nest of birds and was able to fulfill the *mitzvah d'Oraysa* to send the mother bird away from her nest before taking one of her nestlings — and I realized that I must try to help that woman immediately or lose the opportunity that G-d had obviously sent my way.

Why did G-d make sure that I would be in this exact place, the United Airlines counter, early one Wednesday morning, if not to offer that woman assistance when not one other person noticed her immense distress? It had to be that G-d was testing me, a kippah-wearing Jew! So I shot out of my seat next to Gregg, who was still immersed in his laptop, walked over the woman and said, "Excuse me, Ma'am. I couldn't help noticing that you are in some kind of distress. Is there some way I can be of assistance?"

It took her a moment before she managed to blurt out, "I'm in real, deep trouble! You have no idea!" after which she couldn't

---

1. If you chance upon it while on the way.

utter another word as tears coursed down her cheeks and she bit her lips in an effort to control herself.

"Would you mind telling me your name?"

"Mary. Mary…McGuire."

"Mary is a beautiful name," I said, thankful that the announcements of other planes boarding and ready for takeoff provided us with a bit of privacy in that crowded airport terminal. "So," I said, "tell me your problem, and I'll do my best to help you."

"I'm…I'm getting married this Saturday at my church in Columbus, Ohio. It's…it's been my lifelong dream!" She stopped a moment to wipe her eyes and her tear-soaked face, after which she continued. "My wedding gown is in this bag. When I called to make reservations for this flight, I explained that I must be allowed to take my gown on board. I cannot risk having it lost if I check it. It could get misplaced. It could get stolen! I…I can't risk that!" She swallowed unshed tears and then said, "On the phone they told me not to worry! I would be allowed to bring it along with me. They'd take it when I board and hang it in the plane's closet. But…but now the woman behind the counter told me that due to a mix-up with another flight, there is no longer room in the plane's closet. So she said I must check my gown as if it were a regular piece of luggage! I can't! I simply can't!" And then she broke down again, totally inconsolable.

"Listen, Mary," I said. "G-d put me here at this moment, so I feel privileged to help you. Please, please calm down while I speak to the ticket agent." I did not explain to her that to me this was a *kan tzipor* moment, but that is exactly what I was thinking.

I walked over to the ticket counter and quietly explained to the agent that Mary was getting married in a few days and could not risk losing her wedding gown by checking it in. The woman said that she was truly sorry but there was nothing she could do.

"Today, of all days, we simply have no room on the plane for her gown."

"I have an idea," I said. "Mr. Petit and I are traveling on the same flight as Mary. Surely we don't have seats together, so maybe you can ask the three people seated in the plane's first row to take the three seats that would have been ours. If they agree to help a bride get her gown to her wedding unharmed, Mr. Petit, Mary, and I could sit in the first row and lay the gown across our laps for this very short flight. We'll buckle our seat belts and forego having any drinks during the flight so that this can work. Do you think you can arrange that for a very distressed bride?"

"Wow," she answered while clicking her pen, "that's an interesting idea! Only thing is, I don't have the authority to approve that change. I'll have to run it by the pilot."

A few minutes later Ms. Ticket Agent returned to the counter, beaming. "The pilot agreed, and I'll do my best to arrange it, but the three of you will have to board last."

By then, most of those who were on our flight had become aware of what was going on, and many waiting passengers were watching me to see how this would play out. Ignoring all else, I walked over to Gregg and said, "We have a great opportunity to do a good deed for that woman standing over there trying her best to keep herself from crying. And helping her out will also make a good impression of Jewish people on all those around us who, seeing that my head is covered by a *kippah*, realize that I'm Jewish." After I explained what Mary needed and the solution I had suggested, Gregg was immediately "on board" about changing seats. "But," he said, "I have one condition."

Uh oh! "What's your condition, Gregg?"

"That I get to wear a *kippah* as well! Since I'll be doing something good for the Jewish people I, too, want to wear a *kippah*."

"Great!" I said as I handed him the extra *kippah* from my carry-on bag.

I walked over to Mary to tell her that I had resolved her problem. At that very moment they started allowing our flight's passengers to file onto the plane. Ms. Ticket Agent used her mike to summon to her desk three passengers who had been seated in the first row, and quickly arranged with them to take the seats that had been assigned to Mary and the two of us. While passengers lugging their carry-ons walked by us to the sleeve that led to the plane, Mary, Gregg, and I waited on the side.

When everyone else was seated, a grinning Ms. Ticket Agent signaled that the three of us could board. Mary, flanked by a *kippah*-wearing Gregg and me — all of us holding her precious wedding gown as if we were walking her down the aisle to a *chuppah* — proceeded to board. When the three of us stood that way next to our seats and facing the rest of the plane's passengers, whose faces were illuminated by smiles, they all began applauding. It was an unbelievable moment, and I was gratified to notice that Mary looked ten years younger than when I first saw her less than an hour before.

We sat down, fastened our seat belts, and spread the gown across our three laps. Then the pilot's voice boomed over the sound system, "Congratulations to Mary McGuire on her forthcoming wedding! On behalf of the crew of this United Airlines flight we are so happy we could accommodate her and her precious wedding gown on board today. And I want to thank Rabbi Petit and Rabbi Savitsky for their wonderful act of kindness to Mary that allowed this to happen."

That day, Gregg was delighted to be counted among "the Jewish rabbinate," and I couldn't help but smile at the thought that I had just gotten *semichah* from United Airlines, something I don't think any other Jew can claim!

During the flight, as the crew pushed their carts down the aisle offering drinks, the aroma of fresh-brewed coffee was more than tantalizing. Having risen very early to daven Shacharis before leaving to the airport at close to seven in the morning, I could almost taste the hot, invigorating brew. But true to our word, the three of us declined the drinks, ever-watchful that Mary's gown should arrive unblemished. And to reinforce my commitment to that goal, throughout that short flight I ran my fingers over the somewhat rough material of the garment bag that held the gown, in awe that such a simple undertaking could actually be so inspiring.

When we landed in Columbus, we were slated to deplane first since we were in the first row. I asked Mary if she would join us in standing outside the plane's door to express our gratitude to the passengers who had changed seats with us, and all those who had applauded on this very special flight. Of course, she agreed, so as our fellow travelers exited the aircraft, we thanked each one of them, which garnered many congratulations for Mary on her upcoming wedding.

But what touched me most was that seven or eight people who had flown with us, Jews who were not at all visibly Jewish, told us, one by one: "Today you made me proud to be a Jew." "You don't know how good I felt today, to see two *kippah*-wearing men help this woman out, when no one else even noticed her pain." "You restored my faith in being a Jew." "Thank you for showing everyone that kindness and consideration is what being a Jew is all about." And other such comments.

One such woman stood on the side until all the others had gone on their way before approaching us. Then she said, "I want you to know that I grew up in an observant home, but I drifted for many years. Lately, I've been thinking that it's time I became a little bit more traditional, that maybe I should even keep the

Shabbos a bit. Today, when I saw you and what you did, I realized what Judaism is all about, what the Torah is all about. The two of you restored my feelings for what it means to be a Jew. Thank you so much! You have no idea what you've done for me."

After Mary told us that she'd never forget our kindness, she left the airport on a cloud of happiness, and as Gregg drove our rented car to our appointment with the fund manager, I called my wife. "Genie," I said, "I had the greatest day today!"

"How can that be, Steve? Your meeting hasn't even started yet!"

"I know! But this morning I was blessed with a *kan tzipor* moment! This is the first one Hashem sent me since I performed the mitzvah of *shilu'ach ha-kan*, and it happened when I was least expecting it, 'on the way,' exactly as mentioned in the Torah! I know that what Hashem sent my way today, which I'll share with you, G-d-willing, when I get home later this evening, will surely result in the rest of that *pasuk* being fulfilled: *lema'an yitav lach v'ha'arachta yamim*, that I will feel good about this incident as long as I live."

2

A Surprising Double-Header

QUITE OFTEN, AFTER I am invited to speak at a hotel or on a cruise about *kan tzipor* moments, people tell me stories that they feel could "top" the ones they heard from me. Most of the time, those stories turn out to be wonderful instances of Divine Intervention but do not qualify as such moments. However, the story I'm about to share is a genuine example of what *kan tzipor* is all about, although all names have been changed at the request of the people involved.

One day, while at work, one such storyteller, whom we'll call Abe Weiss, received a strange phone call. Abe is a senior vice president in a large advertising company who also happens to be an Orthodox Jew, and the call he received was from a woman who introduced herself as Mrs. Mona Klein.

"You don't know me, I don't know you, and we have never met," she began in a trembling voice. "But I've heard from many people that you're an unusually wonderful person, as well as an Orthodox Jew, and since I have a serious problem that I don't know how to handle, I'm calling you, hoping you'll be able to help me."

My first instinct was to hang up on the woman, since my schedule was full and I simply didn't have time for such calls. But for some reason that I still can't explain, I replied, "I hear you, Mrs. Klein, and I'm sorry for your trouble. How can I help?"

"I thank you for not hanging up on me, Mr. Weiss, especially after my strange introduction, and…and I want you to know that I did not give you my real name because I need to be sure that what I am about to share never gets back to the wrong people. Okay?"

After I assured her that her problem would be held in strictest confidence, Mrs. Klein continued. "I work for a competitor of yours, another large advertising firm. I've been a very loyal, competent employee there for close to twenty years. All of my annual reviews have been highly complimentary, and through the years I've been promoted several times. I've also gotten regular raises and have been told many times by my superiors that I'm a stellar employee.

"About six months ago, my boss hired a new person, Ms. Mary Simpson, to be my immediate supervisor. Unfortunately, Ms. Simpson, as she insists everyone in the company must call her, is a genuine anti-Semite. She constantly harasses me, constantly belittles me in front of others, and does her best to show people that I'm the opposite of a valued employee. This disturbs me to no end, and since she has come on board I am so nervous that I actually cannot perform as well as I used to.

"I'll give you an example. Since her first week on the job, she has come to my desk every Friday right after our lunch break, has plopped a thick folder on my desk, and has announced, 'Mona, this project must be completed by tomorrow or we will lose the account. I was told that you are a religious Jew, which is highly commendable, but this is top priority for our department, so there's no way you can leave early today.'

"When I would respectfully tell her that I cannot stay late on Friday and that my contract states that I am permitted to leave two hours before candle lighting time each week, she would totally ignore me and simply repeat her demand. When I would explain that I stay half an hour later than everyone else Monday through Thursday to make up any missed time and ask her to please hand the folder to another member of our team, she'd answer, 'It's your choice, Mona. You either get a dispensation from your rabbi to remain at work today and pull your weight in our department, or I'll insert a note into your file that not only were you insubordinate, but that you dared instruct me on how to do the job I was hired to do.'

"So my record now contains many of her negative reports, and when it came time for her to give me my annual review, for the first time in twenty years it was negative."

Mrs. Klein ended her call to me by saying, in a tear-laced voice, "I don't know what to do, Mr. Weiss! I'm at my wit's end! I've tried to be nice to her, I've tried everything to make her look good in the eyes of all of our team members — although I have much more experience in our field than she does, and I have no need of her so-called supervision — but it's simply not working. So in desperation, since I know that you're also Orthodox and work in my field as a senior vice president, I thought you might know someone in my company who you can speak to, someone in my company at a senior level who could help me."

I told her, "I don't understand why you are calling me. The protocol in our industry is for you to go directly to the head of your human resource department, so that's what I recommend. They will surely take this seriously and will handle it for you. Trust me."

Mrs. Klein answered, "Of course, that's what I would have done, if I could. But I can't. Ms. Simpson and the head of human resources are best friends; in fact, that's how she got the job here!

And I know that anything I tell the woman who heads human resources will be repeated to Ms. Simpson, which will end up getting me into even more trouble.

"The reason I called you was to explore if there's anything else I can do to protect myself without jeopardizing my job and my career. I am truly desperate, Mr. Weiss, or I wouldn't have reached out to you! Please advise me!"

After jotting down Mrs. Klein's phone number, I told her, "If I can possibly think of a solution for you, I'll be in touch."

My first reaction was, *I still don't understand why Mrs. Klein called me. We have no connection at all, I owe her nothing and, in fact, I work for a rival advertising agency. Her call to me makes no sense.*

Then I remembered the *kan tzipor* story I heard on the cruise we took together, and I thought, *Maybe this is a kan tzipor moment, like the one Mr. Savitsky spoke about! Maybe this is the moment that G-d is sending to me, saying, "Please help this desperate woman!" After all, where is she going to go for help? She called you even though she doesn't know you.*

So, empowered by the talk I had heard on that cruise, instead of resuming work on my current account, I clicked onto Mrs. Klein's employer's website where I began scrolling down the list of those affiliated with that competing firm, from the CEO to the most recent employee. Suddenly, I spotted the name of a senior vice president, Samuel Goldstein, who I guessed might be Jewish. Before I allowed the voice in my head to tell me to stop interfering in another company's business, I quickly dialed Mr. Goldstein's direct line, determined to take this step to help Mrs. Klein, while fighting another voice that whispered to me, *Don't be stupid! Pray that your call goes to his voicemail. He could have a Jewish father and still not be Jewish, so hang up before you make a fool of yourself.*

My luck, Goldstein answered on the first ring, and when I introduced myself and the position I held in our company, which he immediately identified as their competitor, instead of hanging up on me, he was intrigued.

"To what do I owe the honor of your call, Mr. Weiss?"

"I assume that you're Jewish," I said, to which he replied, "And proud to be so! Which charity are you collecting for, Abe?"

I couldn't help laughing before telling him that this was not a cold-call for charity, but rather about a much more serious issue that was unfolding in his own company.

"Seriously?" he asked, sounding more than suspicious. "How do you know what's going on in our company?"

That's when I asked for his word of honor that what I was about to tell him would remain between us, unless he asked for, and received, my permission to share it. When Mr. Goldstein agreed, adding that as a Jew he took such matters very seriously, I took a deep breath and then shared the details of Mrs. Klein's story with him. I also told him why she reached out to me, although I had never heard her name nor met her before.

He asked why I didn't suspect that this was a phony call, a prank being played on me, and it was then that I told him about the speech you gave on that cruise, and how it suddenly occurred to me that perhaps this was my *kan tzipor* moment, when G-d was calling on me to help this stranger with a problem that was ruining her life.

Samuel Goldstein was speechless, and for a moment I thought he had hung up on me. But he hadn't. "I still don't understand why she didn't reach out to our human resources department."

"I asked her the same question, and her answer was that the head of your human resources division is best friends with Ms. Simpson, so that route was not open to her. Mrs. Klein has suffered constant harassment, belittling, bullying, and worse from her anti-Semitic supervisor, and cannot afford to quit her job for personal reasons she was not at liberty to disclose to me. So, Sam — if you'll permit me to be on a first-name basis with you — please advise me how I can help someone who has been a mainstay of your company for twenty years and is now suffering beyond belief."

"I have no problem with you calling me Sam, and I'm disturbed to hear what's going on under our roof. Please give me some time to look into what's happening. I promise you I will protect our employee who identified herself to you as 'Mrs. Mona Klein,' and if your help is needed before this issue is resolved, I'll get back to you. Thank you for entrusting me with this delicate matter."

Since on the phone Sam had sounded like a really stand-up fellow, I was sure that I would hear back from him before that day was over or, at the latest, the next day. But nothing of the sort happened. Days and weeks passed without a word from him and, frankly, I was embarrassed to call Mrs. Klein, since I had nothing positive to report back to her. In fact, the silence from both Mrs. Klein and Sam Goldstein was so painful to me that I simply erased the entire episode from my mind. And when it surfaced at the oddest moments, I took comfort in promising myself that the next time I met you, Mr. Savitsky, I would tell you how I had mistakenly thought I had been granted a *kan tzipor* moment when, in fact, it was not one at all.

And then, a few months after Mrs. Klein's call to me, one day when I answered my phone with my usual greeting, I immediately recognized the caller's voice.

"Mr. Weiss, Mrs. Mona Klein here, calling to thank you sincerely for all you did for me. You have no idea how much you helped me. The very day I poured out my heart to you, the vice president of our company intervened. He summoned me to his office, told me you had reached out to him, and that he had promised you he would never divulge a word of what you two spoke, so I should stay calm, knowing that he would advocate for me in the most careful manner possible.

"I won't bore you with the details, Mr. Weiss, but what Mr. Goldstein did was review my record before Ms. Simpson came on board, which impressed him greatly. He told me to remain calm and to continue doing the exemplary work I had always done. 'Be patient,' he said, 'as it will take some time for me to re-assign you to another division in our company where your skills and talents will be more than appreciated. Remember, this move might take a few weeks. But knowing that your work under Ms. Simpson will shortly come to an end should empower you to endure until I make sure that happens. Deal?'

"He really came through for me, Mr. Weiss, and today is my first day working in another division, where my position is higher than the one I filled under Ms. Simpson, and so is my salary. I can't thank you enough, Mr. Weiss. And please forgive me for not calling you sooner. It's simply that until it actually happened, I feared mentioning what Mr. Goldstein had promised. That's how afraid I was that he might not succeed, given Ms. Simpson's power."

So, Mr. Savitsky, in the end, that did turn out to be my *kan tzipor* moment!

The story doesn't end there. A few months later, Abe Weiss was sitting in a dentist's office where, to keep from being bored until he was called in for his appointment, he picked up a copy of an advertising magazine, *Advertising Age*, geared to those in the industry. He opened to the centerfold, where, to his amazement, he read a short piece about a prestigious company that had been searching for a new CEO for quite a while. The board of directors had decided to halt their headhunting and instead looked internally and decided to promote a Mr. Samuel Goldstein, who had never been a candidate for that position, as their new leader.

Abe Weiss immediately called me and blew my mind by telling me, "Mr. Savitsky! You won't believe it, but the first assurance that those who fulfill the mitzvah of *kan tzipor* will be blessed: 'that it should be good for you,' has already come true!"

And that's when he read the short story from *Advertising Age* to me.

"So you see, Mr. Savitsky, it was truly a *kan tzipor* moment when I called Sam Goldstein. I can't get over how amazing that was, simply amazing!

"And it seems to me that Mr. Goldstein also had a *kan tzipor* moment when he picked up the phone immediately after we had spoken and set the wheels in motion to rescue Mrs. Klein from the trauma she was experiencing in his company. If I'd be a baseball fan, I'd call this a double-header!"

Abe Weiss was so overcome by what had transpired since he took Mrs. Klein's troubles to heart despite his initial reaction not to do so, and especially by the selection of Mr. Goldstein by his own board of directors for his new, prestigious position, that he called Sam Goldstein to congratulate him.

When Sam picked up the phone after his secretary announced who was calling, his first words to Abe were, "You know, I've been thinking about your call to me that led to Mrs. Klein's promotion and raise, and perhaps to my new position as well. I can't help thinking that it was all in the merit of what you asked me to do! When you asked me to speak up on behalf of our long-term employee who was being harassed for her religious beliefs, I immediately, without consulting anyone, said, 'I'll do it.' Because of that, I think, G-d rewarded me by having me selected as the CEO of the company where I've been employed for years, never even dreaming that I could be a contender for that position."

Hearing Abe Weiss's story taught me that a *kan tzipor* moment could even turn out to be a "double-header," as Abe called it. That is why every Jew should become, and remain, what I like to call, an "Observant Jew," meaning, a Jew always on the alert for when G-d might tap him or her on the shoulder. And when that happens, seize the moment. You'll never regret it.

3

A Valuable Calling Card

BARUCH FELDMAN ATTENDED ONE of my lectures, during which I spoke about *kan tzipor* moments. About six months later, he called to tell me the following truly incredible story.

I'm a frequent flyer whose business demands that I travel almost every week. On one such flight, I found myself seated next to a gentleman and, as happens often when I share an armrest with another person and they notice that I'm wearing a *kippah*, they strike up a conversation with me by saying, "I want you to know that I'm also Jewish."

And many times, I have to keep myself from laughing out loud when people mistake me for a rabbi simply because I cover my head! And what's just as amusing is when they let me know, in an off-handed manner of course, that they are "one of the tribe." This fellow told me straight out that he was Jewish, but often they try to imply we have a connection because they are familiar with words that have crept into every English-language dictionary, such as *klutz* or *nudnik*. Then they wait for me to make the next move in their version of the game of Jewish geography that they have begun.

But my seatmate on this flight was too classy to play games. Instead, on the flight on which this story happened, after my seatmate told me he was Jewish, he added, "I travel on business every other week, for two or three days at a time. And you?"

That day I was particularly exhausted from back-to-back meetings that had been particularly grueling, so I said, "It's nice to meet a fellow traveler who understands that someone like me, who travels *every week* for *three to four days,* uses his time in the air to catch up on some sleep."

The well-mannered gentleman smiled, nodded, and said, "Oh, sure! I certainly understand. Be my guest."

Glad that I had been given permission to sleep my way to Kennedy Airport, I switched my seat to its most comfortable position, flexed my shoulders, and closed my eyes. But it was impossible for me to nod off, because this fellow, his face pale as newly fallen snow and his chest heaving, had unbuckled his seatbelt and was now standing in the very narrow space between our row and the one in front of us, clenching his hands and shaking one foot at a time.

Sensitive to the vibrations of his very obvious discomfort, I said, "Sir, is something the matter? Should I summon a stewardess?"

"Oh, no, please don't ring for anyone. And no need to call me 'sir.' My name is Jason. But you're right; there *is* something wrong, and I'm very sorry I disturbed you. You see, even though I must have flown two hundred thousand miles or more, on every trip I take I'm extremely nervous until we land. I know it sounds like the craziest thing in the world, but when I think of being thirty thousand feet up in the air, hurtling forward at a couple hundred miles per hour, I...I'm one bundle of nerves."

I guess simply telling me about it calmed Jason somewhat, because he then sat back down in his seat and buckled up before continuing: "I'm actually jealous of you! I've never been able to relax enough to sleep on any flight I've ever taken. But don't mind me. Go right ahead and do your thing."

That's when I snapped my seat back into the upright position and said, "I'm really sorry to hear of your trouble, and I just remembered that I have something that might help you."

I pulled my wallet from the inside pocket of my suit jacket, extracted a laminated card I had gotten in a mailing from a yeshivah, and turned to my seatmate, who by then was sweating profusely. "I'm about to say a special prayer that I recite every time I travel, whether by car, boat, train, or plane. This prayer, written by great Jewish sages, is called *Tefillas HaDerech*, the Traveler's Prayer. The original version is found in the Babylonian Talmud that was completed more than fifteen hundred years ago, so it's truly authentic and powerful. After I finish reciting it with utmost concentration, I breathe deeply, and feel a great calmness overcome me, knowing that G-d is with me on my journey, and no matter what happens, I will be safely in G-d's Hands.

"After I recite it in Hebrew, would you like me to read you the English translation?"

"Please! Please do!"

After I enunciated each word slowly and clearly in Hebrew, and motioned to him to answer Amen, I read him the English version that was printed on the back:

> May it be Your will, Lord, our G-d and the G-d of our ancestors, that You lead us toward peace, guide our footsteps toward peace, and make us reach our desired destination for life, gladness, and peace. May You rescue us from the hand of every foe and ambush, from robbers and wild beasts on the

trip, and from all manner of punishments that assemble to come to earth. May You send blessing in our handiwork, and grant us grace, kindness, and mercy in Your eyes and in the eyes of all who see us. May You hear the sound of our humble request because You are the G-d Who hears prayer requests. Blessed are You, Lord, Who hears prayer.

I replaced the card in my wallet and put my wallet back into the front inside pocket of my suit jacket. The aroma of brewing coffee enticed me, and I was about to ring for the stewardess to bring me a cup of black java, but realized that that was the last thing I needed right now. Yawning, I glanced at my seatmate. Almost magically, he appeared as calm as I was. I smiled at him, repositioned my seat, buckled up, and promptly fell asleep.

As we were landing, I awoke and noticed that my seatmate was sitting upright with his carry-on carefully placed between his expensive shoes, ready to deplane. I couldn't help asking, "So, my new friend, how did your flight go after you answered Amen to that beautiful prayer?"

He turned to me, smiling from ear to ear. "Truth to tell? It was the calmest flight I've ever had, thanks to you! I can't tell you how much I appreciate what you did for me!"

At that moment, Mr. Savitsky, as we were taxiing to the gate, I remembered hearing your beautiful speech about the mitzvah of *shilu'ach ha-kan*, and I realized that I was facing a *kan tzipor* moment.

And that is when it hit me that had you, Steve, been sitting next to my seatmate you would have asked yourself: *Why did G-d put me on this particular plane, next to this particular man, who was having an anxiety attack on this flight? He just told me that he loved hearing me recite Tefillas HaDerech in both Hebrew and English. Although he doesn't appear to be a man who has had much experience connecting to G-d, reciting this short tefillah seems to have made a huge impact on him. Don't let this moment pass as if it were a random occurrence! G-d is offering you an opportunity to make a permanent difference in this man's life! Don't let this moment pass without trying to do so!*

Immediately, I heard another voice, even louder than yours, Steve, say: *Hey there, Baruch Feldman, you're not Steve Savitsky. You're not a speaker or a scholar-in-residence. You're just a simple Jew. If you say anything that insinuates that you're selling Orthodox Judaism, this Jason guy will surely laugh at you! He might even get insulted and tell you that you have overstepped an invisible boundary that dictates that Americans mind their own business, and they especially don't mix into someone else's relationship with G-d.*

Precisely then, the plane lurched to a halt, the "Fasten Seat Belt" sign clicked off, and all around us passengers were standing up and removing their carry-on luggage from the overhead bins. To my right, across the aisle, a grey-haired woman was being helped by a stewardess to retrieve her belongings, most passengers were using their cell phones to call family or friends, and the chatter of passengers was a familiar and welcome background symphony broadcasting that as soon as the plane's door would open, the line of passengers would start moving forward. I had been seated only two rows from the rear, so it would take several minutes for those of us in the back to exit the plane. But as long as we were safely on the ground, it appeared that those extra few minutes bothered no one.

And as I struggled with myself to ignore the voice in my head that was urging me to mind my own business and do nothing, to forget what I had heard about *kan tzipor* moments, I realized that in one minute we'd be walking into the sleeve that connects the plane to our terminal and I'd never see my seatmate again. If I didn't grab this opportunity to make my experience of sharing a section of a row in the back of flight #1059 meaningful, this moment would be lost forever!

I quickly removed my small *Tefillas HaDerech* card from my wallet and said, "Listen up, my friend. Here's the card from which both of us said that terrific prayer for travelers that helped make this flight the calmest you ever flew. I got it in the mail from a yeshivah — a school where young men study to become rabbis — and I can always ask them for another one. Take it as a souvenir of the flight we just shared. Use it on all your upcoming flights, and best of luck to you."

He said, "Hey, are you sure? You really want me to have it?"

"Absolutely! I'll fly much happier knowing that you'll feel relaxed on all your upcoming flights, fully aware that G-d has your back, that G-d's going to watch out for you."

"Wow! Thank you so much for this gift. I can't believe that a total stranger would do that for me. I'll…never forget your kindness."

And with that, my seatmate exited the plane into the sleeve that led to the terminal, and walked out of my life.

Or so I thought!

For some reason, after that flight I was able to conduct my business without flying for about four or five weeks. I had always made it a point of being at home for every Shabbos, but now my family was thrilled that I was able to spend evenings and Sundays with them as well, and so was I. But then, when I could no longer conduct my business locally without the risk of losing a great deal, I once again found myself on an airplane.

As usual, the first thing I did after takeoff was reach into my inside jacket pocket for my *Tefillas HaDerech* card. Of course, it wasn't there! I had given it to that anxious seatmate and had forgotten to contact the yeshivah for another one. But I knew the *tefillah* by heart, and made a note to myself to call the yeshivah so that on my next flight I would have the printed words in front of my eyes so that I could concentrate on their meaning instead of struggling to recite them from memory.

When I returned from that business trip — which was successful, thank G-d — I called the yeshivah and asked the secretary who answered the phone to mail me one of the *Tefillas HaDerech* cards they usually mail out before Rosh Hashanah. The person who answered the phone said, "No problem, sir, we have a whole lot more, and I'll be glad to mail you one. Give me your name and address and it will be in the mail this afternoon."

I gave her the information they needed, and then I said, "By the way, there's a crazy reason I need you to mail me another card. A couple of weeks ago, while I was flying back to JFK after a long business trip, my seatmate saw my *kippah* and decided to let me know he was also Jewish. When he later admitted that he was terrified of flying, although that was a big part of his job, I recited *Tefillas HaDerech* with him, and he calmed down so much that before we got off the plane he told me that thanks to reciting that prayer, he had been the calmest he had ever been on any flight.

"Right before we entered the sleeve that led to the terminal, I removed the card from my wallet and handed it to this man as a gift. I have no idea who he was, but I assured him that if he recited the prayer when he flew, he'd feel close to G-d and G-d's protection. Of course, I promptly forgot what I had done, and when I reached for your card the next time I flew, it wasn't in my wallet. So I'm very thankful that you'll send me another one."

The secretary who had answered the phone said, "I can't believe you called us! We were wondering who you were! You think what you did was the craziest thing in the world, but listen to what that man did! He knew the name and phone number of our yeshivah, because it appears on each laminated card we mail out. So he called us to thank us for the card you gave him, and to ask for our mailing address, which I gave him. A few days later we received a beautiful letter from him telling us how he got the card — that he had been on a plane and some man who he didn't even know was kind enough to give him this prayer for the traveler, the *Tefillas HaDerech*.

"In the letter he went on to say that this prayer had changed his life completely because now he is very calm on all of the many flights he needs to take. And in appreciation, he enclosed a check for $25,000 for the yeshivah, so we could continue our holy work.

"When we received that letter and check, all of us in the yeshivah's administrative office were extremely curious to find out who had given Mr. Jason Marks[1] our card, but we had no way of finding out. And now, out of the blue, you called! Wait until I tell the Rosh Yeshivah that the man in whose merit we received that large donation is none other than you, Baruch Feldman, and that now I even have your address! I'm so excited that you called, Mr. Feldman! How would you like a few dozen *Tefillas HaDerechs* to take along when you travel?"

---

1. Not his real name.

4

A Most Unexpected Match

ESTHER AND BARRY APPEL, friends of ours whom we first got to know through the condo we own in Florida, came along with us when I was invited to be the scholar-in-residence on a cruise organized by Kosherica. While on that voyage, my audience was captivated when I related one of my *kan tzipor* stories. Afterwards, Barry came over to me and said, "Steve, I'd like share with you something that happened to me that I now recognize as a *kan tzipor* moment, because I think it's truly incredible."

❧

This story began way back in the 1960s in the city of Berdychiv, Ukraine, where a young man named Gedalya Rappaport grew up. Against great odds, and actually almost miraculously — given the regime under which they lived — his great-grandfather and grandparents were still observant and knowledgeable about *Yiddishkeit*. In fact, his grandfather was a *gabbai* in their illegal shul. Gedalya's love of his grandparents and strong connection to them engendered in him strong ties to his heritage. Many decades later, he still spoke fondly of Berdychiv's Pesach matzah factory, davening alongside his grandfathers in shul, and being entrusted to take chickens to the local *schochtim*. And he readily admitted to being fluent in Yiddish thanks to his grandparents, who for years had regaled him in their mother tongue with stories of ancestors who had been adherents of great rabbis and who, despite the many difficult challenges they had endured under tyrannical rulers, remained loyal to their religion, their G-d, and their fellow Jews.

When Gedalya graduated high school, due to the exceptionally high grades he had earned throughout his school years, he won a coveted placement in the University of Moscow. Given the general intellectual, moral, and cultural climate in Berdychiv at that time, and despite the close to 660 miles between his hometown and Russia's capital, there was no way Gedalya's parents would allow him to forfeit that opportunity. So sixteen-year-old Gedalya Rappaport became one of the very few Jews enrolled and studying in that university.

Since his new professors and classmates were openly anti-Semitic, Gedalya's parents warned him to only use his Russian name, Genya,[1] and to make sure to hide his Jewish background. Always an obedient child, Gedalya heeded their warning. This led to a diminished level of Jewish observance, but facilitated his success at his studies, and at the age of twenty he graduated with honors and was licensed to practice dentistry.

But at that time, and perhaps even today, nothing in Russia is given to any citizen without the government demanding payback. Gedalya was not free to return to his hometown and his family, where he might have reverted to Jewish observance. Instead, he was ordered to settle in Gorky, locate 260 miles east of Moscow. At that time, Gorky was a city closed to anyone not specifically permitted entry by the government, because it was there that Russia manufactured its nuclear submarines.

---

1. Pronounced Jzhenyah.

Once again, Gedalya was cut off from everything that had given him joy during his childhood. But the influence and love of his religious grandparents, while not a burning flame, still flickered within him. When Rosh Hashanah approached, Gedalya was determined to locate a shul. After making many clandestine inquiries, he thanked G-d for the scrap of paper on which he had finally written the address of a synagogue. He then set out on the two-hour walk that would bring him there.

What awaited him on the end of his trek was not even a close resemblance of the shul in Berdychiv where he had davened alongside his family. Instead, it was a small apartment where a handful of elderly Jews gathered in fear, determined to connect with their Creator. Gedlaya inhaled deeply and gladly took the empty chair offered to him by Yosef,[2] the youngest member of that "congregation." After Yosef locked the door, he invited Gedalya to join the few men who were able to study *Chumash* together. Despite fear of the KGB[3] and the openly displayed anti-Semitism that ruled at that time, Gedalya now had a means of connecting, in a small way, to his Jewish heritage.

However, when he let his parents know how happy he was to have celebrated the Jewish new year like he had done as a child, they warned him to break all ties with Yosef and to continue living as a non-Jew. That's how terrified they were of the "Russian Bear's" evil empire.

And their fears were not unfounded, because one day the

---

2. Under Communist rule, Jews who endangered their live to teach Torah did not divulge their family names so that none of their students could inadvertently cause their capture and severe punishment.

3. The initials of the Russian name for the Committee for State Security, foreign intelligence, and domestic security agency of the Soviet Union.

KGB came knocking on the door of that small Gorky apartment where that handful of elderly Jews, Yosef, and Gedalya gathered from time to time to practice their religion. They interrogated Gedalya for hours on end, and demanded that he reveal all he knew about Yosef, the relatively young man who, because he dared teach Torah, was part of the "Jewish conspiracy against Mother Russia." When Gedalya refused, they made sure that press releases about him — wild lies that were very detrimental to his reputation — appeared in the local newspapers. And when that didn't break Gedalya's determination not to reveal even the slightest information about Yosef, they warned him that they would do all in their power to make sure that he would be drafted into the Russian army.

That threat almost broke Gedalya's spirit, because it was well known that anyone drafted into the Red army, especially from Moscow, would be posted to Afghanistan, where Russian soldiers, totally unused to the culture and terrain, didn't stand much chance of surviving.

Fortunately, Gedalya's grandfather, who had once been a decorated officer in the Russian army, convinced the powers that ruled with an iron fist in the KGB to switch the city from where Gedalya would be drafted to his hometown of Berdychiv. This was of great importance, since it was in that city that Gedalya's grandfather had many connections. And *b'chasdei Hashem*, not only did Gedalya's grandfather's plan to derail his grandson's deployment to Afghanistan succeed, in the end Gedalya was deemed totally unfit to serve in the army, and he never heard from them again.

Gedlaya thanked his grandfather profusely, but his pure soul recognized that Hashem had orchestrated a miracle for him, and he expressed his gratitude to his Creator by organizing a clandestine class in Berdychiv during which he taught all the Torah he had learned from Yosef in Gorky. And since he had more than a "taste" of the KGB's iron fist, he also began exploring means of leaving Russia before that evil anti-Jewish group caught on, once again, to his "anti-state activities."

That is how, in 1990, he succeeded against great odds to emigrate to Eretz Yisrael. Thirsting to one day be as well versed in his heritage as his beloved grandfathers, he enrolled in Yeshivas Ohr Somayach, and after completing their course of study, he returned to Berdychiv to secretly teach Torah to other young men and women who yearned to be fully observant.

While he was teaching Torah in Berdychiv, Ukraine's government underwent a drastic change that posed a danger to his safety. Once again, possibly in the merit of his grandfathers who by then were no longer alive but must have been advocating for him in the World of Truth, he returned to Eretz Yisrael where he re-enrolled in Ohr Somayach.

There he befriended many students, as well as all of their very special staff members. By then Gedalya was twenty-nine years old, and wanted very much to get married. He recognized that his complicated family and personal background would not make it easy for his *rabbe'im* and Roshei Yeshivah to find him a *shidduch*. When he discussed these issues with his devoted mentors, they gently informed him that in addition to those drawbacks, because he also insisted that his future wife have a Russian background, and be educated, as vivacious as he was, kind, gentle, and attractive, he had to be ready to wait patiently and daven fervently for this one-in-a-million woman to appear in his life.

This is where Part One of my *kan tzipor* moment ends, and what follows is Part Two.

This segment of my story concerns a young lady, Leana Freibina, a Russian girl who immigrated to America with her parents when she was eight years old. They settled in Providence, Rhode Island, because their immigration sponsor lived there. Leana knew very little about living life as a Torah Jew, and when she graduated high school she won a full scholarship to the University of Miami. As soon as she settled into her dormitory room, she began looking for a job because although her scholarship covered tuition, she needed to earn money for all her other expenses. She began networking with anybody she could think of, asking them to help her find employment.

One of Leana's aunts knew me, Barry Appel, and she was aware that I owned hotels in Miami, so it was thanks to this aunt's connection with me that I hired Leana to work in one of my hotels. During her employment interview, after I outlined her areas of responsibility and daily work schedule, I informed her that since she is Jewish she would not be permitted to work on Saturday. Leana's eyes opened wide and her eyebrows shot up into her hairline. Then, apparently unable to control her surprise, she blurted out, "Why in the world do you have that rule, Mr. Appel? What's wrong with working on Saturday?"

When I told her that Saturday is a full holiday for Orthodox Jews, she answered that although this was the first time in her life that she was hearing about this Jewish holiday, she was interested to hear more. My phones were ringing off the hook, and I wished I had the time to give her more details of our Orthodox life, but since the time I had reserved for meeting this young woman was over, and since I had covered all of the important points she needed to know to begin taking full responsibility for the front desk at one of my hotels, I swiftly concluded our conversation, and she immediately went to work.

I was gratified to discover that what had started out as a

favor for Leana's aunt, ended up being a blessing for my hotel. Leana did a great job. She was very inquisitive, which meant she asked all those on my staff how she could improve her performance. She also sought ways to better convey to guests who were checking in or out — and to those who rang the phone at the front desk asking for assistance — that their needs were her top priority and that she would see to it that their stay in our hotel was comparable to what they would have enjoyed in any five-star establishment.

Leana's inquisitive nature also prompted her to ask about the Jewish religion, and it seemed to me and to those who cared to report to me about Leana's progress, that she was truly interested in exploring what it means to live as a Torah Jew.

I started giving her books, articles, and tapes that could answer some of her many questions about *Yiddishkeit*, and a short while after she began working for me, my ever-gracious wife suggested that I invite her to our house for Shabbos. Leana was delighted to accept my invitation, and that first Shabbos she immediately became very friendly with our two daughters. Leana spent Shabbos at our house week after week, and since many things we did and did not do on Shabbos were totally strange to her, she constantly asked for explanations.

Why did Esther cover her eyes with her hands while whispering the blessing during candle lighting? Was there a reason for the number of candles Esther lit? Why did I bless my children when I returned from shul? Why were the challahs covered until we washed our hands and recited a blessing, and why was another blessing required before we ate our slice? Was there a reason for the interesting way we ate boned fish on Shabbos? Was there a verse in the Torah that mandated how many courses each Shabbos meal contained? Why didn't we use hot water to wash the dishes on Shabbos? Why was she not permitted to jot down the answers to these questions on Shabbos, so that she would better remember how to observe the next Shabbos?

Leana didn't ask these questions to challenge or disparage us; she honestly found our way of life intriguing, and after a while, I realized that her endless questions were a sign of her deep interest in the heritage she had been denied.

My wife and I invited Leana to arrive a bit early one Friday afternoon, and as we sat around the kitchen table chatting — while the aromas of chicken soup gently bubbling on the stove, a roast being kept warm in the meat oven, and cinnamon-sprinkled apples for that Friday night's dessert baking in the *pareve* oven created a welcoming, homey atmosphere — we told her that if she truly wanted to learn more about living an authentic Jewish life, she needed to enroll in an Israeli seminary. We assured her that we would pay for everything, and we would even make sure that she had pocket money while she was studying in Neve Yerushalayim, a beautiful seminary for Jewish women that specializes in giving those with little or no Jewish background not only a solid foundation on which they can establish fully Orthodox Jewish homes, but also a love of G-d, His Torah, and His People.

Although her immediate supervisor at the hotel was quite upset that Leana would no longer be covering the front desk, and her parents were appalled that she was dropping her courses at the University of Miami, Leana assured everyone that she was only taking a few months' vacation, after which she'd return and fulfill everyone's expectations of her.

Leana immediately acclimated to Neve's schedule of classes, she was in awe of their teaching staff, and she quickly made friends with many of its students. And the "icing on the cake," as she called it, was that our daughter Ahuva was then studying in Israel as well. After a few months of intensive study, in response to constant blue airmail letters from her parents, Leana returned to her family as she had promised. But when they urged her to re-register at the University of Miami, she told her parents that she could not do so at that point in her life. She begged them to understand that her studies at Neve were so mesmerizing that she simply must return for one more semester. Her parents reluctantly agreed.

When my *kan tzipor* moment happened, both Gedalya and Leana were in Israel at the same time.

While Leana was in her second semester at Neve, my father, Reb Avraham ben Mordechai, *a"h*, a distinguished Chassid of the Vizhnitzer Rebbe, as were my grandfather and great-grandfather, passed away. Since my father had arranged to be buried in Eretz Yisrael, I flew there with his casket. And although I was extremely brokenhearted by my father's passing, the enormity of his death only hit me full force when I saw that he was to be buried in his tallis instead of in a casket, which is the custom in Israel but to me was quite alarming. I was truly comforted by the attendance at the *levayah* by numerous Chassidic cousins who had all put their lives on hold to honor my father and had arranged a place for me to sit *shivah* in Bnei Brak for the few hours before I needed to head back to the airport for my return flight to New York.

As I mentioned, our daughter Ahuva was then in her second semester at a prestigious Israeli seminary. That is how it happened that she came to Bnei Brak to pay a *shivah* call along with Leana, who was in Neve at that time. Ahuva sat close to me, reminiscing about her beloved Zeidy, while Leana sat nearby, unable to converse with any of my relatives since she didn't know Hebrew or Yiddish. But communication is not solely dependent on language, and I was comforted by her respectful presence, her modest dress, and the silent message of condolence that she conveyed with her eyes.

I motioned to her to come closer to where I was sitting, which she did, bringing her chair with her. Ahuva stopped speaking to me to give Leana a chance to recite the Hebrew sentence of comfort that Ahuva had practiced with her as they traveled by bus to Bnei Brak, after which she told me, in English, how sorry she was for my loss. Then, to give others a chance to console me, she returned with her chair to the other side of the room, where Ahuva joined her.

Suddenly, one of my long-bearded cousins who was dressed in full Chassidic regalia, came over to me as I sat on the low mourning chair and asked me in whispered Yiddish, "Who is the girl sitting next to your daughter?" I told him she was a young Russian woman who had been coming to our house quite often, and was now studying at Neve.

He asked, "What kind of a person is she?" to which I answered, "She's unbelievably smart, dynamic, and has a vivacious personality. In short, she's a wonderful young woman."

My cousin then told me that he knew the perfect young man for her. "He's also from Russia, and he's a dentist, so if she's looking for a professional, or if her Russian parents would be happier if she married a professional, this is an absolutely perfect *shidduch*!"

He then looked me in the eye and said, "*Nu*, so what do you say?"

Looking at my watch, I realized that I'd have to leave for the airport in less than half an hour, so what was there to say? Should I inform him that in America, and especially in the newly arrived Russian community, young men and women met each other by chance, not through a third party? Would he even begin to understand what to him would be an outrageous system guaranteed to end in disaster?

There were several more relatives waiting to be *menachem avel*, my back and legs were tingling from sitting on the low mourner's chair they had borrowed from a *gemach*, and my head was spinning from exhaustion. My flight to Israel had taken almost eleven grueling hours, I had arrived at JFK two hours before take-off, and it had taken me over an hour to exit Ben Gurion. Add the time it took to get to the cemetery, the shock and emotional trauma of watching my tallis-clad father being placed into the ground, and then having to converse with many relatives, and you'll understand that getting involved in a *shidduch* at that moment was really beyond my ability.

On the other hand, I was leaving Israel in a very short time, and if I didn't act on the spot, who knew if this prize catch suggested for Leana would ever get to meet her? And, Steve, having heard you talk about *kan tzipor* moments on several occasions, it hit me that this might be the one chance in my lifetime to be involved in this kind of mitzvah.

I said to my cousin, "You know what? Call that young man right now!"

While he was searching for this Russian guy's number, I signaled to Leana to come over to where I was sitting. Then, in one sentence I described the young man my cousin had deemed "a perfect match for her," and asked if she was interested. When her eyes opened wide and she nodded, I told her to return to Ahuva's side, and that I'd update her when we succeeded in reaching this fellow.

Since I was sure that Hashem had placed me in Leana's presence at this precise time so that this particular cousin of mine could suggest this *shidduch*, I fully believed that the whole process would proceed as speedily as possible. But that is not what happened. My cousin reached "the perfect *shidduch*," but he said he simply could not make it to Bnei Brak before I had to leave for the airport. My first reaction to this information was, *Okay, Hashem. I hear You loud and clear. Is this or isn't this a kan tzipor moment?*

But then my cousin shoved the phone into my hand and ordered me to speak to Gedalya, which was this young man's name. Believe me, I was not at my best. In fact, I was afraid I'd fall asleep before I could think of what to say to him. But this guy was on the phone waiting for me to speak, so I shot questions at him in English as if they were coming from a Uzi: "Where exactly do you come from? What languages do you speak? What do you do, learn, or earn, and if you're earning, what do you do? How observant are you? And finally, what type of wife are you looking for?"

After I heard Gedalya's respectful replies. I told him, "Gedalya, I have an absolutely fantastic girl for you, and I think you should meet her as soon as possible!" When Gedalya agreed, I looked at my watch and realized that I had to leave for the airport in not more than five minutes. So thinking what someone in a *kan tzipor* moment would do, I said, "I don't want to leave for the airport until I set up your first date," and that's exactly what I did! As Leana hovered near me, excitement written all over her face, I wrote down exactly where they'd meet and where he would take her, jotted down his phone number in case she needed to contact him, asked for her contact information and gave it to him, and then handed the phone back to my cousin.

Ahuva and Leana rushed to make their bus back to Yerushalayim, I sat down for two more minutes so that the relatives who hadn't yet recited the required words of comfort could do so, and then I rushed out to the car that was to take me to Ben Gurion airport.

I later found out that Gedalya and Leana dated on four consecutive nights, and that at the end of their fourth date they both knew that they had found their soulmate. You might think that all *kan tzipor* moments lead to happy endings with no one involved experiencing any complications, setbacks, or disappointments, but that's not how this *shidduch* went. However, when I returned to Israel about four weeks later for my father's *hakamas matzeivah*, Gedalya and Leana announced their engagement, and I was extremely delighted to sponsor their *l'chaim* and a few days later their more elaborate *vort*.

And that was Barry's story.

Fast forward many years for a report of what Barry has shared with me.

Today Leana and Gedalya Rappaport live in Pomona, New York, located about six miles from the highly respected, countrified, Orthodox enclave of Monsey. He runs a very successful dental practice with unusual hours; at 2:00 p.m. daily he leaves his office and heads to a *beis midrash* where he immerses himself in serious Torah study that will eventually lead to his meriting the title of *Dayan*. Gedalya, who loves learning Torah, is a marvelous role model for all who know him, and especially for his children, each of whom is indistinguishable from kids whose parents were born into religious families.

Gedalya and Leana and their loving family are respected members of the Orthodox community in which they live, which continues to give Esther and Barry Appel much *nachas*. And Barry often marvels that taking immediate advantage of the opportunity to introduce these two special people during the *kan tzipor* moment that was presented to him about an hour after burying his father — a time of extreme emotional upheaval — resulted in two searching souls who had been born under Communist rule establishing a flourishing Jewish family.

As for the *lema'an yitav lach* reward of doing that mitzvah, Barry and Esther continue to invite family members and other visitors to page through the many photo albums they have of their "adopted" couple and their children, so they can see for themselves the beautiful family whose children consider them their spiritual grandparents!

5

A Mother Bird Shooed in Washington, D.C.

IRVING BUNIM WAS ONE of the great American leaders of Torah Jewry during the 1940s, '50s, and '60s. A Renaissance man who was successful in business, his involvement on behalf of American Jewry was legendary, including serving as president of the National Council of Young Israel, actively supporting Vaad Hatzalah whose mission was to save Jewish lives during the Holocaust, as well as generously donating to Bais Medrash Govoha in Lakewood, New Jersey, the renowned Talmudic academy of higher learning familiarly known as the Lakewood Yeshiva.

Mr. Bunim was also a sought-after speaker, who was often invited to address formal dinners held to benefit many other important Orthodox Jewish causes. And if all that was not enough, in his spare time, which was very limited, he authored a beautiful interpretation of *Pirkei Avos*. His book was based on the many years during which he lectured on this topic to various crowds. I felt personally connected to him since he was a friend of my unforgettable father-in-law, Aaron Seif, may he rest in peace.

Years ago, I heard this *kan tzipor* story directly from Mr. Bunim when I had the pleasure of sharing a car ride with him as we returned to New York City from the Catskill Mountains, where we and our families had spent Pesach at the once-popular Orthodox resort, the Pioneer Hotel. Years later, his son, Amos Bunim, included this *kan tzipor* story in his biography of his dad entitled *A Fire in His Soul: Irving M. Bunim, 1901-1980, The Man and His Impact on American Orthodox Jewry.*

In mid-October 1944, with Germany's defeat looming, Recha and Yitzchok Sternbuch, Swiss citizens representing New York's Vaad Hatzalah, who had endeavored since the outset of the war to rescue as many Jews as possible, initiated negotiations with the former Swiss president, Dr. Jean-Marie Musy. They begged him to entice SS leader Heinrich Himmler to release the approximately half-million Jews still under Nazi rule.

That plan fell through due to resistance from the Allies who balked at the specter of absorbing that many Jews into their countries. After further extensive negotiations that stretched to January 1, 1945, Musy had hammered out an agreement with Himmler, who demanded five million Swiss francs "handed to the German Red Cross to aid German civilians." That demand also met resistance from the Allies. Two weeks later, after additional negotiations led by Musy, the Sternbuchs informed the Vaad Hatzalah that for a payment of $5 million they could buy the lives of 30,000 Jews. To demonstrate Germany's intention to honor their part of this "deal," after another round of negotiations, on January 25, 1945, 1,210 Jews were released from the Theresienstadt concentration camp and transported via train to Switzerland, where they arrived on February 7. In an attempt to continue these efforts to save additional Jews, the Sternbuchs secured five million Swiss francs, equal to about $1 million, from private donors, and asked the Vaad Hatzalah to transfer to them an additional $1 million[1] for the liberation of all of the remaining European Jews.[2]

As soon as the Sternbuch's report was received by the Vaad, they realized that this was an opportunity that could not be allowed to slip through their fingers. However, despite vigorous fundraising during the previous months, they were short $937,000 of the required $1 million. Their only hope was a loan from the Joint,[3] so the Vaad immediately requested an appointment with its board of directors.

Although Irving Bunim[4] arrived for his meeting at the Joint headquarters well-armed with facts and figures, and clearly presented all of the details of the "Musy Plan" utilizing every ounce of his formidable powers of persuasion, from the facial expressions and body language of his audience he realized that his pleas had not been sufficiently convincing. And after Moses Leavitt, the Joint's executive vice-chairman, cavalierly voiced his organization's unwillingness to partner with this rescue plan, Bunim realized that he had no choice but to utilize the last tactic in his arsenal, which is when he told the group that their refusal to cooperate would force the Vaad to publicize to the Joint's major Orthodox donors exactly what he had proposed, and that he had been turned away empty-handed.

---

1. An amount equivalent to $14,600,000 today.
2. The previous two paragraphs are based on *Witness to History*, the monumental textbook on the Holocaust written by Mrs. Ruth Lichtenstein, p. 503.
3. American Jewish Joint Distribution Committee, America's leading global Jewish humanitarian organization.
4. This section is based on *Soul on Fire*, pp. 143–146.

At that point, Leavitt, in the name of the other board members, agreed to lend the Vaad the $937,000 they were missing, but only on condition that the US government would grant the Vaad a license to transfer the funds to Switzerland, and then, through the Sternbuchs, to the Germans. This was a condition Leavitt was certain the Vaad could never meet, since such a transfer was illegal at the time.

As Bunim rose to leave the meeting, Paul Baerwald, a German-Jewish banker and top Joint official, wagged his finger and said, "Mr. Bunim, even if you get the license, what you are really asking for is permission to trade with the enemy. Our government will demand to know what you intend to do with the money, and once you tell them the truth, your request will be categorically denied, because sending money to Germany is tantamount to paying ransom!"

Bunim replied, "If we have to, we will storm Washington, where we have many contacts and sympathizers. Rabbi Aaron Kotler, head of Lakewood's Beth Medrash Govoha; Rabbi Abraham Kalmanowitz, head of Brooklyn's Mirrer Yeshivah; and I will use every contact we have and, with G-d's help, we will succeed." Irving Bunim's words were more a prayer than a promise, but he left that meeting determined to do his utmost to save the remnant of his Jewish brethren.

And there was no time to waste. As the three representatives of America's Orthodox Jewry headed to Pennsylvania Station for their train ride to Washington, Bunim thought, *This is the Vaad's greatest rescue opportunity. Hundreds of thousands of Jewish lives are at stake, and we have nothing more than a grudging promise of Joint support. Our only hope is to convince the powers-that-be of the life-and-death issue at hand, but can I fully count on the persuasiveness of the two Gedolim accompanying me, when neither of them speaks English? May Hashem be with us every step of the way.*

Their plan was to go directly to the top, to President Roose-velt himself. However, when Bunim called the Oval Office for an appointment with the president, instead of succeeding, he was referred to Henry Morgenthau.

Although Morgenthau's willingness to act on behalf of Europe's beleaguered Jews had changed somewhat since his first encounter with the Vaad, Bunim could not count on the Secretary of the Treasury's goodwill, even when the lives of hundreds of thousands of Jews depended on his government's approval to transfer $937,000 to American agents in Switzerland. But he was their only hope.

After the Secretary of the Treasury respectfully welcomed the delegation to his office — where they chose to stand although they had been offered seats — Bunim concisely articulated the "Musy Negotiations" and told Mr. Morgenthau exactly what had prompted their journey to Washington.

Secretary Morgenthau gazed steadily at the three men who had insisted on standing before him: at the clean-shaven Mr. Bunim, the man who had so earnestly pleaded their case; at the bearded Rabbi Kotler, whose short stature belied his giant intellect and even greater heart; and at Rabbi Kalmanowitz's tall, regal appearance that demanded instant respect and whose reputation was that of an untiring fighter for the rescue of European and Russian Jews who were being obliterated from the face of the earth. Then he calmly uttered the reply that had been predicted by the men Bunim had met with at the Joint. "Are you serious, Mr. Bunim? Surely you know that the United States' motto is, 'Millions for defense but not one cent for tribute.' We simply cannot do it!"

During such meetings, Bunim usually translated for the rabbis, who did not understand or speak English, but Morgenthau's tone and facial expressions were so clear that there was no need.

As Bunim attempted to hide his disappointment and frame a response, Rabbi Kalmanowitz's tears coursed down his cheeks, unchecked, into his long, silvery beard, and Rabbi Kotler fought visibly to hold back his emotions. Rabbi Kotler, already in his sixties, stood shaking like a short, sturdy tree that had been hit by hurricane-force winds. His blue eyes blazed as he pointed a finger at Morgenthau, one of the most powerful men in the United States. "Bunim," Rabbi Kotler snapped in rapid-fire Yiddish, his words coming in agitated bursts, "tell him that if he cannot help rescue the remnant of his fellow Jews at this time, then he is worth nothing, and his position is worth nothing because even one Jewish life is worth more than all of the positions he aspires to in Washington!"

Although Morgenthau did not understand Rabbi Kotler's words, there was no mistaking the intensity of the elderly man's fury. After an awkward moment of silence, Morgenthau asked Bunim to translate.

Sensitive to the protocol involved in speaking to top-level officials, Bunim decided to take the edge off of a difficult situation. He cleared his throat and told Morgenthau that Rabbi Kotler had said, "Perhaps because of your high office in government you cannot force the issue. But please understand that in this case there are mitigating circumstances. Perhaps something might yet be worked out."

When Morgenthau looked relieved, Rabbi Kotler realized that his powerful message had not been conveyed accurately. "No, no!" he shouted in Yiddish. "Bunim, tell him *exactly* what I said!"

Morgenthau looked quizzically from Rabbi Kotler to Bunim.

Bunim exhaled slowly. He knew their chance to save countless Jewish lives had all come down to this moment. It all depended on what he was about to say, so he spoke slowly and deliberately, never taking his eyes from Morgenthau's face. "Rabbi Kotler thinks that you may be unwilling to help us because you are afraid of losing your position in government. He wants you to know that one Jewish life is worth more than any office."

Morgenthau, his arms crossed on his desk, leaned forward and gazed at Rabbi Kotler's fiery stare, Rabbi Kalmanowitz's anguished tears, and Bunim's quiet determination. Then he lowered his head down onto his arms. Minute after minute went by in the silent room, until Bunim began to fear for Morgenthau's health.

And now came the *kan tzipor* moment that Irving Bunim had referred to when he began telling his story to me. Although many years have passed since then, I still recall every word he said, which I will now convey.

While Mr. Morgenthau's head rested on his arms, I realized that he was contending with a huge inner struggle. Henry Morgenthau, who at that time was fifty-three years old, had served as President Franklin Delano Roosevelt's secretary of the treasury for his twelve years in office, during which Morgenthau had supervised without scandal the spending of $370 billion — three times more money than had passed through the hands of his fifty predecessors combined.

As head of the treasury, Morgenthau was an industrious and effective administrator who surrounded himself with an able and dedicated staff, and insisted on high standards of departmental efficiency. He was frequently torn between his intense loyalty to the president and his conservative conviction that a balanced budget was essential to the national welfare. In the end, loyalty prevailed, and he threw himself wholeheartedly into the task of financing Roosevelt's ambitious New Deal domestic program and the nation's enormous fiscal responsibilities in World War II.

Almost two decades earlier, Morgenthau had become a close friend of Roosevelt, whose Hyde Park estate was near Morgenthau's farm in Dutchess County, New York. He had assisted in Roosevelt's political campaigns for both governor of New York and president of the United States. During Roosevelt's governorship of New York (1929–33), Morgenthau served as state conservation commissioner and as chairman of the governor's agricultural advisory committee.

Despite his many achievements, Morgenthau's record as a Jew who cared about his religion, or his co-religionists anywhere in the world, was quite weak. Although born Jewish, he had lived his life totally unaffiliated. Now, most unexpectedly, a relatively unknown Orthodox rabbi from Lakewood, New Jersey, and an impressive rabbi who was a known valiant fighter for Jewish survival had dared him to face his Creator, something he had never once before done.

The three Orthodox men were waiting for his answer. He had no one with whom to consult, and if he misspoke now, he would never have the opportunity to replay this moment. Having lived his entire life honestly and ethically, albeit never Jewishly, the rabbi's correctly translated statement awoke in him something he did not understand, but could not deny. After many moments of contemplation, Henry Morgenthau stood up to his full height, looked directly at Rabbi Kotler, and said with great dignity and emotion, "Mr. Bunim, tell the rabbi that I am a Jew. And tell him that I am willing to give up my life — not just my position — for my people."

By that time, we had stopped at the toll booth to the George Washington Bridge, so when I glanced at Bunim, I noticed him smiling. "That is when I managed to breathe normally for the first time since Morgenthau had rested his head on his arms. He had been challenged by a *kan tzipor* moment, and had stepped up to the plate. He would exert his best efforts to see to it that the license we sought would be forthcoming. I knew that Morgenthau had a difficult task before him. But going forward, he would be our advocate.

"The outcome would be in Hashem's Hands, as everything in This World is, but this man would never again be indifferent to the needs of his people. What more could the three of us ask?"

I am not sure, to this day, to what extent Morgenthau succeeded. I could look it up in a history book, but whether *lema'an yitav lach* and *v'ha'arachta yamim* were fulfilled in This World or not was ultimately decided On High. What is important for us to know is that in response to Rabbi Kotler's challenge, a totally unaffiliated and distant Jew chose to stand with his People, no matter the consequences.

Leap of Faith

TO FULLY CONVEY THE enormity of another of these *kan tzipor* moments, I need to relate a bit of personal history. I was privileged to serve as president and chairman of the board of the OU from 2002 through 2014. One of the most important subdivisions of the OU is NCSY (National Council of Synagogue Youth), the largest *kiruv* organization in the world, which services close to 25,000 teenagers every year. NCSY runs summer camps, *Shabbosonim*, and an incredible number of other programs. For decades, in almost every community to which I've ever traveled, I've met somebody who told me that either they, their parents, or their grandparents had become *ba'alei teshuvah* thanks to NCSY, which proves the enormous effect this organization has had on North and South American Jewry. I would not be exaggerating by calling it the crown jewel of the Orthodox Union.

Although I fulfilled myriad responsibilities at the OU, interacting with NCSY is something that I especially loved doing, so I traveled the length and breadth of America to observe, firsthand, the inspiring work being done with its young members. Those trips led to an expansion of the NCSY programs begun by my predecessors, taking them to ever-higher levels and, during my tenure, introducing them not only in Israel, but in additional countries with considerable Jewish communities.

One such country that interested me to a great degree was Argentina; with close to 250,000 Jews, it is one of the largest Jewish enclaves in the Diaspora. As exciting as that number was, the other side of that coin pained me greatly: the rate of assimilation in Argentina was close to seventy percent. While others might have despaired, to me that meant only one thing — Argentina was ripe for NCSY. With much effort on the part of my wonderful, devoted staff and, of course, with G-d's help, the OU succeeded in establishing a small NCSY chapter there. The program was meeting with some success, and after a few years of hard work, the people in charge of that initiative made a huge breakthrough: the ORT[1] school system embraced our activities. ORT had been founded by Jews, and about eighty to ninety percent of its students are Jewish. Surprisingly, their curriculum contained almost no mention of religion, yet, possibly as an answer to the prayers of many of our devoted leaders, they finally agreed to offer their students a chapter of NCSY.

And that is how I came to be invited to take the eleven-hour flight from New York, where I live, to be the guest speaker at NCSY's first major event in Buenos Aires, Argentina. I, along with six members of the OU's board of directors who joined me on that trip, were eager to take a firsthand look at what we might accomplish there. The agenda we received before takeoff was daunting. We'd be arriving on a Wednesday night, and

---

1. A non-governmental organization devoted to education. Founded in 1936, it serves Jewish communities throughout the world. There are two ORT technical schools in Buenos Aires, as well as a post-secondary Institute of Technology, and a School of Integration of Technology, Management, and Business. ORT Argentina employs almost 900 teachers, and its student body exceeds 6,000.

experiencing a whirlwind of activity on Thursday, Friday, and Shabbos before flying home on Sunday night. And that's exactly how it played out. I still can't figure out how we managed to meet all the rabbis, laymen, and women who were the backbone of the program, as well as the students, and student wannabes.

The very first day we landed, after I delivered something akin to a keynote address in a synagogue called Sucath David, someone mentioned to me that there was a unique program, funded by two philanthropists, taking place on the building's third floor. There, separate groups of college-aged men and women were paid for the hours they spent being introduced to the texts and tenets of their Jewish heritage.

I was intrigued, but also torn. In five minutes I was expected to participate in an NCSY program in another part of that building, and many of my colleagues had already begun making their way there. But unable to resist at least glimpsing a group of modern young adults with almost no knowledge of authentic Judaism seriously studying ancient texts, I bounded up the three flights of stairs, found the room, and was both astounded and gratified to see thirteen or fourteen *kippah*-wearing young men, eyes glued to a rabbi, whose passionate delivery, in Spanish, seemed spellbinding.

As I was about to make a U-turn and sprint down those three flights of stairs two at a time so as not to miss the next item on our agenda, the rabbi noticed me, rose from his chair with his right hand extended in the classic "*Shalom aleichem*" and said in perfect Hebrew, "*Baruch haba!* Welcome! I heard that a group of Americans was going to visit us today. Please come in and say hello to everybody."

The rabbi's demeanor was so welcoming that I couldn't refuse, but I told him, "I only have a minute, and I don't speak Spanish." Then in English, I asked the room at large, "Does anyone here speak English well enough to translate for me?" One tall, sweet, good-looking young man raised his hand. I shook his hand, and right after he introduced himself as Martin Leibovich, I spoke for about one minute in rapid-fire English explaining who I was and why our American delegation had come. Martin translated to the small class, we all exchanged warm smiles, and I headed back to the staircase, accompanied by my translator who kept up with me as I bounded downstairs.

Although I knew that he wouldn't want to miss the rabbi's lecture, and that I was by then most probably late for our next session, after breathlessly thanking him once again for his service, I couldn't resist asking, "Where did you learn to speak English so beautifully?" For about half a flight it didn't appear to me that he wanted to converse with me, but then, ever so shyly, as our feet beat a drum-like sound on that staircase and I did my best to control my breathing, he told me that he was quite a good basketball player. In fact, he had played on Argentina's national team, and had even traveled around the world playing for Maccabee teams. One thing led to another and he was awarded a basketball scholarship to Florida's Barry University, where he learned to speak English.

By then we were outside the hall in which the next phase of our visit was unfolding. I peeked in and was gratified to see our group mingling with the local NCSY staff members, so I was free to continue my conversation with Martin for an additional minute. "Wow," I said, "that's amazing. But from what I recall, Barry University is a Catholic school! What is a fine Jewish young man like you doing in such a place?" When he shrugged shyly, I heard myself blurt out, "I guess you came back to Buenos Aires for the summer, and somehow found yourself covering your head with a *kippah* and studying Torah. Do you enjoy the learning?"

"You bet! I love it!"

"So what will happen when you get back to Florida? How, after seriously studying Torah here in Buenos Aires, will you be able to endure living on a Catholic campus?"

Martin was so quiet that I could almost make out what those who were conversing behind the closed doors to the event room were saying. Martin stared at me, his face frozen in concentration.

And then I noticed tears leaking from his eyes onto his cleanly shaven cheeks.

That's when I realized, once again, that I was being offered a *kan tzipor* moment. G-d was presenting me with a rare opportunity, another such moment. It was so clear: G-d had orchestrated that I meet this tall, sweet, sincere young man at the time when I was expected to lead the next part of our mission to Argentina. G-d seemed to be testing me to see if I would grab this unexpected opportunity to do all in my power to save this young man's *neshamah*, or if I would choose to ignore our "chance" encounter, shake his hand, wish him well, and go on with my life.

Why had this very special moment been presented to me when I was busier than I had been in many weeks? I hadn't flown down to Buenos Aires as a tourist, to learn to tango and take in the sights. My goal during this mission was to encourage and support this Jewish community, which truly needed the Orthodox Union's leadership and services. So what I should have done was wish Martin well, make a grand entrance as I strutted into the packed meeting room behind those closed doors, and lead our delegation to a successful conclusion of our vital communal goal. By nature, I almost never allow myself to be distracted from what needs to be done.

I had assumed responsibility for the success of this trip to South America, and I owed it to my colleagues to do just that. But what I did at that moment was turn to Martin Leibovich and say, "I don't know you and you don't know me. We have just met. But somehow I feel that there's a magical bond between us, and that I have an answer to what might be tormenting you."

Wiping his damp cheeks, Martin whispered, "You…you have answers for me?"

"Yes. I know how you can be a Torah Jew while continuing to play basketball, how you can lead a normal life while learning Torah and observing the commandments. In fact, I have the perfect solution for you."

By then, totally intrigued, he squared his shoulders and stood even taller than he actually was, if that was even possible. "What are you talking about?" he asked. So I told him — in as few words as possible so that I could rejoin my colleagues as quickly as possible — about a school located in Manhattan named Yeshiva University. "It's a place where they not only teach Torah, but they also offer a superb academic program and have several sports teams, including basketball."

And then, challenged by Martin's apparent skepticism, I said, a bit sarcastically, "But I'm not sure if you're good enough to make the Yeshiva University basketball team, since until now you've only played for Division Two teams!" I was kidding, of course, because I had a feeling he was a real star. So I continued, "Listen, all kidding aside, I think you might really enjoy being part of YU." And since this conversation took place long before smartphones were invented, I added, "Go home and Google the words 'Manhattan's Yeshiva University.' But before you go, stay put for one minute while I call someone who might be able to make this happen."

I punched into my cell phone the number of Jonathan Halpert, a dear friend of mine who also happened to be the coach of Yeshiva University's basketball team. And although often, when I dialed someone while in Monticello during the summer nothing happened due to poor reception, somehow even though I was thousands of miles away in Buenos Aires, Jonny's phone rang clear as a bell.

Incredibly, Jonny picked up immediately and I said, "Jonny, it's me, Steve." His voice boomed into my ear, "Steve, what's up?" I said, "Jonny, I'm calling from Buenos Aires, Argentina. I'm standing next to a really lovely young man who's also a great basketball player, and I think Yeshiva University could be a tremendous place for him. Do you have time to speak to him for a moment?" When Jonny agreed, I handed my phone to Martin, and they spoke for less than a minute. My friend told Martin a bit about YU's academic program, and that they offer Torah classes on many different levels, so that even if a student didn't know much about Judaism, he could quickly catch up on any missed Torah knowledge. It didn't take more than two minutes before Jonny hung up, after which Martin looked at me and said, "Wow, that was nice of your friend, but...but he didn't ask me anything about basketball."

"There was no need for him to do so, Martin! I think that after my introduction, he understood that if you want to enroll in YU, you will most certainly play on his team. So why don't you think about it a bit? We just met, we don't really know each other, and here I am trying to change your life because I truly believe G-d sent me to Argentina to experience a *kan tzipor* moment, which will end up being a life-changing moment for you."

That was kind of heavy for Martin to absorb, so he said, "I've got to think about all of this! It's not as simple as it seems..." Of course, it wasn't! So I said, "Saturday night our mission will be sponsoring a gala *melaveh malkah*. Lots of kids are going to attend, and I hope you'll be one of them." His face broadcasted his hesitation before he uttered his next words, which were: "I...I heard about that Saturday night party and was thinking about coming by, but now I'm not really sure. But I'll think about it."

Not wanting to pressure him into anything simply because I had decided that this was another of my *kan tzipor* moments, I backed off a bit. "That's exactly what you should do. Think about it over the weekend. Today is Thursday, so you have until Saturday night to decide. Deal?"

He nodded, shook my hand, gave me a million-dollar smile, and bounded up the stairs to rejoin his Torah class, while I slipped into the nearby meeting room where the discussion group we had organized was proceeding most successfully.

Later on, during a short break, I called my wife and told her about my latest *kan tzipor* moment. "I don't know what's going to happen, Genie. I really have no idea. But this young man, whose name is Martin, has the sweetest disposition, and during the few minutes we spent together he impressed me as being exceptionally refined! Can you imagine? He actually cried when I asked him what he was going to do about all the Torah he was studying during this summer break when he goes back to that Catholic university!"

After an incredible Shabbos, during which the seven of us OU representatives did our utmost to bring a taste of genuine, warm, and welcoming Torah life to those who joined us, it was Saturday night, and time for our gala *melaveh malkah*. The venue had been fantastically decorated, the sound system blasting traditional *melaveh malkah* songs was soul-stirring, and the aroma of delicious food prepared to perfection was a fitting backdrop for our meticulously planned program. And to top it all off, our guest speaker was Rabbi Yisroel Leshak, whose inspirational presentation in Spanish made a huge impact on all who attended.

Obviously, I had no idea what he was saying, since my entire

Spanish vocabulary consisted of not more than five words. But from the response of the four hundred young men and women, and the many NCSY staff members who comprised his audience, it was clear that they would follow him to the moon, which meant that inviting him to speak had greatly advanced our mission's goal.

I should have been elated, which in one sense I was, but at the end of the evening, as much as my eyes raked the room from north to south and from east to west, although I saw waiters clearing tables and folding tablecloths while others on the caterer's staff were deftly stacking chairs and sweeping the highly polished floor, I did not spot Martin, which caused me great pain. Despite what I thought had been a deep connection between us, he had simply not shown up.

Although quite let down, I pretended to be a most elated host. After I had smiled a sincere good night at most of the young attendees, as well as at the men and women who were the backbone of NCSY's Argentinian initiative, which I hoped expressed my genuine pleasure and satisfaction with that evening's program, I headed toward the double doors that led out of the ballroom. And that's when I spotted Martin coming toward me in the company of a young woman who was dressed like a typical non-Jewish, or totally unaffiliated, college girl. When we stood about two feet from each other, Martin introduced her to me as Pamela. Not having mentioned her family name, I had no clue whether she was Jewish, and I was genuinely amazed a few moments later when I discovered that she was! I turned to Martin and asked him if he had made a decision about what we had previously discussed.

He replied, "Truthfully, Mr. Savitsky, I've been thinking about your offer from the moment you and I parted on Thursday. In fact, I've thought about little else. But I'm simply not sure.

My parents are divorced, and each of them remarried. I'm very close to both of my parents, and to their spouses, and I don't think they're going to want me to go to school where, when I finish, I'm going to end up being a rabbi. They have always hoped that I would pursue a career in medicine, law, engineering, or politics — whatever field speaks to me. They will be against your plan, big time."

Determined to turn my *kan tzipor* moment into an eternal lifeline for Martin, I said, "The school I suggested to you offers tracks that will qualify you to pursue any of the professions you mentioned. Of course, if you want to obtain *semichah* and serve as a rabbi, that option would be open to you as well. But you could also become a doctor, a lawyer, an accountant, or an investment banker. Why would your parents and their spouses object?"

Pamela stood at his side, not uttering one word, but offering Martin emotional support through her presence. He took a deep breath and said, "I hear you, Mr. Savitsky, but it's all too much, too rushed. I need more time to think it over."

"Fine!" I said, "No problem. I'm flying home tomorrow. Here's my email address and my phone number. Call me any time. I'll always be there for you, Martin, because meeting you has been the highlight of this trip."

As soon as I returned to our New York home, Genie wanted to know what had happened with Martin Leibovich. All I could say was, "I don't know what's going to be with him. He's a truly lovely young man, and looking back on our encounter, I realize that I pushed a lot on this kid in a very short time. In fact, I actually presented him with a plan that would change his whole life. So I'm not at all sure what he'll decide."

The next week, as I was still in the midst of catching up with all the work obligations I had placed on hold while I was in Argentina, I got a phone call from Martin, who said, "How are you, Mr. Savitsky? I know you'll be happy to hear that I'm doing great. I can't stop thinking about the opportunity you offered me, but I don't think the answer can be yes. My parents absolutely don't want me to come to New York. They don't think it's a good idea, and what's also on their minds is that at Barry University I was awarded a totally free education. In two more years, I'll be finished with the school I'm in now, after which I can go on to pursue whatever career I choose. So right now, I don't think it's going to work."

Hearing the heaviness in Martin's voice, hearing that he was close to tears as he spoke to me, I said, "Answer this question for me: Do *you* want it to work?" After a silence so long that I feared he had hung up on me, he said, "Yes, I *do* want it to work. But I can't fight my parents." So I said, "Are you calling from home?" When he said he was, I asked to speak to his parents. And that is how I, with my wife on the kitchen extension, spoke to Martin's father and stepmother. We explained what Yeshiva University is all about. We described the kind of life that Martin would have, studying to be a Torah Jew, an observant Jew. We explained that he could be "normal," and do everything everybody else was doing, but that, in addition, he'd have something priceless in his life, namely, spirituality.

After our conversation with the elder Leiboviches went on for a while, they finally admitted what was uppermost in their minds. "Listen here, Mr. Savitsky," Martin's dad said. "Right now Martin has a full scholarship. If this YU place matches that, maybe we'll seriously consider it." I could hardly hide my elation. Genie and I told them that we fully understood their concern, and that we would explore all available financial options. Then we bid them farewell, and not a minute later I was on the phone with my friend Coach Jonny.

I shared the whole *megillah* with him, after which he said, "Steve, first things first. Let's get Martin's transcript. We don't award basketball scholarships, but if he qualifies academically, maybe we can wrangle a financial-need scholarship." I called Martin, who had his transcript sent to me and, thank G-d, it attested to the fact that he was a great student with an exceptionally high grade-point average, and some excellent recommendations.

Over a five- or six-week period, we went through a frustrating process during which each week, YU's administration pointed out that Martin was "missing this or that course," so his application swung back and forth, back and forth. And during those weeks, each time I spoke to Martin it seemed to me that his determination to enroll in Yeshiva University was wavering. Once he told me, "I don't know what to do, Mr. Savitsky. Maybe I should simply remain in Barry! It sounds like it will be impossible to make up for my poor educational background in Judaism." Another time he said, "I don't know if this makes any sense!" And as the first day of that academic year loomed, it wasn't easy for me to keep encouraging him.

Finally, however, Martin admitted that although my plan was a life-changer, when he thought of dropping the whole idea, he was extremely unhappy. In the end, he agreed that he would enroll in YU, no matter the challenges. And as if by magic, once Martin expressed his full commitment, Yeshiva University confirmed that all of their requirements for Martin Leibovich's scholarship had been approved, and that the administration was offering a ninety percent scholarship. Elated, I committed to financing anything not included in their package so that Martin's parents would not be asked to pay one cent.

However, we were far from having scored a slam dunk. I had advised Martin not to mention the possibility of his leaving Barry University to his coach or to anyone connected with that school, in case the deal with YU fell through. No way would I have allowed Martin to end up worse off than before we had met! But now I said, "Martin, at this point you have to let your coach and student advisor know that you will not be returning for the coming semester. It's the beginning of August, and it's only fair to inform them as soon as possible."

Martin told me he would immediately compose an email to his coach. When he showed me a copy, I asked if I could keep it, that's how impressed I was that at the young age of twenty, he was able to express himself so beautifully. This is what he wrote:

Dear Coach Gonzales,

Unfortunately, I am writing to give you some very, very sad news. It's extremely hard for me to write this email to you. But I know, deep in my heart, that there's no other way for me to go than to tell the truth. As you know, I am Jewish. And as a Jew, there are certain things I can and cannot do. I was raised in a secular family, and never got involved with Judaism. As I grew up, I started to learn about my religion, and hoped to make small changes in my life. I was getting more involved, but obstacles were always placed in my path that did not allow me to pursue my Jewish identity.

Let me give you a few examples of the things I was trying to achieve. I was determined that one day I'd only eat kosher food, keep the Sabbath, and study Torah. At Barry University, these goals are almost impossible to achieve. I had just about given up hope, but one day, Mr. Steve Savitsky, the president of America's Orthodox Union, came to my study group. He was visiting Argentina on a mission and told me about a special university in New York called Yeshiva University. There, everybody is Jewish, and they will enable me to lead a completely Jewish life, studying Torah with great rabbis, eating kosher, and keeping the Sabbath.

I know that apologizing is not enough to make up to you, and to those who invested so much in me and believed in me, for my leaving. But I hope you understand my situation. I have been offered an opportunity to make a dream that I've had for some time of living as a Torah Jew come true, and I simply must "catch that ball and make that basket."

I will always be grateful to you, and I wish you a successful season, now and always,

Martin Leibovich

Reading Martin's email proved to me that during my *kan tzipor* moment in Buenos Aires, I had met a *neshamah* that had been silently calling out to Hashem saying, "Help me! I want to find a way to become a Torah Jew. But no matter what I do, it just doesn't work. Please, G-d, help me!"

Not long after Martin shot off his email to the coach, he received Mr. Gonzales's response:

Dear Martin,

I was extremely surprised to hear about your decision. We had great plans for you this season. As a coach, I am disappointed. But as a person, I understand that you are following your heart and your religion. May G-d bless you! I hope you achieve your goal of becoming a Torah Jew.

Good luck in New York!

After that, we made the final arrangements. Martin was scheduled to land in New York on either August 27 or 28, so he'd be settled in time to start the new school year at YU. My entire family was thrilled because they knew Martin's whole story and could hardly wait to meet him. I was so excited about having played a small part in Martin's religious journey that I imagined that along the entire east coast of America, the sun would be dancing high in a cloudless sky, and gentle breezes would help every tree in sight wave their branches in welcome to my hero, who was flying north from Argentina.

But that was not meant to be.

We woke up that day to find that all of what people call nature was in turmoil, as if all the plagues of Egypt had descended on America's entire eastern seaboard: dark storm clouds, ferocious hail, ear-splitting thunder, and dangerous lightning. It was beyond belief. Flights were canceled one after the other, and instead of looking forward to our trip to the airport to welcome Martin, I sat, with one cooling cup of coffee after another abandoned on the kitchen table, as I fretted to Genie, "This isn't a joke! After all we had to maneuver to make this miracle of return happen, and all the time and heart we invested, Martin will be stranded in some far-off airport, alone, without kosher food, and with no end in sight?"

I finally calmed down a bit when he called to let us know that he had landed safely in Miami, but his next sentence sent my blood pressure soaring once again. "Mr. Savitsky, thanks to G-d I'm in America, but they just announced over the loudspeaker that my flight from Miami to New York has been canceled. You told me when I started this journey that the *yetzer ha-ra* and the *Satan* would do their best to stop me. Well, they're doing a spectacular job, because here I am stuck in Miami. I don't have much money on me, so I can't buy a ticket for any other flight. And even if I did, every plane seems to be grounded."

I said, "Martin, don't worry. We're here for you. Stay on the phone while I try to get you to New York ASAP." From our second line, I called JetBlue Airlines and asked if they had any flights at all from Miami to New York scheduled for that day, and nearly jumped out of my skin when the ticket agent answered, "We do, but what's available is only one seat." "Book it for me right now," I said, as I simultaneously thanked G-d, pulled out my wallet, and extracted a credit card. After I rattled off the card number, she added, "But sir, it's a middle seat, all the way in the back of the aircraft." I told her that middle seats are great, that this passenger absolutely loves middle seats, all the while thinking, *He's six-foot-four. There's no way he'll be able to fold himself into that cheap airline's tiny, middle seat!* But we had no other options. It was as if G-d had saved that one seat for Martin on the one plane out of Miami that day!

Martin managed to squeeze into that seat, and I met him at Kennedy Airport around one o'clock in the morning. This was the second time I was seeing him after meeting him for perhaps a total of five minutes while I was in Buenos Aires. And there he was, looking worn out as he strode forward, head and shoulders above a sea of exhausted fellow passengers who were flowing like a tired river toward the exit doors. A moment before Martin reached me, I realized that only I knew that the difference between him and all of his fellow passengers was far more than what was apparent due to his height. The changes he had agreed to undertake to draw closer to G-d separated him from that surrounding mass of humanity, in the same way that pure olive oil rises above water.

Martin searched his surroundings, trying to pick me out of those waiting to greet the other passengers in a way that reminded me of films I had watched where, accompanied by appropriate background music, a military hero, returning from fighting against great odds to help win a country's freedom, can hardly wait to be embraced by his elderly father. As the music rises to a crescendo, they lock eyes, their lips part in a smile that could light up Manhattan on a pitch-dark night, and they run toward each other and embrace. The moment Martin and

I hugged each other that night was one I will always remember, no matter how many years on Earth G-d blesses me with. And at that moment I could finally define the entire meaning of the phrase "spiritual son."

The next morning, after we went to shul together and ate the hearty breakfast that Genie had lovingly prepared, I drove him to YU, where I helped him register for some classes. Then we strolled a bit on Amsterdam Avenue where I recognized Richard Joel, the president of YU, who is an old friend. He took one look at me, then eyed Martin from his shoes to his *kippah*, and said, "Aha, so this is the kid who is the future star of the Yeshiva University basketball team!"

As we shook hands, I replied, "Although that's true, you are actually now looking at the future chief rabbi of Argentina!"

It didn't take long for Martin to hit his stride at YU, where he was incredibly successful. He excelled in his Torah studies, he loved all of his other classes, and he outdid all of his previous records when playing on their basketball team. I can't even count how many awards he won. I will always remember the first time I watched him on the basketball court. Martin came out dribbling like the professional that he was, but all I noticed were the eighty-five bobby pins with which he had attached his *kippah* to his head to make sure that it wouldn't fly off when he played.

Whenever Martin played in New York, as much as possible, my family and I made a point of cheering him on from the bleachers. And through the years he was at YU, when I spoke to him and also to his parents — who were very proud of his stardom in basketball — I made a point of reminding them that when Martin played for YU, he wasn't just a kid doing what he loved and what he excelled in; he was playing for the Jewish people, for all Jews who needed his wins to give them a reason to hold their heads up high.

Our granddaughter Shira, who back then was a little girl, had a sign taped onto her bedroom door that read: "I'm Martin's youngest fan!" We loved going to his games, where he always scored incredibly. But he was so much more than an exceptional sportsman. Martin was an incredible human being. He came to our house so many times that he became a *ben bayis* by us. He won awards in sports, but also in learning; in fact, one year he was honored at YU's Chanukah dinner for being one of their outstanding scholars. Over those years Martin thrived. He loved being *frum*, and he grew ever closer to me and my family.

When Martin graduated from YU, he decided to become an investment banker. Since he excelled in everything he did, he also landed a great job in his chosen field, and did very well for himself. And since this exceedingly successful young man was our *ben bayis*, people naturally called us about *shidduchim* for him. But whenever my wife broached the subject, Martin appeared to be totally uninterested or, we thought, perhaps it was simply that the young women Genie mentioned to him were not what he was looking for.

After graduating and working for a while in New York, Martin decided to return to Buenos Aires for a short vacation and to reconnect with his family. When he arrived, his old friends were thrilled, "Martin, how are you doing?" "Martin, you look great!" "Martin, have you seen your old girlfriend Pamela lately?" When he replied that he and Pamela had completely lost touch during the time he was studying in New York, they said that while he was at that Jewish university, she had visited Israel where she had been influenced by the huge spiritual step he had taken and had also reconnected to her heritage. She had become a full-fledged *ba'alas teshuvah*.

"What? You have got to be kidding!" is what he *told* them, but what he immediately *did* was look her up. He needed to hear about her journey to a Torah life, and to share his story with her as well. One conversation led to another, and before long Martin was engaged to Pamela, after which they got married and decided to remain in Argentina.

Since we continued our close connection, despite the thousands of miles that separated us geographically, it was not long before Martin became affiliated with NCSY and, as time marched on, he got increasingly involved with running some of our programs in his homeland. The young men were in awe of him, and the young women were thrilled to adopt Pamela as their role model. In time, thanks to their charismatic and dynamic personalities, Martin and Pamela Leibovich became a most incredibly sought-after couple.

Before long, Martin told Pamela, "I think I want to do something a little bit different with my life. I no longer want to be just another successful investment banker." Ever the devoted wife, and totally on the same page as her husband, Pamela supported his decision to explore how he might make that happen. And today, Martin Leibovich is the director of NCSY in Buenos Aires, Argentina, changing the lives of countless young men and women in the city of his birth.

Martin sent me a note a few years ago. He wrote:

> Zeidy,[2] remember the room where you first met me? I returned to that room, and I'm now giving a Gemara *shiur* there to college guys. It's almost exactly like it was ten years ago when you met me learning in that very same room, but now I'm the rebbi!

---

2. He calls me Zeidy.

Everything about Martin and Pamela is incredible. That he ended up marrying Pamela is incredible! And that they have three wonderful children is even more incredible. NCSY runs a *semichah* program; Martin enrolled in a rabbinic student *kollel* program as well. To celebrate Martin's milestone of earning *semichah*, a gala ceremony was held in New York, and I was privileged to attend. Aside from the *simchas* in my own family, that was the most touching evening I've ever attended, all thanks to that *kan tzipor* moment I had so many years before.

Today, Martin is changing the lives of countless Jews in South America. He is also running a Michlelet TJJ seminary program in Israel for hundreds of Argentinian girls; there's nothing he can't do once he makes up his mind. He's a genuine *talmid chacham* who has retained his sweet personality to such an extent that everyone who meets him, everyone who interacts with him, can't help loving him. And through the years, despite a truly demanding schedule and his dedication to striving ever higher, he has continued to play basketball whenever possible.

From time to time, I think about what Martin's life would have been like, what Pamela's life would have been like, what would have been with all the young adults that he, and she, have brought back to their heritage had I not sped up those three flights of steps while on my mission to Argentina. Back then, I was sure I knew the reason for my trip to South America, and it did not call for me to appear on the third floor of the Sucath David synagogue. But G-d had a different plan: He presented me with a *kan tzipor* moment.

To give me that opportunity, while my colleagues made their way downstairs to participate in the next segment of our mission, something drew me up to the third floor of that synagogue. And, as they say, "The rest is history."

Had I not grabbed that *kan tzipor* opportunity when I connected with this young man who cried, I'm sure G-d would have chosen someone else to reconnect Martin to his roots. But after my 120 years here on Earth, I would have been told: "Savitsky, you felt you were a real big shot when you traveled to South America on that mission, but the truth is you missed a great opportunity to change the life of a refined, tall, young Jew. I put him right in front of you so you could change his life, but you were too full of yourself to realize what I was offering you! How sad that you weren't open to becoming My messenger."

When I think about what Martin has accomplished in his life, and what he will continue to accomplish with G-d's help, I cannot thank G-d enough that I recognized the golden opportunity He was offering me during that *kan tzipor* moment: to change the life of an incredible young man, and through him, the Jewish world.

7
My Small-Yet-Great Moment

A FRIEND SENT ME this touching story written by a non-Jewish taxi driver who experienced a special moment. When I read it, I immediately realized that unbeknownst to the cab driver, he had lived through a *kan tzipor* moment, whose details were heartwarming. Having "read between the lines," I feel I understood much more than he was able to express, and I am pleased to include his story — in first person, which is how he wrote it originally.

I arrived at the Manhattan address I had been given by my dispatcher and honked the horn, certain that my passenger would hurry outside to the curb to prevent me from driving off into the night. This was New York City, where that kind of discourtesy happens all too often.

Don't get me wrong. I fully understand my fellow cab drivers who pull away after waiting only one minute, because we only earn money when we're driving, and we never know if the person who ordered the taxi was a teenager, or even a troubled adult, who was having fun placing prank calls.

But my mom brought me up to give people the benefit of the doubt, so after waiting a few minutes, I honked again. Still no one showed up. Since this was going to be my last job for that night, I shifted my cab into "park," walked up to the door, and knocked. "Just a minute," answered a frail, elderly voice.

I could hear something being dragged across the floor, and after a long pause, the door opened. A short, frail woman in her nineties stood before me. She was wearing a print dress and a pillbox hat with a veil pinned onto it, and looked like somebody out of a 1940s movie. At her side, a small, well-used suitcase, constructed from fabric, sat on the floor.

She was so short that it was easy for me to peer over her head into the apartment, which looked as if no one had lived in it for years. All of the furniture was covered with sheets, there were no clocks or pictures on the walls, no knick-knacks or utensils on the kitchen counter that was fully visible from where I stood. In one corner, I could see a half-covered box filled with framed photographs and some glassware.

Her shaky voice cut short my mental inventory. "Would you please carry my bag out to the car, young man?" she asked.

I carried the relatively light suitcase to the cab, smiling to myself for being mistaken for a young man when I was far, far from that! Then I returned to assist the old woman, who might have been anyone's dearly beloved grandmother. She took my arm for support, and we walked slowly to the curb. "Grandma," as I called her in my mind, kept thanking me for my kindness.

"It's nothing," I told her. "I try to treat all of my passengers the way I would want my parents to be treated." I didn't say, "...the way I would want my grandmother to be treated," because Mom had taught me that women are very sensitive about their age, and I didn't want to embarrass or hurt her.

"Oh, you're such a good boy," she said. The smile that lit up her face seemed to erase at least one decade of her wrinkles.

When we settled into the taxi, she gave me the address where she wanted to be taken, and then asked, "Could you drive through downtown before dropping me off?"

"It's not the shortest way to where you're going, and since the meter will be running you will end up paying quite a bit more than if I drove you directly there," I answered.

"Oh, don't you mind, young man," she said. "I'm in no hurry. You see, I'm on my way to move into a hospice."

I looked into my rearview mirror and noticed that her eyes were glistening. And I couldn't blame her. Although I am not in the medical field, even I know that a hospice is where people go at the end of their life, a place from which they are taken to their final resting place.

"I don't have any family anymore," she continued in a soft voice. "My devoted doctor says I don't have very long left."

Shivers ran down my back as I imagined that it was truly my grandmother sitting behind me. How would I react if Granny was sitting back there and she had just told me that her days were numbered? That she had just closed and locked the door of the apartment she had called home for many years, and that once she entered the hospice she would never be returning there again?

As I drew up to a red light, I inhaled deeply to keep myself from crying. Mom used to tell me that grown men didn't cry, so I forced myself not to. And anyway, my tears would not make this elderly woman's last journey any easier. As the light turned green, I kept driving at the slowest speed possible without causing an accident.

My wife and grown kids were waiting at home for me. The kids had already eaten supper, but Cheryl would be waiting for me to come home, tell her about my day, and eat supper together with her. But how could I tell this little old woman that I didn't have time to drive her around town? How could I tell her that I'd take her directly to the hospice, and that if she wanted to take one long, last ride around the city, she could do so tomorrow, driven by another cabbie who would be glad to earn a ton of money? I wanted to tell her that I had to get home to my wife, but something kept me back from doing so.

Those were the days long before cell phones, and although I might have pulled over at a pay phone and called home at that moment, I had connected to this old woman's pain, and couldn't imagine breaking the spell we were both under. Thank G-d I was sure Cheryl would understand a delay of an hour or so. I hoped that the story I would tell her about this last ride of my shift would make her proud of me. So I quietly reached over and shut off the meter.

"What route would you like me to take?" I asked as gently as I would have wanted someone to speak to my mom, had she been alive.

For the next two hours, we drove through the streets of New York City. She pointed out to me the building where she had once worked as an elevator operator. Then we drove through the neighborhood where she and her husband had lived when they were newlyweds. Next, she asked me to pull up in front of a furniture warehouse that once had been a ballroom, where she had gone dancing as a girl. Sometimes she asked me to stop in front of a particular building, or at a certain corner. As she sat staring into the darkness, saying nothing, totally immersed in thoughts of long ago, I knew that these places held precious memories for her.

When I realized that Cheryl might be worrying, I asked Grandma permission to make a phone call at the next pay phone

I spotted. Apologizing profusely for taking so much of my time, Grandma handed me the quarter necessary for me to place my call. And realizing what it meant for her to be able to pay her own way stopped me just in time from saying, "No thanks, I have plenty of change in my pocket."

And so it went, hour after hour, with Grandma telling me where to go next, and me taking her there. Sometimes she shared why that particular place was meaningful to her, other times she didn't. But as the night drew to an end, and I could hardly see any more twinkling stars in the sky, her voice sounded a bit stronger than when we first met, which made me very happy to have been given this opportunity to perform this kindness for her.

At the first hint that the sun was kissing the horizon good morning, she suddenly said, "I'm tired, so let's go now."

We drove in silence to the address she had given me. It was a low building that looked like a small old-age home, with a driveway that passed under a portico. Two orderlies came out to the cab as soon as we pulled up. They were attentive and intent, watching her every move. They must have been expecting her.

I opened the trunk and carried her small suitcase to the door. Grandma was already seated in a wheelchair. "How much do I owe you, young man?" she asked, reaching for her purse.

"Nothing," I said.

"You have to make a living," she answered.

"There will be other passengers," I said. And then, instinctively, I bent down and gave her a hug.

She held onto me tightly, and said, "You gave an old woman a gift of many moments of joy. I will never forget you."

I squeezed her bony hand and walked into the dim morning light.

Behind me, the door of the hospice shut. To me, it sounded like the closing of a life, but it also sounded like the building had just hugged that little old lady, as I had, promising to make her last days as easy as possible. I didn't pick up any passengers on the way home. Lost in thought, I was surprised when I recognized our front door.

Cheryl understood that I needed to sleep before I shared what I had experienced. But a few hours later, when I sat at the kitchen table hugging a mug of hot coffee with the two hands that had recently hugged that frail old grandma, Cheryl's raised eyebrows invited me to speak, to share, but I found that I couldn't. In fact, for the rest of the day, I could hardly talk.

All I could do was think.

What if that woman had gotten an angry driver, or one who was so impatient to end his shift that he treated her roughly? What if I had refused to take the run, or had honked once and then driven away? Thinking back on that night, I know that I have never done anything more important in my life. We're conditioned to think that the great moments in our lives come wrapped in packages of heroism. That night I learned the falseness of that idea. Great moments often catch us unawares, beautifully wrapped in what others would mistakenly consider just another ride.

Thank you, Grandma, for that lesson, which has so enriched my life.

8

An Unexpected Blessing

YAAKOV HAGLER, A VERY good friend of mine, is an exceptional *ba'al tefillah*. I've had the great pleasure of standing next to him along with another friend, Lazer Blisko, during the *Yamim Nora'im tefillos*, as we accompanied him in an attempt to infuse our congregation with ever-greater religious spirit. By now, I know all of Yaakov's *niggunim*, and he is the indisputably best go-to person in our community when it comes to questions of *tefillah*.

Yaakov leads davening on the first night of *Selichos* in Aish Kodesh, one of our community's extremely popular synagogues. In fact, videos of Yaakov dancing afterward with Rabbi Moshe Weinberger, the shul's notable rabbi, have gone viral. And whenever he and his family spend time in a hotel that caters to an Orthodox Jewish crowd, he's usually invited to lead services due to his reputation for having a repertoire of soul-stirring tunes that inspire all who are fortunate enough to daven along with him. So it's no surprise that I admire him, and the power he has to elevate any davening.

Yaakov has been blessed with a loving family, amazing brothers, a plethora of delightful relatives, an exceptionally good marriage with his devoted Ruchy, great joy from his children and grandchildren, a wonderful social life, and business success — along with many challenges that led to another one of my *kan tzipor* moments.

The story I am about to share took place when Genie and I were marrying off our dear, youngest daughter and last child, Esti. The occasion was especially meaningful to me not only because this would be the final wedding Genie and I would be hosting for our family, friends, fellow congregants, neighbors, and business associates, but also because Esti was marrying an amazing young man from a wonderful family, Yehuda (Jud) Berman, from Cleveland, Ohio. His father, Nate, *a"h*, was a *talmid chacham* devoted to *Daf Yomi*, who passed away much too young. His mother, Rochel, is a social worker and marriage counselor who has helped countless people. Both of the Bermans were very involved in NCSY, which increased our joy and made this wedding of our youngest child all the more meaningful.

I longed for Yaakov to come to the wedding, but unfortunately, at that very time, when he was in his early forties, he was extremely ill. He had recently been diagnosed and endured a series of debilitating treatments aimed at curing his leukemia. Understandably, it was extremely important for him to be isolated, so that he wouldn't be exposed to infections, the slightest of which could end his life since his immune system had been highly compromised. In fact, his doctors forbade him to leave home during the month between his last treatment and the following one.

But Yaakov was a dear friend and wanted to attend some part of the celebration. So to everyone's surprise, and especially mine, on the weekend before the wedding, against doctor's orders and I'm sure without his wife's consent, Yaakov showed up in shul on Friday night, looking pale, drawn, and weak, but beaming a thousand-watt smile. But no matter how much he wanted to enhance our joy, he could hardly walk to his usual seat, and family members had to quickly borrow a wheelchair to get him home after the service.

While attempting to absorb the shock of the sacrifice Yaakov had made to come to shul, I greeted him warmly, wished him a full, speedy recovery, and said, "Dear, dear Yaakov! I am terribly saddened that you can't make it to Esti's wedding. Believe me when I say that you will be sorely missed, but I fully understand, and I will be davening for you as we stand under the *chuppah*!"

"Steve," he said, as he fought to keep the tears in his eyes, "I'm scheduled to return to the hospital early Monday for Round 2 of these debilitating, but totally necessary, treatments. I'll have to remain there again for over a month as they zap me with more of the same poison aimed at eradicating the last vestiges of this killer disease. And, of course, they insist on strictest isolation. You can't imagine how sorry I am to be missing your *simchah*, to miss hearing you recite a *berachah* under Esti's *chuppah*. You and I have been waiting for this, davening for this…"

By then both of us were fighting to hold back tears, so I began pushing the wheelchair out of the sanctuary to the door that led to the street, where a family member took over and wheeled him home. Before they left, I gently squeezed his bony shoulder in a gesture of camaraderie, and then joined my family members on our walk home.

Once the others had gone to sleep, Genie and I marveled to each other about the strong ties that bound Yaakov and me. And then we opened our *Tehillims* and prayed our hearts out for the full recovery of my very dear friend, who was admired by all.

That Sunday was Esti's long-anticipated wedding day, and every member of our immediate family began our last-minute preparations. I was tasked with making sure I would be able to settle financially with the caterer, photographer, musicians, florists, and many others whose services we had engaged to make this event one that Esti and Jud would remember their entire lives. I was also responsible to see to it that the personalized *bentchers* we had ordered were placed in the trunk of my car, and that the list of those who would be called upon to recite the *sheva berachos* and who would read the *kesubah* was available to hand to the relative who would announce those honors. I had also undertaken to arrange that the officiating rabbi who would marry our precious young couple would be brought to the wedding hall early enough so that the ceremony would begin at the exact time printed on the invitations.

All of the women in the wedding party were busy that day having their make-up professionally applied and their hairdos expertly coiffed. They had also insisted on being in charge of placing their gowns and all of their accessories and jewelry into various cars that were to transport these precious items to the hall, where they would be getting dressed. And finally, who else but the women-folk could be entrusted to see to it that each one of the children, from toddler grandkids — as well as those still-single young adult family members who would be repeatedly wished, "G-d-willing, soon by you," because they were "next in line" — were dressed in their finery and be picture perfect for the photography shoot that would begin about two hours before the first guests were scheduled to arrive.

Shouts of, "Has anyone seen the cases of liquor?" and "Help! I can't find the box of *bentchers* that was delivered yesterday!" and "Make sure that the seating cards aren't left at home!" and "What time, exactly, did the photographer say we must be at the hall?" were that day's "background music" in our home.

As the hands of the clock that seemed to be racing from hour to hour — more quickly than on any other day — indicated that it was time to actually leave the house, Genie, Esti (who was fasting), and I could not stop thanking G-d that I would soon merit to recite one of the *sheva berachos* that would "tie the knot" — may it be an eternal one — between Esti and Jud.

Before I could figure out where each of the hours of that longed-for day had gone, we arrived at the wedding hall. I checked that everything that had been placed in the trunk of my car was safely in the Bride's Room. Then, after too many poses to keep track of at the photography session were over, and I had caught one private moment to wish my dear life partner, Genie, a most heartfelt *mazal tov*, the familiar Jewish wedding music filled the air, signaling that it was time for the reception to end and the program to proceed to the actual ceremony.

By then my right hand was limp from returning the clasps of hundreds of well-wishers, and all too soon I had already accompanied the groom, his father, and many exuberant friends to where my princess, Esti, was sitting on an ornate white, throne-like chair. Jud had lowered a veil over his future wife's face, and I had raised my hands over her regally bejeweled headpiece and recited the age-old blessing with which Jewish fathers bless their daughters before the actual ceremony begins.

The groom, having glimpsed his bride before lowering her veil to make sure she was his intended, escorted by all of his male relatives as well as his many spirited yeshivah friends, and accompanied by joyful traditional wedding music, proceeded to the Groom's Room where he would don a pure white garment under his wedding suit jacket, and then wait to march down the aisle, accompanied by his parents.

Next, our Esti, flanked by her mother and future mother-in-law, proceeded to the Bride's Room, to await being summoned to march down the aisle between me and my wife in the section of the hall where the ceremony would take place.

Once all of the guests were seated — men on one side, women on the other, with the red-carpeted aisle between them — the ceremony would begin with the groom being escorted down the aisle by his parents. The *chuppah* had been erected directly under an opening in the ceiling large enough to allow the starry heavens above to twinkle their blessings on the new couple as they committed to a lifetime of fealty, love, and devotion. While the groom and his parents stood silently praying under the *chuppah*, and the hundreds of guests whispered prayers of their own, Genie and I, supporting Esti's arms, awaited the hall manager's signal that it was time for us to begin accompanying her down the aisle.

In those fleeting moments, I kept reviewing in my mind the *berachah* that I would be reciting under the *chuppah*. I knew that I would be handed a card with the *berachah* printed in large font so that I wouldn't stumble, but I wanted to be able to recite the age-old words without needing the "crutch" of reading from the card. While I uttered those holy words, not only would their meaning be crystal clear, but I could also bestow G-d's blessings on our youngest, most precious child for a lifetime of good health, happiness, and achievement, as well as generations that would bring her and Jud not only joy but also spiritual delight.

Focused as I was on those fatherly thoughts, I was amazed at the silence in the room as each guest continued to silently recite personal prayers from the printed cards that had been placed on each chair, and by the aura of sanctity achieved by the whisper of traditional music that filled the room. Glancing at Genie, whose eyes were closed and whose lips were silently moving, I was gratified to see that this last moment we had with Esti before giving her over to Jud was as meaningful for her as it was for me.

Looking back, I thank G-d that Esti's wedding took place before the COVID-19 pandemic, so that we were surrounded by hundreds of family members and friends. Then, suddenly, the music that Esti had chosen to accompany her down the aisle began, and the three of us glided down the plush, red carpet to the three steps that led up to where Jud and his parents were already standing under the *chuppah*.

The officiating rabbi and two witnesses were called up to the stage from among those who were seated and took their preordained positions, as the photographers and video crew covered the event in the most unobtrusive manner possible.

While that was happening I silently gestured to the male family member who had happily agreed to announce each person, from the bride's and groom's sides, who would be honored to recite one of the *sheva berachos*. He slowly waved the typed list I had handed him earlier in a gesture meant to let me know that I could relax. Everything was in place for the ceremony to proceed without a hitch.

Once again, I quickly reviewed the *berachah* I would be reciting, and I was gratified that I knew it perfectly by heart. This was a moment I had looked forward to since the day Esti was born, and I could not thank G-d enough that I had merited to actually reach this milestone.

And it was exactly then, while I was standing under the *chuppah* — with Jud and his parents, Esti and Genie, the rabbi and the two witnesses — that I turned a bit to see what could have caused a rustling of the drapery behind me, and I spotted my dear friend, Yaakov.

I didn't know how he had made it to the wedding hall and, frankly, I couldn't believe that he had actually arrived. He looked like a man who had clearly endured a very serious medical challenge, but also like a man who had mustered his last strength to do something that was particularly meaningful to him.

And that's when I said to myself, "Steve, this is a *kan tzipor* moment!" I knew beyond certainty that this was a moment of *ki yikarei*, a Magic Moment that G-d was giving me, totally without warning. I would either grab the mitzvah or forever lose this opportunity. No time to think, no time to consult anyone; it was either now or never.

Thankfully, the entire hall was in darkness, with the only lights in the room focused on the *chuppah* stage, and I was standing right near the edge of the men's side of the platform. I whispered to some friends who were standing nearby to immediately help Yaakov emerge from behind the curtain that formed the backdrop of the *chuppah*, to the side where the relative assigned to announce those who were being honored with reciting each of the *sheva berachos* stood. When my dear friend was within earshot, I whispered, "Yaakov I'm going to honor you with reciting my *berachah*."

As his eyebrows shot up until they almost reached his hat, he whispered back to me, "You can't do that, Steve! It's *your brachah*; Esti is *your* daughter! I simply could not miss this *chuppah*, so I convinced Ruchy to bring me here, and I want to get back to my place behind the drapery, away from anyone who might be contagious!"

I didn't answer him so as not to disturb the two witnesses who were examining the ring, as was the custom, and Jud was about to place it on Esti's finger. Thank G-d, I didn't miss that moment! Then the revered rabbi honored with reading the *kesubah* was called up, and as he made his way to the *chuppah* stage, I said to the officiating rabbi, "I have something important to share with you. When we attend weddings as guests, we are often given a list of names of sick people who need a *refuah she-leimah*, and we do it gladly. I don't recall ever having a very sick person actually present on the *chuppah* stage when that happens. But tonight Hashem has presented me with such an opportunity, and I feel that I cannot allow it to slip through my fingers!" My speechless rabbi nodded his consent.

When my name was called out to recite the *berachah* I had been waiting to chant since Esti was born, I faced all of those seated on both sides of the red carpet, took the mike in my shaking hand, and addressed the assembled guests: "I want you all to know that since our daughter Esti was born I was looking forward to tonight, so that I could recite a *berachah* for her, as only a father can, under the *chuppah*. But I just realized that all of us have been presented with a rare opportunity, perhaps a once-in-a-lifetime opportunity, and I cannot allow it to slip by. Right now, not only can you daven for a sick person who needs a huge *refuah sheleimah*, but right now such a person, a very dear friend of mine who needs such *tefillos*, is right here with us. I don't know how he managed to get here or how long he can remain with us tonight, probably only for five or ten minutes, but he made it here because he was determined to participate in our *simchah*. I invite all of you now to stand up, and as Yaakov Hagler comes forward (most of the guests knew who he was) I want you to begin davening for his *refuah sheleimah*." And that is when I announced his full Hebrew name, and that of his mother.

Yaakov walked up the steps to the *chuppah* excruciatingly slowly, and he recited "my" *berachah* in a voice that many in the audience recognized from the times he had led them in prayer. It was an emotional moment for me, for Yaakov, and for all the wedding guests, those who knew him and those who didn't. I was more than gratified to see all of our guests silently davening with extreme fervor that Yaakov should be completely healed.

When he finished reciting "my" *berachah*, I loosely embraced him and whispered to him, "Yaakov, a year from now, on the anniversary date of tonight's *simchah*, you're going to be with me again. You and Ruchy, as well as Genie and I, will go out for dinner, and then you're coming back to our house where we're going to watch the video of this *chuppah*. Please mark down today's Hebrew date, and remember to reserve time on this date next year for us to celebrate your *refuah sheleimah*."

Yaakov nodded because he was too overcome emotionally to speak, so I added, "Say Amen!" which he did. And then he left the hall, assisted by his wife.

During that year, Yaakov went through many treatments, procedures, and setbacks, as he was truly very sick. But *b'chasdei Hashem*, little by little he improved, regained his strength, and was given an increasingly hopeful prognosis.

And before we knew it, it was time for Esti's first anniversary. I called Yaakov and said, "My dear friend, we have a date coming up next week!"

"You don't know how much I've been looking forward to this call from you, Steve," he replied. "While I was in the hospital, in pain and in isolation, all I kept thinking about was that *berachah* you gave me under Esti's *chuppah*. Thinking about that *berachah* and about all those hundreds and hundreds of people standing up and davening for my *refuah sheleimah* infused me with the strength I needed in order to survive. So, my friend, tell me, what's the exact plan?"

The next week, the four of us went out for dinner, after which we watched Esti's wedding video. We had a great time and thanked G-d for allowing us to celebrate Yaakov's recovery together.

Many years passed. Yaakov was weak, but he continued to work, and he continued to lead congregations in heartfelt *tefillos*. He not only functioned as best he could, but he also retained his great sense of humor. Everything was going well, but little by little his kidneys began failing. Yaakov was well-aware that he was facing yet another medical challenge, but he put off facing his fate as long as possible. Eventually, however, his doctor told him, "One day, very soon and without much warning, your kidneys are going to totally shut down. If you want to reach your next birthday, we must schedule a kidney transplant as soon as possible."

A search began for an appropriate donor, and they eventually realized that his son Yosef was the perfect match. Once again, Yaakov was in the hospital for many weeks, and his recovery was excruciatingly slow. No one saw him for quite a while, but *b'chasdei Hashem*, eventually he was discharged and able to mingle with people.

One Friday night, while I was in shul, in walked Yaakov; it was his first time back in shul since his surgery. People swarmed to his regular seat, eager and so happy to welcome him back, but very careful not to place him in danger of catching even the slightest cold. "We're so glad to see you!" and *"Refuah sheleimah!"* resounded from the shul's walls that had absorbed years of his heartfelt prayers, his lilting *niggunim*, his robust singing.

I waited for my turn to greet my dear friend, and when I was within arm's reach, unlike to everyone else, he gave me a hug, and he whispered in my ear, "Hey, Steve, you think you can make another wedding?"

I appreciated his way of thanking me for my *kan tzipor* moment, gently rubbed his bony back, and returned to my seat so that others could greet him, all the while whispering my gratitude to G-d that I had recognized that *kan tzipor* moment and had fulfilled that mitzvah opportunity to the best of my ability.

Thank G-d, today, Yaakov Hagler still leads the davening — not only in our shul, but whenever and wherever he is asked to do so. He is not at all the man he was before illness struck him down, twice, but not only will Yaakov Hagler always remember that *kan tzipor* moment, not only will his wife and family always treasure the memory of it, but so will I, my wife Genie, our daughter Esti, and all the guests who attended Esti's wedding.

Believe it or not, people still remind me about Esti's unusual *chuppah*. That night, we all realized once again that G-d works in mysterious ways, and that when He wants you to do a very special good deed it will be presented to you when you least expect it. Such opportunities challenge you to overcome your natural tendencies, and you are given no time to consult with others or hesitate; either you react as G-d wishes you to, or that moment evaporates as if it never existed.

A person cannot orchestrate such a moment for himself, or for others; it must be "stage-managed" by G-d Himself. And when that happens, there's usually only one moment when the person to whom it's presented from On High can either *carpe diem*, seize the moment, or regret it the rest of his or her life.

If such an opportunity is presented to you, remember this true story, and go for it. Trust me, you will never regret it.

9

The Mensch of Malden Mills

PROBABLY THE MOST INTRIGUING *kan tzipor* moment that I know of occurred amidst a tragedy.

The Feuerstein family is extremely well known in New England as founders of the Boston Jewish community, and especially of the Young Israel of Brookline. It is an old-line family that became prominent in the early 1900s and remained a pillar of America's Orthodox Jewish world to this day.

Recognized as successful businessmen, the Feuerstein family-owned Malden Mills, a company that manufactured a full line of fabrics used worldwide to produce all types of cloth and cloth products. Located just outside of Boston near Lawrence, Massachusetts, Malden Mills was famous for its manmade fiber and silk, for weft knit and nonwoven fabrics, lace, and warp knit. Malden Mills was forced to declare bankruptcy in 1981, but came back strongly with a lightweight Polar fabric they invented, called Polartec. Recognized worldwide for their moisture resistance and thermal qualities, Polartec fabrics are in great demand by manufacturers of gloves and ski equipment. That extraordinary innovation in itself spurred the plant's 200% annual growth during the 1980s and 1990s. In fact, when tragedy struck their firm, Feuerstein's Polartec fabric was being used in garments sold by Eddie Bauer, LL Bean, Timberland, and a host of other popular clothing companies.

The company, founded in 1907 by Mr. Henry Feuerstein, an immigrant from Hungary, was eventually led by his son Samuel, who had started working in his father's business at the age of thirteen, and finally by his grandson, Aaron, the hero of our story. Throughout the twentieth century, the Feuersteins were major philanthropists who contributed generously to many organizations. And Aaron's brother Moses (Moe) Feuerstein, one of the leaders of Torah Umesorah, was elected president of the Orthodox Union in 1954 while continuing to be a great supporter of many Jewish causes.

In 1995 the Feuerstein businesses were booming[1] despite the fact that so many manufacturing plants were leaving "factory towns" all across America. The Feuerstein family, well-known for treating their employees in the best possible manner, looked forward to continuing to grow their business and to investing additional time and money in their philanthropic endeavors.

And then, on the night of December 11, 1995, that empire of business, community service, and philanthropy came to a crashing halt when a boiler in one of the factory's five plants exploded. The force of the explosion wrecked the state-of-the-art sprinkler system that had just been installed, and outside winds of forty-five miles-per-hour instantly turned the fire into a raging inferno that spread at amazing speed to three other company buildings.

It took firefighters almost sixteen hours to extinguish the blaze in which more than thirty people were injured. This tragedy obviously also affected Feuerstein's almost 3,000 employees, who

---

1. They did close to $400 million in sales that year. That amount, adjusted by inflation, would be worth about $729 million in 2022.

were certain that this catastrophic industrial accident foretold the end of Malden Mills — the last large textile company in Massachusetts — and the end of their livelihoods. Their fears were not exaggerated because by then most factories that had dotted New England for almost 200 years, faced with competition from lower-wage states and cheap imports, had either closed or moved production out of the state, so Feuerstein's employees had little hope of finding employment elsewhere.

Simultaneously, as that fire raged on, Aaron Feuerstein found himself facing the greatest challenge of his life. From a wealthy and very respected and beloved CEO of a thriving company he was now a man facing ruin. He was insured, but he suspected that it might take years to convince the insurance company to honor his claim, since such huge amounts are not handed over without thorough investigations and numerous, lengthy delays. So for Feuerstein, this was a true *ki yikarei* moment, a life crossroads he never anticipated and did not relish. But a person doesn't choose his or her life challenges, and on December 11, 1995, Aaron Feuerstein found himself out of business and with very little time to decide how to react.

He did not call a meeting with his accountants, production managers, and human resource people in a frantic attempt to share the responsibility of the decision of how to go forward. This was his empire, the over-ninety-year-old empire he had inherited from his father and grandfather, and the responsibility was his and his alone.

And on his own, while facing a vastly unknown future on his seventieth birthday,[2] when most other wealthy individuals have

---

2. Since the fire broke out on his birthday, he might have considered it a message from Above that this was his personal challenge, and his alone.

long retired and devoted themselves to other pursuits, Aaron Feuerstein decided to pay all of his employees their weekly wage and to keep them on board as he set about rebuilding. Although the insurance company would ultimately award him millions of dollars, he would not use any of that windfall to spend the rest of his life pursuing personal objectives. Instead, he made the incredible, instantaneous decision to stay the course and provide his employees with a secure livelihood.

On that day, after Aaron Feuerstein publicly announced his decision to his employees, over 1,400 workers lined up to pick up their paychecks.[3] He also announced that he was planning to rebuild, and that he was going to continue paying them for the next several months so that they could celebrate their end-of-year holiday without financial concerns.

When word of Feuerstein's decision became public knowledge, his generosity was publicized in newspapers nationwide. The story was celebrated to such an extent that he was featured on national programs such as "60 Minutes," and the *Boston Globe* dubbed him "The Mensch of Malden Mills."

About six weeks after the catastrophic fire, on Tuesday, January 23, 1996, Aaron Feuerstein, a proud Orthodox Jew, attended President Bill Clinton's State of the Union address, to which he had been invited, where he was seated next to the First Lady.

Feuerstein's greatness wasn't only recognized by those in high office. His magnanimous decision was a story closely followed by the local newspaper, *The Eagle-Tribune*, which nearly won the publication a Pulitzer Prize for its coverage. Here's what Albi Cameron of Salisbury, one of Feuerstein's employees, told them:

---

3. The other 1,600 employees showed up in the coming days.

On Sunday, December the tenth, I finished a shift at my "ten-ter" machine, that stretched cloth. The next day me and my cousin were shopping for our end-of-year holiday in Methuen Square when we saw smoke in the direction of Malden Mills.

The whole hill was lit up because of the fire! I stood there starin' at the black smoke, holdin' my son, who's autistic, so I couldn't stop the tears runnin' down from my eyes. Imagine! Two weeks to our biggest holiday of the year and now I'd have no way to pay the rent and put food on the table, let alone buy gifts and all the other stuff that make that time special!

I was a nervous wreck until Aaron, the big boss himself, told me, "Albi, don't you worry for even one minute. All of you will get your paychecks no matter what. Malden Mills is a family! Don't worry about a thing. You're going to have a great holiday!"

Not only did Albi Cameron receive pay and benefits, but Feuerstein's company gave him free tickets to a holiday ice show so he could entertain his son.

Cameron was so grateful, he volunteered to help clean off the machines from Fin 2 and move them to another location, where manufacturing could resume until a new building was erected. Cameron worked for Malden Mills for eighteen years, and later described it as the best job of his life, where people were proud of what they produced.

And as the weeks went by, Aaron Feuerstein kept extend-ing his generosity to all of his employees despite the fact that they did not show up to work, since no production lines were running. For three entire months, they were able to pick up pay-checks without having to show up for work, and he paid for their health insurance to continue for six months. He took the hun-dreds of millions of dollars of the insurance money he would ul-timately receive and invested it all in rebuilding the plant exactly as it had been before, so that his faithful workers could continue supporting their families with dignity.

Aaron Feuerstein's only concern was that the people who had worked for him faithfully for so many years should not find themselves destitute. That was a genuine fear, because they lived in Massachusetts, a state that had seen its manufacturing employment numbers crash from 225,000 in the 1980s to about 25,000 when the fire occurred.

About three months after the fire, in the spring of 1996, the Orthodox Union dedicated their annual dinner in his honor. Many hundreds of people attended, not only because at the time Aaron Feuerstein was a celebrity, but because he was a man worthy of honor. I was fortunate to be that dinner's chairman, which afforded me the pleasure of talking to him before and during that memorable event. I can personally attest that he was an extremely humble, intellectual person who truly loved to learn Torah and to quote our Sages.

Part of that dinner's program was the screening of a five-minute video tribute clip the OU had commissioned. I stood up at the head table and announced that the lights were going to be dimmed so that the entire, huge crowd could enjoy our high-tech tribute to a man whose example of *kiddush Hashem* and *chesed* was worthy of emulation.

The room went dark, and the larger-than-expected audience was pin-drop silent.

But nothing happened. Absolutely nothing.

I asked that the lights be turned on and, gazing at the stunned audience and the frantic technicians, I announced, "If Aaron Feuerstein could rebuild Malden Mills after a terrible fire, we at the Orthodox Union can get this clip to be screened!" When the thunderous applause that ensued died down, I called out to the technicians who were located at the back of the room and asked, "So fellas, are you going to get this fixed?" And they replied with a resounding, "Yes, we will!"

Thank G-d, a minute or so later, the clip came on, and Aaron Feuerstein received his due respect. Later, characteristically, he laughed off the glitch, saying that all along he had been sure that it would all work out.

And it did.

Aaron Feuerstein's magnanimous decision resulted in an instance of incredible *kiddush Hashem*. Worldwide, the talk continued about the decision that this Orthodox Jew had made to stand by his employees. In that one critical moment, he changed the negative perception of Jewish people prevalent in the minds of so many. But only we, and Hashem, recognize what he had done as an incredible *kan tzipor* moment.

As the fire raged in Aaron Feuerstein's fabric mill, as his life work was literally going up in smoke on his seventieth birthday, Hashem was tapping him on the shoulder, testing him to see how he would react, to see what was truly most important to him.

And because I knew Aaron personally, I am convinced that his decision resulted in *lema'an yitav lach*, because Aaron lived the next twenty-five years of his life in the same aura of positivity that he had displayed at the OU dinner when that video clip honoring him refused to behave.

What we also learn from Aaron Feuerstein's *kan tzipor* moment is that such stories don't necessarily have to have "happily-ever-after" endings to be hugely worthwhile. It is true that using the money he received from the insurance company and taking additional bank loans allowed him to rebuild his entire business. It is also true that he made sure that his employees suffered the least possible financial loss. However, unfortunately, both of these decisions forced him to accumulate a huge amount of debt.

Then, due to America's economy plummeting to historic lows in the ensuing years, and with many customers deciding to manufacture their products in the Far East and other areas where laborers worked for extremely low wages, it became almost impossible for him to remain competitive.

So eventually, unfortunately, Aaron Feuerstein was forced to declare bankruptcy. He lost many millions of dollars that could have lined his own pocket had he taken the insurance money, abandoned his employees, and retired. Because Aaron Feuerstein chose communal benefit over personal profit, he lost his business, but that *kan tzipor* decision designated him forever as an incredible figure in American Jewish history.

By facing his *kan tzipor* moment so bravely and selflessly, Feuerstein became an instant national hero in the country that had been so good to his family for almost a century. And no one can dispute that he also merited *v'ha'arachta yamim*, since Aaron Feuerstein lived to the ripe old age of ninety-five. He died on 29 Cheshvan 5782/November 4, 2021.

May his memory be a blessing.

10

Operation Save His Soul

I HEARD THIS STORY on a cruise, after I had given my *kan tzipor* speech. A man we'll call Baruch came over to me and said, "I experienced my own *kan tzipor* moment, and I can hardly wait to share it with you. I don't mind if you share it with others, as long as you don't use real names." Naturally, I agreed, because there's nothing I like better than to hear about such moments, and I assured him that I would not divulge the identities of those involved. We settled ourselves in a small alcove, where we had as much privacy as you can expect on a cruise ship, and this is what "Baruch" told me.

When this story began, my name was Brian Friedman. I was a nice Jewish fellow, but because I had been raised in an extremely secular home where my parents never even celebrated my bar mitzvah properly, as I matured I didn't feel particularly Jewish. A bright and eager learner, I practically sailed through my college years, after which I was accepted by Downstate Medical School, located in Brooklyn, New York.

It was there that I met my roommate, Danny Cohen, a brilliant, religious young man from a warm, loving family, who became my best friend. We enjoyed many serious, deep conversations about life, goals, and dedication to others. We also delved into many aspects of fulfilling one's obligations to one's country, one's community, one's family, and one's self.

When Danny realized that I was a deep thinker, he began lending me books on Judaism that he had found compelling, and he also invited me, his closest friend, to spend Shabbos with him and his family in their home that was located in the Flatbush section of Brooklyn, not far from Downstate. The first time I accepted his invitation, the contrast between how my parents and I spent our weekends and what I experienced in Danny's home was so great that I was speechless for most of the twenty-five hours I was their guest.

To me, it seemed as if I had been transported to an entirely different planet. Almost everything Danny's parents, two sisters, and two brothers did appeared foreign to me: from how differently they dressed on Shabbos than on weekdays to how they comported themselves; from the strange, albeit delicious, food Mrs. Cohen served to the respect the children displayed to their parents; from the many activities forbidden on that day to the happiness with which they all seemed to accept the many Shabbos restrictions. In short, nothing I had experienced before prepared me for my first visit to Danny's Orthodox Jewish home.

And what puzzled me most of all was trying to figure out how Danny, having lived this type of life since he was born, could now be one of the top five medical students at Downstate. How could someone who seemed so happy while living with what seemed to me to be hundreds of laws that prohibited everyday activities — rules of behavior that I knew that both my paternal and maternal grandparents had rebelled against two generations ago — be so normal?

But along with that puzzlement also came great happiness. After my first Shabbos with the Cohen family, I couldn't wait to be invited again. And invitations were extended every few weeks during which, without realizing it, I began to feel like one of the family. Little by little, the strangeness of all the Shabbos laws began to wear off as every one of Danny's siblings was happy to explain what was second nature to them, and beyond strange to me.

That first Shabbos morning, I went along with them to shul, despite being unable to read the Hebrew prayer book, and not understanding one word of the two-hour service. Danny, ever sensitive to my feelings, volunteered to teach me to read Hebrew. When I protested, he said, "Brian, it's a totally phonetic language that's much easier to learn to read than English, despite its being read from right to left. Give it a try, my friend. You'll see I'm not fooling you!" And to my surprise, after several months of reading practice on Shabbos afternoons with the youngest of Danny's siblings, I felt at home in the shul as well.

When I reached that milestone, Mrs. Cohen baked her signature chocolate cake, and all of the Cohens celebrated my achievement. Danny's dad blessed me at that time that I should continue to find happiness in Judaism, my rightful heritage. It was no wonder that I couldn't help thinking, *I've come to love Danny's entire family thanks to the love that they constantly shower upon me.*

From then on, during my Shabboses at Danny's house, for at least one full hour and sometimes longer, Danny handed me an English-translated *Chumash* and we studied some of that week's *parashah* from the original text. I treasured those learning sessions which, while sometimes difficult, were always inspiring.

At the end of one Shabbos meal, Mrs. Cohen entered the dining room carrying a platter of cut-up melon, pineapple, and strawberries that she had arranged to look exactly like a beautifully decorated cake, which she placed in front of me. "Today," she announced, "we Cohens are all celebrating your first anniversary with us, Brian! We can't thank Danny enough for having gifted us with you. You've become our child-by-choice!"

When I was sure no one would notice my tear-filled eyes, I said, "I'll never be able to repay all of you for the love and caring you've showered on me during this most wonderful year of my life. And in the future, if I ever have the opportunity to do for someone else what you have done for me, as a merit for all of you, I'll do my best to succeed." And when I finished expressing my gratitude to those wonderful people, I couldn't help thinking, *This is the kind of family I want to have one day.*

But that *one day* to which I aspired seemed years away to me. It felt as if I would never succeed in learning all there was to know about *Yiddishkeit*, which I knew had to happen before that day would come.

I shouldn't have been so pessimistic, because by the time my best friend Danny and I graduated medical school, I felt ready to begin dating so that I could find the person who would help me build a Torah family of my own. I had started steadily wearing a *kippah* after the Cohens celebrated my first anniversary as their guest, and I had been gradually adopting more and more mitzvos, so I didn't feel there was any longer a reason to delay getting on with my life.

Once I had decided to eat only kosher, I could no longer eat in my parents' home because my mom didn't see any reason why she should *kasher* her kitchen. Yet further distance was created between me and my parents when a Shabbos or Jewish holiday prevented me from joining them on one of their many short, spontaneous vacations. Over time, although I loved my parents and I was sure that they loved me, their only child, our calls to each other became increasingly rare. I made a point of visiting them on their birthdays — always bringing along a high-end kosher cake with which to celebrate — and they never failed to call to wish me happy birthday. But after they proudly attended my medical school graduation, I understood that until I "recovered from this religion madness," our continuing relationship was on hold.

A half-year prior to our graduation, by which time I was a genuine *ba'al teshuvah*, I entered what Danny called "the *parashah*," the period of my life when I dated with a single aim in mind: to find the soulmate with whom I would build a Torah home. Danny's dad mentioned to people in shul that I was "available," and some of them suggested possible suitable matches. I dated several young women recommended by congregants, but it was Mr. Cohen who ended up being my unofficial *shadchan* when he introduced me to my future wife, Rebecca Silver.

A week after I graduated med school, the Cohens hosted a gala engagement reception in the shul's social hall for me and my *kallah*. Danny was elated, and at that party, when he was called upon to make a speech praising me, the very fortunate *chassan*, he put his whole heart into it, as well as his sense of humor, which added much to the festivity.

About eight months before graduation, both Danny and I had applied to several hospitals whose residency programs were truly outstanding. Danny, who was single and not yet interested in marriage, hadn't been accepted by the internship program he so badly coveted, but he was fortunate enough to be invited to join a very prestigious hospital on the west coast. He flew to San Francisco, where he became such a rising star that he chose to complete his residency there as well.

Right before my marriage, which took place not long after I graduated from med school, I told those who knew me that I wanted to be called Baruch. And not long after our wedding, we settled into a small Flatbush apartment, not far from the Cohens, who continued to be there for me as if I truly was their son. I knew they missed Danny tremendously, but I was so busy with both my internship and later my residency — which I was fortunate to land in Borough Park's Maimonides Hospital — that I simply did not have the amount of time that today, looking back, I know I should have devoted to them.

I'm sad to report that as the years melted one into the other, Danny and I lost touch with each other. I never forgot the bond that we had shared for so many years, but with no daily interaction and given our geographical distance, our friendship simply withered. I missed Danny's friendship, but frankly, at that point in my life, Rebecca was my closest, dearest friend, which made us both very happy.

About five years later, totally unexpectedly, I got a call from the man who was once my very best friend. "Danny," I shouted into the phone, "I can't believe that it's you on the line! I almost didn't recognize your voice! But I want you to know that I'll always remember the great times we shared, and the very special Shabboses I spent with you and your family. How are you, and how's your practice doing?"

To cover up my curiosity as to what had prompted his call, I gave him regards from his parents, who Rebecca and I had recently visited as they hadn't yet seen our second child, but in the middle of one of my sentences, Danny interrupted me. "Brian—"

"My friend, I'm sure you remember that since my wedding I go by the name of Baruch—"

"Sorry, but to me, you'll always be Brian. And I didn't place this call to schmooze about old times. I'm calling to tell you something that I haven't told my family yet because I don't know how." Danny inhaled and then continued in a whisper, "It's like this. I met a woman here in San Francisco who is everything I've always wanted in a wife. She's gorgeous, she's intelligent, she's caring, and…and she's not Jewish. I'm about to propose to her, Brian. I'm determined to marry her, and I want very much that you should fly out here for my wedding. It won't be held in her church. We're looking for a lovely chapel, and a justice of the peace will officiate. I—"

"Danny, I don't believe what you're telling me! This can't be true! And if you insist that it is, please, please don't ask this of me, I—"

"Don't interrupt me, Brian. I won't have anyone else celebrating with me, because I'm quite sure that my parents won't come. I haven't spoken to them in a while, but by now I'm sure that they know I'm no longer religious, and that I've been dating a woman who isn't Jewish. I realize that they can't approve, so I haven't yet told them about my wedding plans. They're too narrow-minded to accept that I have the right to live my life for myself and not simply to please them. Although I call them once in a while to say hello, we have very little left in common anymore. I refuse to live with their total disapproval of the life I have chosen, and I'm sure that my sisters and brothers feel the same way, so who do I have left to stand at my side when I marry Christine but you?"

I had no trouble answering Danny's skewed question. "Who do you have left? Your entire extended family, that's who. Both sets of grandparents, your uncles, aunts, and cousins! If you're serious about this, if this isn't a Purim joke you're pulling on me, then it's a huge tragedy. I know the loving family you come from, Danny! I'm not that close to your folks anymore, but I still love them, and I love you. All I am today, all I have today, is thanks to all of you! Danny, what you've just told me is insane!"

"I love you as a brother, Brian, and that's why I want you to come to my wedding."

I was so shocked that I instinctively inhaled and then concentrated on exhaling slowly, to prevent myself from saying something that would make this horrible situation even worse. My first reaction had been to make light of Danny's bombshell, and my second thought had been to argue it out with him. Both had not worked, so what should I do?

I'm embarrassed to admit that at that moment the upbringing I had for the first twenty years of my life invaded my mind. A loud inner voice from my past jumped into the fray and tried to convince me that if Danny wanted to take this drastic step, I had no right to tell him what to do. *This is America, not a backward Eastern European shtetl of two hundred years ago! As the American saying goes: "Danny is free and over twenty-one, so no one has the right to tell him how to live." If you asked Danny, he would send you an airline ticket so that you could fly to California to stand by your old buddy at his wedding. Danny told you that it wasn't going to take place in her church, so what's the big deal? Isn't that what friends are for? Didn't you just now admit to Danny that all you are today and all you have in life — your wife, your kids, your happiness — are only thanks to him? How can you even think of turning him down?*

And that, Mr. Savitsky, is when I experienced my own *kan tzipor* moment. It was then that a Torah-based inner voice, that had been nurtured in me since I had become a Torah Jew, demanded equal time. *Baruch*, it said, *this isn't a joke! Hashem is calling out to you to prevent Danny from cutting himself off from his People. Danny is dead serious, but his telephone call to you was prompted by his Jewish soul begging you to keep him from committing spiritual suicide. It's now or never, Baruch: a race against time! You can't allow this to happen! You can't give him up to the forces of darkness without fighting to save his neshamah! You owe it to him,*

*to his parents, and to his siblings to drop everything on your calendar
and fight the devil that has Danny in its clutches! Hashem had him
call you because that's His way of challenging you to demonstrate
to what extent you are ready to go out of your comfort zone to save
another Jew, like Danny saved you. And time is of the essence!*

When I recognized that it was now or never, it was me
or no one else, I suddenly was filled with the courage to heed
Hashem's call.

I said, "Danny, are you still on the line?"

"Of course! I can't forget that you always were a deep thinker,
Brian, so when you suddenly stopped talking, and I suspected
that the line had gone dead, I knew that if I waited long enough
you'd decide to do the right thing."

Doing my best to lighten what had become a very painful
conversation, I faked a hearty laugh and said, "How right you
are, my friend! So here's the deal. I can't attend your wedding
unless I meet you first, so—"

"If you're planning to talk me out of marrying Christine,
forget it!"

"That's not my plan at all, Danny. All I meant is that I'll fly
out to California for your wedding, but first I need to meet you,
alone, just the two of us like old times, before your big day. Are
you willing?"

"You deserve that much, my friend! You don't know how
happy you just made me! I knew I could count on you. Thanks
so much, Brian. Do you want to make up a day and time now,
or—"

"I see that you've got to learn a few rules of life before you get
married, Danny, so I'll teach you the first one right now: never,
ever decide to fly across the country before checking dates and

times with your wife. So, after I do exactly that, I'll get back to you, okay?"

"No problem at all! And you're right, Brian. It didn't occur to me, because I've been alone for so long and made all of my decisions alone for so long. So speak to your better half and then get back to me. Soon."

After assuring Danny that I'd make this my top priority, I ended our connection and immediately dialed my adoptive parents, the Cohens. Hashem had presented me with an incredible opportunity and I was determined to succeed. I wasn't going to ask Danny's parents for permission to meet their son, because Hashem had just tapped me on the shoulder and had given me the opportunity to pay them and Danny back for having lovingly drawn me into the world of Torah. And after my initial hesitation, which I attribute to my early upbringing, there was no way I was going to walk away from this G-d-given challenge.

My only problem was that I had no idea what my next step should be.

After the Cohens answered the phone, they got on two telephone extensions so that they could enjoy a rare three-way conversation with me. It hurt me to have to cut their chit-chat short, but I felt that I must be entirely open with them, and the sooner the better. I said, "I would love to visit with you over the phone, especially since we haven't touched base in much too long, but the reason I'm calling is that I must ask you about Danny."

Both of his parents suddenly clammed up. Distressed when imagining what they were thinking and feeling at that moment, I simply kept quiet until Mrs. Cohen said, in a pain-filled voice, "Baruch, neither of us can answer your questions, which I'm sure are coming from a place of caring, because truthfully, we don't talk to Danny that much anymore. Word has gotten back to us that he…he has met someone out there…a young, non-Jewish woman. I don't know how that relationship has developed since we first heard. He hardly calls us, and when we reach out to him, it feels as if he is determined to cut himself off from us, and from the life he lived until he flew to the west coast to complete his medical degree. We've consulted our rabbi and have been advised to keep the lines of communication open, but…it's not easy to sustain what has become a one-way relationship."

I tried to control my sadness as I waited for one of Danny's parents to tell me how I could help, but all I heard during our telephone connection was their pain-filled silence, which spoke louder than any words they could have uttered. For a minute or two I hoped against all hope that Danny's parents would come up with a plan, and during that time my own thoughts flew in one direction only: *Baruch, if you didn't realize it until now, now you know: it's all up to you. Danny's suffering parents can't think straight because they are the closest ones to him and their pain has impaired their ability to solve this very perplexing problem. So it's totally up to you! Of course, once you devise a plan they will be eager to play any role you assign them, but don't expect more from them.*

So I thanked them for allowing me to share their pain, and assured them that I would do everything in my power to bring Danny to his senses. "All I ask of both of you is that when I call upon you to play your parts in any plan that occurs to me after I pour my heart out in *tefillah* to Hashem, you'll do so enthusiastically."

After Danny's parents assured me that they would, I called my wife and shared with her where I was and what I needed to do. With her blessings ringing in my ears, I then drove to the shul where I had first encountered Hashem's greatness. I entered the darkened sanctuary, turned on one row of ceiling lights, took a well-used *Tehillim* from a shelf, sat down near the *aron kodesh*, and cried my way through the entire *sefer*. Totally spent, but also filled with a serenity that I didn't recall ever feeling before, I returned home for a few hours of rest, and then drove back to the shul for the earliest Shacharis minyan.

After the service was over, I approached the elderly rabbi and requested a short meeting with him. I felt comfortable baring my heart to the rabbi, who clearly recalled the first time the Cohens had brought a young medical student named Brian Friedman to his shul. When both of us were seated in the rabbi's study, I wasted no time with niceties. Time was of the essence, and I needed to discuss with this wise man the plan that had popped into my head while I drove to shul that morning.

A short while later, encouraged by the rabbi's warm blessing, as well as his promise to play to the hilt his part in my plan, I drove to the Cohens' home. After enjoying the delicious, hot breakfast Mrs. Cohen served to me and her husband, I outlined my plan for giving Danny a second chance at leading a meaningful life, which I had discussed with their rabbi. When I told them that Rabbi Gershonson had approved wholeheartedly, and that the evening before I had cried my eyes out while reciting the entire *Sefer Tehillim* as I begged Hashem to help me save my best friend from severing himself from his People, both of Danny's parents blessed me that I should succeed and assured me that they would be davening for my success as well.

Two days later, with my wife's full support, I boarded a flight to California. While jetting westward across America, I took out a pen and a small notebook and made a list of exactly what role each of the "players" in my plan would need to perfect to prevent Danny from marrying out. Before leaving New York, I had let Danny know when my plane was landing so that he could meet me at the airport and drive me to a motel where I had booked a room for us. Although by the time I landed I was exhausted, I called on every bit of adrenalin I could summon to energize myself so that I would be in top form when attempting to get Danny to agree to the first step in what I had named "Operation Save His Soul."

After all, I thought, *years ago Danny orchestrated Operation Save His Soul for my benefit; I can only hope that I will succeed as well as he did!* My immediate goal was simple: to convince Danny to return to his parents' home one last time before his marriage and spend three days there, being the loving, devoted son that his family remembered. *If I achieve that limited goal,* I thought as I made my way into the airport reception area, *it's possible that the rest of the pieces of this very complicated jigsaw puzzle will interlock to create a most pleasing picture.*

Danny drove up to the United Airlines terminal just as I walked out through its revolving doors into the hot California sun. When I was safely buckled up into the seat next to him, it seemed to me that my friend was extremely tense. "See here, Dr. Cohen," I said, "relax! I reserved a room for us at the nearby Travelodge, so we can spend some time together there before I catch my flight back home later this evening. For the longest time, we haven't had time to unwind with each other. I'm sure it will do both of us good! And my wife packed and sent along with me enough delicious food for us to feed an army."

"How can I relax when I'm sure you spent almost six hours on the plane here figuring out how to convince me not to marry Christine?"

"Danny, that was the furthest thought from my mind!" I assured him. "I want to convince you of something, but it's something else completely. Oh, look! I think that's the entrance to Travelodge's parking lot! Wow, that *is* close to the airport, isn't it?"

While I approached the reservation counter to check in, Danny paced nervously around the well-appointed lobby. When we reached our room, we tossed our jackets onto the huge bed, loosened our ties, and popped the lids of cold cans of Diet Coke that we had removed from the room's miniature refrigerator. We sat facing each other in the twin upholstered armchairs that book-ended the sliding doors to our patio, and Danny confronted me. Still insisting on calling me Brian, he demanded to be told why, exactly, I had undertaken to fly almost 6,000 miles, round trip, without even spending the night.

"It's simple. I love you, Danny, and I love your parents and siblings. You were always such a caring and devoted son, such a loving and kind brother, that I cannot imagine you setting out on your own path in life knowing that you had not reconciled with them so that you could build your new life on a solid foundation of peace. That's not the Danny I remember."

"The Danny you remember, Brian, no longer exists! I run a thriving medical practice here, and I haven't observed Shabbos, eaten kosher, or wrapped *tefillin* in about two years. So that Danny is gone, Brian. Dead!!"

"All of the things you mention not observing any longer are between you and G-d. I'm talking about the Danny whose heart was, and I am sure still is, overflowing with compassion. In fact, that's what drove you to choose the medical profession, isn't it?"

Danny couldn't deny the truth of my words, and he realized that I had not even once touched upon the topic of his upcoming marriage, many of the defenses that he had erected around himself began melting away. And yet, he hesitated, so I needed to press him a bit.

"Danny," I said, "if you agree to spend three days in your childhood home over Yom Kippur, with your heart open to a loving reconciliation, I strongly believe that at the very least, your parents might agree to attend your wedding, since it will not be held in a church."

My words excited Danny, who seemed to be impressed by my sincerity. By the time we headed to the airport so that I could catch my flight back to New York, Danny had agreed to schedule a three-day visit with his family.

During our short ride back to the airport, Danny told me that he wanted to get this visit over and done with, so he'd fly to New York the next week. I immediately protested: "Danny, my plan is better. Trust me! If you come next week, you won't have quality time with those you love most. All of your extended family members will insist on visiting and entertaining you, and before you know it, you'll be traveling back to your medical practice without having spent any quality time with those you most love."

"I see your point, but—"

"No buts about it! You know both sets of your grandparents, your uncles and aunts, and your uncountable cousins better than I do, so you know I'm right. That's why you need to book a flight to arrive in New York very early on Tuesday morning, the day before Yom Kippur! No one goes visiting on that day, absolutely nobody. You'll have your parents to yourself, and I guess they'll invite your siblings and their kids as well. Yom Kippur you'll all be in shul, and right after the fast, you'll enjoy your mom's great cooking again. That leaves only Thursday to contend with those of the 'tribe' who manage to visit. But mostly they won't, because those who work will have already taken off two days, the day before Yom Kippur and the actual fast day."

Still on the defensive, and still trying to figure out why I had refrained from even once attempting to talk him out of marrying Christine, Danny attempted to torpedo my proposal by claiming that since he hadn't davened in a shul on Yom Kippur for several years there was no way he could sit through that end-less day of fasting and prayer. I let him talk and didn't reply, hoping he'd simply drop it. But as Danny swung onto the ramp leading to the departures terminal he must have realized that I was one-hundred percent right. If he decided to reconcile with his parents during his rare visit to their home, my plan would present the fewest problems for him, making his "suffering" through a dif-ficult Yom Kippur a cheap price to pay for a lifetime of freedom from his former life.

Still, as I exited the car, Danny told me that although he needed time to think over this entire so-called "visit of reconcil-iation" before committing himself, I should call him when I got home, at which time he would tell me whether he would actually spend the upcoming Yom Kippur in Flatbush or not. Although I had hoped to elicit Danny's compliance before I boarded my home-bound flight, I had to be satisfied with my friend's assur-ance that he would seriously consider all that I had suggested, which I had convinced him was the only way that might get his parents to attend his wedding.

To help that dream of his come true, Danny said, "Brian, do me a favor, and save me from having to convince my parents to accept your idea by letting them know that if I can make the arrangements in my practice, they can expect me early Tuesday morning two weeks from today."

"Your request is my command, buddy!" I replied. "And in exchange, can I ask you a small favor?"

"Are you about to ruin the very pleasant time we've just spent together?"

I laughed, slammed the car door shut, poked my head into the open car window, and said, "Not at all! Would asking you to start calling me Baruch ruin the great time we had today?"

Danny was so relieved that he burst out laughing at his

unfounded fears and promised me that from that moment onward he'd do his best to remember to call me Baruch.

When I landed in New York, I headed immediately to shul,
where I davened Shacharis. When the service ended, I met
with the rabbi and after informing him about my meeting with
Danny, I respectfully instructed him exactly what to say before
Kol Nidrei began on the evening of the fast day, which was the
most-attended service of the entire year.

"I don't have to write your speech for you, Rabbi Gershonson," I said. "You've been addressing the congregation for enough
decades to do a superb job. When you welcome Danny back to
the shul, just remember to mention your first impressions of the
very young Danny Cohen who was a most obedient and respectful son and loving brother, and the wonderful memories you
have of preparing him for his bar mitzvah that took place in this
shul, after which he volunteered to read from the Torah whenever the regular *ba'al koreh* needed to be away. Talk about the
compassion you noticed in him from a very young age that inspired him to become a devoted and caring physician, and make
a big deal about his magnificent friendship with me that changed
the entire trajectory of my life. And please alert the *chazzan* to
choose Danny's favorite tunes when chanting the parts of the
service that lend themselves to song."

Then I drove to the Cohen home, where I told Danny's parents that their son would be arriving early on the morning before
Yom Kippur for a three-day visit, and that while he was back
home, they must do all in their power to make those three days
the best days of his life. Mrs. Cohen was to shower him with
love and prepare a variety of the special foods that Danny enjoyed, and she was to plate large portions for him during the

two customary pre-Yom Kippur meals, as well as the one served immediately after the fast day.

Mr. Cohen was to treat his oldest son with immense respect and show genuine interest in every facet of the successful medical practice Danny had established. The siblings and their children were to join the parents and Danny only for the first pre-Yom Kippur meal, to give him a chance to enjoy a closeness with his parents and family that he had missed while living in San Francisco. An important Yom Kippur theme is reconnection to, and with, our Father in Heaven, and Chazal teach that for that spiritual "homecoming" to take place, individuals must first appease anyone they may have hurt, knowingly or inadvertently. Danny's visit would be a magnificent opportunity for the Cohen family to lovingly reunite, which would surely elicit untold blessing from above.

They were to reminisce about their happy days with him, they were to shower him with utmost love, and they were to completely refrain from even hinting at the news of his plans to marry out of the fold. In short, Danny was to experience everything he would be giving up if he actually married Christine.

My wife and I would be invited to join Danny and the Cohens for the post-Yom Kippur meal, during which Danny would get to meet my two children for the first time. In any case, that meal is a quick event since everyone is usually tired from the day's fast, and Mr. Cohen would want to begin building his sukkah a short while later, with Danny's very appreciated help, of course.

I had also alerted Mrs. Cohen that even at that somewhat abbreviated meal she should serve some foods that Danny especially enjoyed, as a further demonstration of how much she had missed him during his years on the west coast. And during that meal, everyone, including me, must comment on how beautifully Rabbi Gershonson had welcomed Danny to the shul, and how he had reminded the several hundred congregants who had filled every available seat in the sanctuary and the upstairs women's gallery of why all of them had been proud of Danny since he was a very young child, and wished him well in the future.

The next day of Danny's visit, Mrs. Cohen must make sure that in addition to the two sets of grandparents, who should arrive around noon for a lavish good-bye lunch — bearing gifts worthy of loving grandparents — any other relatives who wanted to shower Danny with love should be scheduled for half-hour slots, so that there would never be more than four to six people at one time. That way, when I would drive Danny to the airport, all he would remember then, and forever, would be the absolutely wonderful visit he had had with his family, and the successful reconciliation that would be the foundation on which he could build his future home.

In answer to G-d presenting me with that special *kan tzipor* moment, I had meticulously orchestrated a perfectly successful three-day visit. And that's exactly how it went. Every person involved played his or her part to perfection — from the parents, siblings, nieces, nephews, and both sets of grandparents, to me, the shul's rabbi, the *chazzan*, and the congregants.

When I drove Danny to the airport that Thursday night, I didn't mention a word about any forthcoming wedding, and certainly not about Danny doing the right thing and calling it off. We hugged each other before we parted, and I thanked Danny profusely for not calling me Brian even once during his visit.

In the days and weeks that followed, I kept myself back from calling Danny, half to demonstrate to Hashem that I trusted

Him to bring Danny back "home" where he belonged, and half afraid that Danny would demand that since he had acquiesced to my idea that he return home for one final visit, it was now my obligation to get his parents and siblings to accompany me to San Francisco where they would all attend his wedding to Christine.

I was sure that Hashem had presented me with a once-in-a-lifetime opportunity to make a difference in Danny's life, but as day after day went by without hearing from Danny, I was increasingly tormented by thoughts that I had failed, that I had squandered my *kan tzipor* moment.

About six weeks later, when I noticed Danny's number on my cellphone screen, I dreaded that my constant davening for my friend had gone unanswered, and that I was about to be called upon to go against everything that I believed in by showing up in a non-Jewish chapel and witnessing Danny's final severance with his G-d and his People.

But I knew I must answer this call, and this is what I heard: "Baruch, my friend! I know that you are still grateful to me for influencing you to explore your heritage, which led you to wholeheartedly connect to G-d and the Torah. What you don't know is that since my phone call to you a few months ago, during which I invited you to the wedding I planned with Christine, I've had a huge change of heart. I wish there was one person I could name who brought about this change in me, but I wasn't as fortunate as you were, Baruch. I have no one person who cared enough, loved me enough, to do for me what I did for you.

"But I'm sure you'll be delighted to know that not long after my visit home I broke off completely with Christine. I've also decided that now that I've set out to find a Jewish wife with whom to raise a family, I want her to be open to the possibility of both of us observing some Jewish traditions. Exactly which ones, and to what extent, will depend on who I marry. But one tradition I will insist on is that we get married in a Jewish ceremony, officiated by a rabbi.

"The reason I'm calling you, Baruch, is that I want you to be the first to know, and to tell you that my next call will be to my parents."

That's the story of my *kan tzipor* moment, Mr. Savitsky. And the reason I wanted to share it with you, and have you tell it to others — as long as you don't use our real names — is that I want people to know that when a person realizes he or she is in a *kan tzipor* moment and seizes the opportunity to do this mitzvah, not always are there immediate results of their effort. And sometimes, their efforts on behalf of others don't end up exactly as they hoped. But the reward of *lema'an yitav lach*, promised by Hashem, is guaranteed no matter the result, and *that* is certainly worthwhile.

As President Harry S Truman said, "It's amazing what you can accomplish if you do not care who gets the credit." I think that the *kan tzipor* moment I just shared proves the truth of that saying as well.

When Only One of
Us Heard the Call

AS PRESIDENT OF THE Orthodox Union, part of my responsibility was to be involved in political life and to try to advocate for the Jewish People as much as possible. Throughout the years, I traveled extensively to Washington to meet with many members of the Senate and House of Representatives, with cabinet members, and with countless others in the administration.

In September of 2008, the last year that George W. Bush was president of the United States, I received a call from Nathan Diament, the director of the OU's Washington, D.C., office. He informed me that our organization had been invited to the Oval Office to spend an hour or so with the president before he was to deliver his Rosh Hashanah message wishing America's Jewish community a healthy and happy new year.

Naturally, I was very excited to head the OU delegation on this historic occasion. After all, how many people are granted the opportunity to meet the president with no reporters present, with just a small number of Jews sitting with him and informally talking about life? I had been a great admirer of George W. Bush, and had met him previously on several occasions, so this was an event to which I eagerly looked forward.

Naturally, when any organization receives such an invitation, there are limitations to how many people can be included, but it was extremely difficult to decide who would accompany me to the White House. We went through many iterations of who would receive a coveted invitation and, eventually, we agreed to include only those who had been most active in the Orthodox Union. Thus, in addition to myself, those who received passes to the Oval Office that day were Emanuel Adler, Mitch Aeder, Harvey Blitz, Nathan Diament, Allen Fagin, Charlie Harary, Simcha Katz, Jerry Schreck, Roy Spiewak, William Tenenblatt, Rabbi Steven Weil, Rabbi Dr. Tzvi Weinrib, and Stanley Weinstein.

We traveled to Washington hoping to solidify the president's positive impression of America's Orthodox Jewish community. It never occurred to me that one of our group might experience a *kan tzipor* moment in the Oval Office, but that is exactly what happened.

As we were led into the president's office a mere four days before Rosh Hashanah of 5769, each of us was shown to an exact place where we were expected to stand until the president entered the room. And what an impressive room it was, with the president's massive desk situated in front of three floor-to-ceiling windows accented by olive-green drapes that were flanked by a tall American flag and its "twin," the presidential flag. A bowl of fresh flowers had been placed in the center of the table that spanned the windows between the flags, two cream-colored couches faced each other across the room's oval carpet, two upholstered armchairs faced the president's desk at right angles to those two couches, and several side chairs were placed around the room so that as soon as the president arrived and sat down, each of us would find seating in a circle that would facilitate our chat with the president.

As a grandfather clock tick-tocked the seconds before the most powerful man on Earth made his entrance, I reflected on the meaningful words of the *tefillah*, *K'vakaras ro'eh edro ma'avir tzono tachas shivto*, that equates standing individually in prayer on the holiest days of the Jewish calendar with lambs that pass, singly, in front of their shepherd as he conducts an official counting of his flock. I also thought about the fear of HaKadosh Baruch Hu that overtakes us on Rosh Hashanah, and compared it to the tension we were all experiencing as we awaited the arrival of the president of the United States. And I couldn't help thinking that perhaps we had been summoned to this very room at this particular time to impress upon us how much more awe it would behoove us to experience when we would shortly be meeting the *Melech malchei ha-melachim*, the King of the world Who appoints all earthly kings, on the day when the fate of each of us would be decided for the coming year.

While we stood silently waiting for the president to enter, I was fully aware of how our appearance in the Oval Office was a fitting preparation to what every Jew would experience in a mere ninety-six hours. In light of this perspective that would still be fresh in our minds, just as I couldn't imagine arriving late for this meeting, I couldn't imagine any of us arriving late to shul on Rosh Hashanah. And just as each of the invitees was dressed in their finest clothing, as was befitting the reverence fully expected of every person who had been granted the opportunity to step into Mr. Bush's inner sanctum, I was sure that Jews worldwide would take even more care to dress appropriately when coming to shul. If I gained nothing more from this journey to Washington, in those fleeting minutes before President Bush joined us, I experienced a fitting introduction to the reverence and veneration with which I hoped to greet the upcoming Days of Awe.

As soon as the president entered, he invited us to find seats, and because by nature he was a warmhearted, easygoing, and spiritual fellow blessed with much personal charm, all of us relaxed and knew that this would be an event to remember for its utter positivity. When we were seated, President Bush said, "Well, folks, what do you want to talk about?" From the moment he made that very human opening comment, the talk flowed, ranging from what it felt like to be president to what it took to lead a community famous for its divergent opinions and its outspokenness; from our feelings for the very beleaguered State of Israel to how the strict observance of our Jewish faith enhanced our lives. Every member of our group was given a chance to be heard, and the atmosphere was extremely congenial.

Before traveling to Washington, as we prepared for this auspicious meeting, we debated what type of gift to present to the president. We wanted our gift to be meaningful, but also knew that because by law he was not permitted to keep any gift for his personal use, whatever we gave him would end up in his presidential library and museum after he left office. During those somewhat heated discussions, it was mentioned that although the president didn't *need* anything, to honor him we wanted to purchase and gift him with something very meaningful and appropriate to have been presented to him by a Jewish organization.

During those discussions, someone mentioned that when Jews brought *bikkurim* to the Beis HaMikdash, although G-d had no use for those fruits or for the baskets in which they were presented, only the finest, most luscious first fruits were brought and presented in the most befitting baskets the bearer could afford. We decided to purchase a beautifully framed copy of the speech that George Washington had given to the Jews of Newport, Rhode Island, when he visited its famous Touro Synagogue.

Since I had been honored with the coveted task of actually giving Mr. Bush our gift, I had prepared a very short speech. Even though I am an experienced extemporaneous speaker, this occasion did not call for off-the-cuff words, so I had typed out and placed in my jacket pocket the few lines that would express the sentiments that accompanied our gift. But now, as we all stood about and I held the framed speech Washington had given in one hand, I only had my other hand with which to fish out my prepared remarks, open the folded paper, and glance at the exact words I wanted to say. And there was no way I could do all of that with my one free hand!

Immediately noticing my discomfort, President Bush said, "Steve, forget about the paper! Just speak from your heart!" So that's what I did. I said, "Mr. President, you recently returned from Israel where its people demonstrated the love and respect they have for you because of all you've done to help them stay safe. Israel is a tiny country surrounded by enemies determined to wipe her off the map, yet when a visitor walks the streets in various towns and cities, you see little kids riding their bikes, waiting for school buses, and frolicking in their many playgrounds, thanks to the partnership between Israel and America. Despite the Arab world's uprisings and war of terror, after 9/11 the people of Israel have hope for their future, thanks to the feelings you expressed in your speech to the Knesset. That speech reminded us of the speech made by our very first president to the Jews of Newport, Rhode Island, words that have set the tone for the religious freedom we have enjoyed in America until today. So what more meaningful gift could we give you than a framed copy of that speech, in gratitude for the Knesset speech you recently made?"

The president loved our gift and appreciated that I had compared his recent address to the Knesset to Washington's famous speech, both of which had positively impacted history.

After the president accepted the gift and walked across the room to place it on his desk, I remembered that I had a copy of the speech he had given at the Knesset with me, since it had arrived at OU headquarters from the White House. My friend Jerry Schreck, the very literary and accomplished person I had selected to be in charge of the OU's *Jewish Action* magazine, had also brought that speech with him. Although each of us had been instructed not to bring in anything for the president to sign, inexplicably, both of us had taken along a copy of President Bush's speech, hoping against hope that somehow we'd get him to autograph them!

When the president rejoined our group, both Jerry and I said, almost in unison, "Mr. President, would you mind signing this?" President Bush asked, "What is it you want me to sign?" When we answered that we had each brought along an official copy of the speech he had given at the Knesset, he commented, "Ah, I love that speech! It really captured how I feel about Israel." And then he proceeded to sign mine — which will forever be a treasured memento of my visit to the Oval Office — as well as Jerry's. All in all, every one of us who had been fortunate enough to attend that meeting felt that it had gone extremely well.

As our allotted time with the president was drawing to an end, Mr. Bush said, "That's about it for now, gentlemen, since I'll be leaving in five minutes to meet with somebody I think you know pretty well." When we sent each other puzzled looks, he continued, "My next scheduled meeting is with Mahmoud Abbas, the head of the Palestinian Authority."

And that's when my friend Jerry Schreck had a *kan tzipor* moment.

At that exact moment, Jerry recalled that I had spoken about *kan tzipor* moments, so he asked himself, *Why did G-d place me right here in the Oval Office, exactly five minutes before President*

Bush will meet with the leader of one of Israel's sworn enemies, the Palestinian Authority? Should I simply walk out of this room as if I didn't hear what he said, or should I take a cue from what he told Steve: "Talk from your heart!" and say something that might benefit my fellow Jews?

One of the criteria of a *kan tzipor* moment is that it must be an opportunity that lasts for one swift moment, which, if you don't grab that opportunity, will be lost forever. Another criterion is that doing so must be something that forces you out of your comfort zone. Most of us had barely heard the president announce who he was about to meet, and those of us who did were not standing as close to President Bush as Jerry was, so this *kan tzipor* moment was definitely his.

And Jerry realized that because he was part of our organization and his words would have more power behind them than if he were speaking as a private citizen, he had to be extremely careful what he said. He must speak with total respect and diplomacy while delivering a powerful message that might increase the possibility of peace with the Arabs, while letting them know that they would be held accountable for any breaches of the tentative peace that existed at that time. So Jerry said, "Mr. President, I just heard you tell Steve to forget about his prepared gift-presentation speech and speak from his heart, so I hope you'll accept what I am about to say as words that come directly from *my* heart.

"Mr. President, I also hope that when you meet with your next guest, you remember the powerful speech you gave in the Knesset during your recent visit. If you do, it won't be difficult for you to make Mr. Abbas understand in no uncertain terms that he must immediately cease and desist monetarily rewarding terrorists for killing innocent Israeli citizens, and that he must never again use inflammatory language when addressing Arab audiences while two-facedly speaking only words of peace and reconciliation when talking to non-Arabs."

Jerry's remarks caught the president off guard. His brow wrinkled as he thought what to reply to Jerry, and during that fleeting moment Jerry was thinking, *You just signed my copy of that speech. Please, please remember it when you meet with Abbas!* A split-second later President Bush said, "I'll never forget that speech, Jerry. Never!"

Jerry replied, "Mr. President, I hope that you and Abbas don't agree on anything that you might regret later on in life," to which the president responded, "Jerry, you don't have to worry. There are two things you have to know about Mahmoud Abbas. One, he's an extremely weak leader; and two, he's afraid to take any action toward peace because he's afraid that if he makes peace with Israel, he will be assassinated by Hamas. So don't worry. As long as I'm in the White House, the United States will continue to be Israel's strongest ally."

Each of us had lined up to say farewell to the president and to thank him, but it was Jerry Schreck who had just had a very meaningful *kan tzipor* moment.

Ki yikarei. Here Jerry was, of all places and times, as the president of the United States was about to meet with the head of the Palestinian Authority. Jerry immediately realized that this was a very special moment, and without thinking to protect his reputation as an "unbiased, even-handed journalist," and without allowing thoughts that any of us might be upset with him for speaking out of turn, he took advantage of the opportunity to speak up for our brothers and sisters in Eretz Yisrael.

Jerry, of all the Jews who had gathered there at that time, was the only one who did not allow that moment to slip by. *Lema'an yitav lach, v'ha'arachta yamim.* Whenever the topic of *kan tzipor* is mentioned, Jerry remembers that day and shares that he still thanks G-d that he grabbed that fleeting opportunity to stand up for G-d's homeland and for G-d's People by reminding the president of his magnificent speech in the Knesset.

HaKadosh Baruch Hu had orchestrated a "tapping-on-the-shoulder moment," but only Jerry heard Hashem offering him an opportunity of a lifetime. And every time I recall what Jerry did, I remind myself that one never knows when He's going to gift you with an opportunity to experience your finest moment. *Ki yikarei,* He constantly calls out to us. Maybe He had been calling out to each of us, but it was only Jerry who heard the call.

12

A Moment in Overland Park, Kansas

MY WIFE AND I love to visit small Jewish communities, where there's a certain vibrancy not found "in town" and everyone knows they have to be there for each other. Because those who live in small Jewish communities appreciate that they are a valued part of their congregation, nobody "hides in a corner," and nobody is marginalized. It's a wonderful quality of life. Additionally, having always lived in the greater tristate area, I know how difficult it is for so many people to be able to afford living here, due to the high cost of housing, the taxes, the tuitions, and all-too-often the loneliness, so I'm a real proponent of out-of-town communities.

After a while, I began asking myself: Why not encourage people to relocate to smaller Jewish communities where they would be deeply appreciated, where the cost of living is lower, and the quality of life is so much greater? *Baruch Hashem*, the OU has been successful in assisting many people to move not simply to another tristate enclave teeming with observant Jews, but to small Jewish communities across America.

Because there were so many locations in which such families settled, it was almost impossible for me to visit each community more than once in several years. Even though I wanted to go back and they, thank G-d, wanted me to return to spend a Shabbos with them, it was difficult. There were just a few such places that we actually visited more than once.

One of those was the community of Overland Park, Kansas, a truly lovely place to live.[1] From our previous visit we were aware that the neighborhood had gone through several rabbis since I had been there last, and that they were blessed with a vibrant old-time shul, which had merged with several other synagogues during the last eighty to one hundred years. The cost of housing was extremely affordable, and their yeshivah building hosted an active Jewish Community Council. The *kehillah's* leadership was innovative, and they had a special way of making my wife and me feel at home.

On our first Shabbos there, between Shacharis and Musaf, I had described the many programs offered by the OU, and in the afternoon I had given my *kan tzipor* speech, during which I shared stories to illustrate that concept. I enjoy giving that speech because I believe it is an awareness all Jews should attempt to adopt. Afterward, people came over to me, introduced themselves, and told me that they had been inspired, which is always gratifying. But as I had major responsibilities at OU headquarters in New York, after Shabbos we flew home, happy that we had taken time on Friday to view the tall, imposing, and impressive Clock Tower Plaza in the city's downtown area.

About three years later, they invited us to return so I could serve as their scholar-in-residence for another weekend. Since

---

1. Niche, an organization that analyzes public data and reviews to create rankings, report cards, and more, recently released its annual "Best Cities to Live in America List," and Overland Park, Kansas, landed the No. 5 spot!

Genie and I had enjoyed ourselves there so much, we decided to accept the invitation. And for that second visit, as a special treat we took along one of our grandsons, who we were sure would appreciate the relaxed atmosphere of that lovely out-of-town community, as well as the beautifully landscaped homes, the pristine streets, the many parks and public buildings, and the nearby Deanna Rose Children's Farmstead.

We arrived on Thursday night, and Friday morning our grandson Yoel Schreier, a student at Yeshiva University, was surprised that there was only one minyan for Shacharis. He had been raised in Woodmere, New York, one of the "Five Towns," and was used to having several shuls nearby that ran minyanim every half-hour or so. He couldn't believe that there are Jewish communities where if you miss the morning minyan, there isn't another one until the next day!

Of course, I made sure to arrive at the one morning minyan with our grandson a bit early. We came into the shul, where I recognized one man from our previous visit, although I didn't remember his name. He kept looking at me, then he motioned to me, and I understood that he wanted to talk to me during the few minutes we had before davening began. I nodded to him to come right over.

As I prepared my tallis and tefillin for the upcoming service, the man I'll call Irving Schneider, a long-time community member, said, "I've got to tell you something really important. Actually, Steve, I want to apologize. Since I saw you last, I experienced my own *kan tzipor* moment. When it happened, I thought about you, because I wouldn't have reacted as I did had I not heard your speech, and I should have called you, but I kept putting it off 'for a better time,' and I simply never got around to it. I'm sorry."

I assured Irving that there was nothing for which he owed

me an apology and asked him to share his story with me after Shacharis.

The following is what he told me.

Kansas City, which is about a twenty-minute drive from Overland Park, is blessed with a very large medical community, with leading hospitals and some exceptional medical programs and physicians. People from all over the country, probably from all over the world, come here for treatments. It's not uncommon for those who are Jewish to temporarily stay in Overland Park when they have serious health issues that require extensive treatment.

Well, one day I came into shul and noticed a man, already in his tallis and tefillin, who I'll call Yisochor Green, who clearly did not belong to our community. I went over to him, introduced myself, extended the usual "*Shalom aleichem*," and asked what had brought him to our shul.

Mr. Green, who looked quite forlorn, said, "My...my wife suffers from a very serious illness and the doctors in our hometown recommended that I bring her here for special treatments. So we're going to be in Overland Park for about sixty days. This won't be easy, but thank G-d we have older children who are able to handle life on their own for a while. Of course, I had to give up my job, at least until we return home, and I have to daven that my boss takes me back when we get back. You know how it is; once my boss sees that he can manage without me, there's little incentive for him to welcome me back, but that's also in Hashem's Hands.

"I'm a salaried worker, and after the out-of-pocket medical expenses we've had to pay over the last months, our savings have been all but depleted. But we need a place to stay while we're here, so I'm scheduled to meet with a realtor this morning to discuss available houses to rent."

My first reaction to Mr. Green's mention of the word "realtor" was one of surprise, because although I wasn't about to share my private life with him, I, too, had an appointment with a realtor that day, for one o'clock! We had been renovating a new, much smaller house for many months and had moved into it the previous week. Now it was time to sell the old one, along with much of our still-usable furniture, if possible, and a friend had recommended a Mr. Moynahan as a competent, honest, real estate agent. To someone else, that this Green fellow and I would both be consulting realtors in a few hours might be considered a coincidence, but our rabbi had drilled into us that everything in this world is orchestrated On High, so I was simply surprised.

Hiding my surprise, I focused on what Mr. Green was saying, hoping I hadn't missed anything important while my mind had wandered. "...So as I was saying, in addition to that, my wife will have enough stress from her illness, the treatments, and being separated from our family. When each day is over I need to provide her with a calm, quiet home where she can rest up until her next round. I am going to daven very hard this morning that this realtor will be able to help us quickly, as the inexpensive motel we're staying in is too far from this shul to walk to and not at all the calm atmosphere that she needs in order for her to suffer the least from this illness. Thanks, Mr. Schneider, for even noticing me."

This man's plight was truly touching, but since there was no second minyan and we both had to begin davening, at that moment I returned to my regular seat. I watched as he, too, began to daven, and I truly hoped that his prayers would be answered.

To my surprise, during the entire morning service, I found it difficult to concentrate on the meaning of the words I was saying. I fought with myself to focus, but I'm embarrassed to admit that it was extremely difficult for me. I kept remembering the speech I had heard from you on your previous visit about a "magic moment" when someone — or something — comes along, presenting a person with a fleeting opportunity to do a mitzvah. While my mouth was uttering *"Yishtabach Shimcha,"* I kept hearing your voice, Steve, exclaiming: *"Ki yikarei."* I shooed it out of my mind and managed to concentrate on the meaning of the words I was saying until I got to *"Ezras avoseinu Ata Hu mei'olam,"* when your voice from that past Shabbos intruded again, telling me that this might be **my** *kan tzipor* moment. And suddenly I knew it was true, and that as soon as davening had ended, I must step up to the plate.

What else could it be? There I was, in shul. Nothing unusual about that; I come to shul most every morning. But out of the blue, I meet this Yisochor Green, who tells me that he must live in our neighborhood for sixty days. He tells me that although he has little left of his savings, he's going to meet a realtor in the hope of renting a house or an apartment for two months. Then he says he's going to daven that Hashem should help him. Great. But having lived in Overland Park forever, I know that it would take a miracle to find anyone willing to rent to anybody for such a short term. And suddenly I felt like stopping right in the middle of davening to tell him that I have the perfect solution for him.

But then I heard another, much louder voice telling me, *Come on, Irving, who are you kidding? Steve wasn't talking about plain folks like you! And even if he was, all you have to do to cover all possibilities is to get Mr. Green's cell phone, let him meet with the realtor, and later today call and find out if he was successful. If he wasn't, you have plenty of time then to share the brainstorm you had while davening. Most probably it was your yetzer ha-ra that interrupted your concentration, right? It couldn't be otherwise! Your mom always told you that no one ever regretted not saying something, while jumping into a half-baked plan, which is what's disturbing your concentration now, might get you into real trouble.*

And although I'm ashamed to admit it, Steve, that's how it went during that entire Shacharis. Two voices were fighting in my head for dominance. To say I was torn is an understatement. You certainly could not have meant that Hashem was calling out to me with this once-in-a-lifetime mitzvah when I was supposed to be speaking directly to Hashem during Shacharis! I understood that thought as proof that all I should do is get the man's contact information

By the time the last Kaddish was over I was sweating bullets, and before my eyes, as if in Technicolor, I envisioned Mr. Yisochor Green and what I imagined how his very sick wife looked, standing in front of a third-rate motel with two suitcases at their feet, totally homeless.

After that, I quickly removed my tallis and tefillin, while keeping my eye on Mr. Green to make sure he was doing the same, which he was. When we were both finished, and the only two men left in shul, I called out to him and said, "Mr. Green, do you have a few minutes for me before you leave?"

When he nodded, I headed toward him. And as I walked, that first, loud, and strident voice that had disturbed me throughout davening was back again! *Irving, it's true you have a house to sell because you and your wife just moved into a new one. Firstly, you really don't want to allow total strangers to live in it, even temporarily, because although this fellow you just met told you his wife's treatments will take sixty days, there's no guarantee of that. And secondly, once they're living there, face it: you might not be able to evict them! So simply wish Yisochor Green well with the realtor and at most, give him your home phone number and tell him that if he needs anything he should call you. You're not obligated to do more, trust me!*

In the few seconds it took me to sit down next to Mr. Green, my thoughts yo-yoed up and down, up and down. *Should I speak up? Should I remain silent?* And right before Mr. Green turned to me, ready to hear me out, I heard another, even stronger voice that sounded as if it was coming from a much higher place say, *This man came into your shul this morning with a problem that you can resolve. You have an empty house that you intend to sell, now that you've settled into your new one. It's true you could use the money, but it's also true that it won't make a great difference in your financial position if you put the house on the market in sixty days from now. Grab the opportunity to do this mitzvah, Irving, now! How will you face Steve Savitsky if he ever returns?*

And that is what I did, Steve. I told Mr. Green that he doesn't need to call a realtor because I was about to hand him the keys to our empty house, where he could live with his wife as long as she needed treatment. His first question was, "How…how much is the monthly rental? I don't even want to go see it if it's beyond our budget." When I told him that they didn't have to pay me even one red cent, that this would be our mitzvah, the smile that lit up not only his face but his eyes, and somehow helped him sit up straighter, prompted me to also tell him, "And, my new friend, not only am I about to hand you the keys to the house, I'm also going to give you another set of keys. They fit the car that is parked in the driveway of that house. It's the car we let the married kids drive when they fly in for visits, and its tank is full of gas!"

Yisochor Green's eyes shone with unshed tears when he said, "I can't believe the *chesed* that you're doing for me and for my wife, who is starting her treatments today. That you approached me, listened to my plight, and now are offering your own second home, plus a car, is truly overwhelming, Mr. Schneider. Especially since I'm a total stranger here! *Mi k'amcha Yisrael!*"

I smiled at him and said, "Here are the keys to both; I'll drive you over there now and show you around. Enjoy your next sixty days in our community, and I hope your wife gets better. Strike that! I don't hope. I *know* that she'll have a *refuah sheleimah*. We have wonderful doctors here, and I know of many miracles Hashem has done here. Don't worry about anything. Just concentrate on helping your wife get through this tough time."

Then Irving Schneider said to me, "That was my *kan tzipor* moment, Mr. Savitsky! I've thought about this many times since it happened, and I wanted to share it with you. I knew it was an incredible *kan tzipor* moment, when I had to make a hasty decision, or Green would have met the realtor and heard that what he sought was not to be had, and he might have been too beaten by his plight to approach anyone from our shul, which would have been of great detriment to his wife's recovery. I did the right thing, *lema'an yitav lach*. Afterward, every time I saw this man in shul, I felt so good about what I had done. As a matter of fact, he still calls to thank me, and to give me a progress report on his wife, who left with him after the sixty days were up and seems to be holding her own, thank G-d.

"I'm glad you returned to our community, Mr. Savitsky, because the only reason I stepped up to the plate that day when I saw this downtrodden husband was because you taught me what to look out for, what a *kan tzipor* moment is! And that it doesn't have to be something earth-shattering, something unusual, to earn great merit.

"So, Mr. Savitsky, was my magic moment a good story for you to tell others?"

I said, "Irving, it was worth the trip down here from New York just to hear what you told me now. I haven't even yet held one speech in your shul, and already you made our trip to Overland

Park truly meaningful. Because I usually never learn what happens after I speak about *kan tzipor* moments until those who have heard my speech share their stories, I sometimes doubt that what I'm doing is of value. By coming back to Overland Park and listening to your incredible tale, I'm inspired to continue sharing this concept with other communities. Thank you, Irving. I appreciate it so much. What a wonderful way to begin our second Shabbos in Overland Park."

It was only then that our grandson, Yoel, who had been sitting at my side, riveted to every word Irving had said, took my hand and said, "Zeidy, no wonder you travel all over for the OU. You get to hear really great stories! Do you think you'll ever write a book about them?"

And back then, the only thing I could truthfully answer was, "Only Hashem knows!"

13

Taken for a Ride?

THEY SAY YOU CAN'T go home again, but I was fortunate a little before the COVID-19 pandemic hit America, in the spring of 2020, to be invited back to one of my former synagogues, the Young Israel of Queens Valley in Kew Gardens Hills, New York, where I spent the first twelve years of my married life. I was very active in that shul because I felt close to my fellow congregants, and most of all to the rabbi, Rabbi Peretz Steinberg, *shlita*, who has since retired.

They invited me to come back for their Partners in Torah Shabbos. The rabbi's *drashah* that morning was about Partners in Torah, and when they asked me to give a speech on Shabbos afternoon I decided to give my *kan tzipor* speech because I love the topic, and I had new stories to illustrate its innovative concept.

After I spoke, a man I'll call Shlomo Asher came over to me and said, "Mr. Savitsky, I want to share with you what I consider my very own *kan tzipor* moment."

Often, when I go to a synagogue, people tell me a story that is a beautiful example of *hashgachah pratis*. They're lovely stories of *bashert* and quite inspirational, but they're not *kan tzipor* moments. Unexpectedly, Mr. Asher's story actually fit the bill, and it shows how sometimes it takes a while to realize if an incident is truly a *kan tzipor* moment.

156

You might disagree with my conclusion, but the only way you'll know is by reading what he told me that day.

❧

I'm a *shomer Shabbos* taxi driver, Shlomo Asher told me, who comes to shul every Shabbos, and whenever I can do so during the week. Once, since I had just dropped off a fare in the neighborhood, I got on the taxi line at La Guardia Airport, which is located here, in the New York City borough of Queens, to wait for any passenger who might need a ride. Almost immediately, the dispatcher on duty motioned to a man that my cab would take him to his destination, so he opened the back door of my taxi and sat down. I asked where he needed to go, and after hesitating somewhat, he said, "To Brooklyn. Do you have a problem taking me there?"

I know that many taxi drivers don't like to go to Brooklyn, but I didn't mind, so I told him, "Not a problem. What's the exact address?"

After the passenger gave me the address, which was someplace in the Flatbush section, we both settled in for the ride that usually takes about forty-five minutes to an hour, depending on traffic. I asked the fellow his name, which was Shimon, and since I recognized from the man's accent that he was a fellow Israeli, I began speaking to him in Hebrew, which prompted my passenger to feel very much at ease. Within a minute, Shimon and I were chatting away a mile a minute in our native Hebrew.

Within minutes of leaving the airport we hit heavy traffic, which is one of the reasons many people avoid flying in to La Guardia, but since it gave us time to schmooze, neither I nor my passenger, Shimon, minded. When I asked him what business he was in, he said he was "in diamonds," and when he didn't specify if he processed them or was a salesman, I didn't pry.

"Are you returning from a business trip?" I asked, to which Shimon replied, "Yes."

Sensing that my passenger was no longer eager for conversation, I pushed a button that resulted in Avraham Fried's mellow voice filling my taxi, and both of us enjoyed the CD until we found ourselves on Ocean Parkway, passing Avenue P, headed toward the higher avenues of Flatbush.

On Avenue S I swung left and began driving towards the higher street numbers. As we neared Shimon's destination, I slowed down, and when we reached the exact address, I announced, "Here we are."

Shimon glanced at the meter and handed me three $20 bills. While I was distractedly preparing the change, I asked Shimon, "Which floor do you live on?"

"I live in two rooms in the basement."

"Really? Wow! You told me you have a wife and two young girls. How do you all fit in?" I asked as I turned to hand the change to my passenger.

Our eyes met. As Shimon accepted the change he lowered his eyes, and when he didn't lift them I faced forward so as not to embarrass him further. Then I purposely didn't say another word, waiting to see if Shimon would open the taxi door and leave, or remain to continue our conversation.

A full minute elapsed before Shimon said, in a somewhat strangled voice, "Actually, I'm in the process of getting divorced now, so I moved out of our apartment several months ago. I took this apartment because it was the closest one available to where my wife and two daughters live. I want to be close to my two daughters, no matter how distasteful my apartment is. I have a very good relationship with my two girls. And frankly, I don't have a bad relationship with my former wife either. Actually, she's still my wife. We're not divorced yet, but we had to separate. It just wasn't working out."

Hearing the pain in Shimon's voice, I was torn. Should I tell him I have to find another passenger so he'll get out, or should I spend the time it might take to encourage him to stop being a fool and return to his family? I am not a trained counselor, and my personal history doesn't make me a good role model. Maybe in Israel it is acceptable to mix into someone else's private life, but here in America, "Mind your own business" is almost a law, so why should I make a fool of myself?

One part of me told me to ask him to leave my taxi and forget about him, but the rabbi of our shul had spoken just that previous Shabbos about *kol Yisrael areivim zeh ba-zeh*,[1] every Jew being responsible for every other Jew since we are all descendants of our Three Forefathers, so how could I not try to help this man?

Yes, no. No, yes. I couldn't decide. What if he got angry? What if he got aggressive? But how could I face my rabbi if next Shabbos he asked us if we had passed up an opportunity to help a fellow Jew? Could I lie to him? The answer to that question empowered me, and the next thing I heard was myself asking Shimon, "So tell me, what happened? Why are you getting divorced?"

I was shocked that my passenger didn't get angry or aggressive. In fact, just the opposite. His next words were spoken in a voice that sounded relieved that he had someone to whom he could unburden himself. So I turned and faced him while he did just that. "My wife and I were never really all that observant. We both grew up in *chiloni* families, we got married, and then we moved to America.

"When our two daughters were old enough to go to school, we didn't want them mixing with all the riff-raff, so we decided

---

1. *Shavuos* 39a.

to enroll them in a school with observant Jewish kids. And, of course, they began coming home with songs and stories about Shabbat and *kashrut* and all kinds of other things, including *chagim*. It was nice, it was cute, and neither I nor my wife had any problem with it. It was all kids' stuff.

"But as the girls grew older, it wasn't just songs and games and stories. Starting from when the older one was in third grade, both of the girls started asking us why we, their parents, were not religious, and if that was the best way to live, without Hashem in our world. By then, my wife had no problem taking on more mitzvot, so she started lighting candles on Friday nights and buying kosher food. I had no problem with that, as it had nothing to do with me. Then she started praying, going to shul, and dressing in skirts instead of pants.

"That's how, slowly but surely, I realized that my wife and I had grown distant from each other. She was going in one direction, and I was stuck in another direction. After a while, we realized we weren't that compatible anymore, so several months ago I decided that it was time for me to move out. That's what I did, and now I live alone in the basement of this house."

When Shimon finished sharing his sad tale, I said, "I want you to know, your life story mirrors mine. My wife and I also were not all that religious. And when we came to New York from Tel Aviv, we also enrolled our kids in Beis Yaakov because we didn't want them going to school with the lower classes and learning from them to do drugs and other terrible things.

"Then, also because of what our children were learning in their Jewish school, little by little, together, my wife and I started to become more observant. It took a long time. We took three steps forward and two steps back, always realizing that what we were doing was building a meaningful life together for ourselves and for our children. The more I got into the religion and the more I got into Torah learning, the more I felt a purpose in life and the happier I was, and it was the same for my wife.

"Today I go to shul on a regular basis, and I don't drive my taxi on Shabbos. We're not yet perfect with all the laws, but we're certainly much farther along than we were when we decided to preserve our family. It was a process that wasn't always easy. My wife and I didn't always agree on everything, but we agreed on one thing: we really love each other, and we greatly love our children, so this was going to be the best thing for us in the long run.

"Listen to me, Shimon. I hope you don't mind me calling you by your given name, because by now I feel close to you. You told me that you kind of get along with your wife, right?"

"No, I don't mind you calling me Shimon . And yes, I said we had a wonderful marriage until this religion thing broke us apart."

"Right, that *is* what you said. So listen to me: Go back to your wife, go back to your two sweet daughters, and tell them you're going to try to make your marriage work. It will surely be a slow process. I know because 'I've been there and done that'! But in the end, you will succeed. Before that success you'll certainly have many failures. Don't let them scare you, and don't allow them to derail you. Tell your wife and daughters that what you want most in life is to be together with them. Friday night you want to eat dinner together. You want to give them a blessing before you recite Kiddush. Love them and do all you can do to make them happy and proud of you.

"Do all the things that you *can* do and then, if for a while you still have to work on Shabbat, do it secretly. Never drive away from in front of your apartment. When you drive your car or take a cab on Shabbos, park or get into your car or taxi two blocks away. Do what you feel you have to do secretly, until you can bring yourself to stop, but be careful never to embarrass your wife or confuse your precious daughters.

"About kosher food: Listen, you now live in Brooklyn, home to plenty of kosher restaurants and tons of kosher takeout food stores. You can buy almost anything kosher that you used to buy non-kosher. You can even get kosher sushi, and all types of kosher Chinese and Italian food. And when you crave actual non-kosher food, then eat it, but never in your home and never in your neighborhood where anyone who knows your wife and kids can see you. When you take the wife and kids out to eat, always choose a strictly kosher restaurant. And make sure that when you take the kids for pizza, it's to a strictly kosher dairy place.

"Encourage your kids to be religious and respect your wife for being religious. Tell them that you appreciate them going to yeshivah and studying Torah. When you meet with the rabbi, make sure you wear a *kippah*. Following my advice, little by little you'll get closer to your wife and kids, and you'll see, after a while, that you won't need to rebel and go against G-d. You'll be so happy that you'll feel that being religious and keeping all the negative as well as the positive mitzvot is a small price to pay for the joy you'll have. You shouldn't be living in a basement all by yourself, Shimon. That's not the kind of life you deserve. You're better than that. You truly are."

Shimon the diamond dealer — or whatever he did in diamonds, I never really found out — was in shock. "I...I don't know. I'm not sure I'm ready to do all of that. I was never a good actor, but I'll think about it."

And with that, Shimon got out of the cab and ran up the driveway to the entrance to his basement apartment...totally forgetting to tip me.

And that was the end of the story. I didn't hear another word from the man. Sometimes I wondered what had happened to Shimon, but since he had never mentioned his last name, I had no way of finding out how his story had ended.

Until last summer.

When my daughters were in Camp Sternberg, my wife and I drove up to the mountains on visiting day, and while I was strolling around the campgrounds with our kids, I thought I saw a man who reminded me of Shimon, the man I had driven from La Guardia to Flatbush. But, no, it couldn't be; this guy must be what's called a *Doppelganger* of the man I once drove. But then that person broke away from his family and walked over to me, and as he came closer I was sure that this was the guy!

"Shimon, is that really you?" I cried out.

The man ran the last few feet that separated us and gave me a big hug. Then he said, "Yes, it's me, Shimon, the man you drove from the airport to Flatbush! And what happened to me is that after giving your heartfelt words much thought over several days, I listened to you. I called my wife and told her about the ride I got from a taxi driver who picked me up at La Guardia, and the conversation we had when I reached my basement apartment. I shared the story of your life with her and told her that you urged me to do all in my power to save our marriage. Then I explained exactly the plan you had laid out for me, and asked her if she was willing to accept me on those terms. When she agreed, I moved out of that basement and back in with my family.

"It's been years since that taxi ride, and little by little it's working. I'm not there yet one hundred percent, but oh so slowly, I'm getting there. This is the first year we've sent our daughters to Camp Sternberg, and here you are, the person who influenced me so positively."

He gave me a friendly slap on my back, then he turned, took out his wallet, and handed me a five and a ten. "As soon as I got into my apartment I realized I hadn't tipped you," he said. "Take this. It's yours!" And with that, he walked quickly back to his wife and daughters, and I never saw him again.

"So tell me, Mr. Savitsky, was that a *kan tzipor* moment I had in my cab or not? When I just heard you speak about *kan tzipor* moments, it sounded as if you were describing exactly what I experienced with Shimon. I could have ignored his sad story and driven off to find my next fare; there was enough reason for me to do so. But I overcame my hesitancy and obeyed what my rabbi had spoken about the Shabbat before I picked him up: *Kol Yisrael areivim zeh ba-zeh.* That's what gave me the courage to spend almost an hour convincing him that he should go back to his wife and kids.

"And now that I heard your speech, I feel like, wow! What I did was truly special because despite my great hesitancy I took advantage of that one moment and allowed that little bird-story to fly into my life. *Ki yikarei…lema'an yitav lach.* It had to be orchestrated by Hashem, because if it wasn't, what were the odds of picking up a Jewish man whose life almost paralleled mine, so that my words could help save him and his family?

"Please tell me that this was a *kan tzipor* moment, Mr. Savitsky! It's a great message, and people should know that one never knows when overcoming their hesitancy and saying the right thing at the right time to someone who has to hear it ends up being an instance of *ki yikarei…lema'an yitav lach, lema'an ya'arichun yamecha.* I'm not sure I'm quoting the Torah correctly, but if I made a mistake, I'll eventually learn to say it right."

That taxi driver who heard me speak in the shul in which I had davened during the first twelve years of our marriage couldn't wait to tell me his story, which he strongly believed was a genuine *kan tzipor* moment — and I agree.

If One Is Good,
Two Are Better

THE SECOND INTIFADA STARTED in September 2000 and continued until February 8, 2005. This was a very frightening time in Israel. Buses were being blown up. People were afraid to go to restaurants. Tourism was way down, and so were the spirits of Israelis, especially since there seemed to be no solution to the constant civilian deaths or to the plummeting economy.

In the summer of 2001, the Orthodox Union decided to conduct several small missions to Israel, each of them consisting of thirty to fifty people. We would spend one week there, consoling families who had sadly lost someone in a terrorist attack. We would visit the almost empty stores and purchase as many items as we could take home with us. And we would meet with political leaders, all in the hope of showing support and solidarity with *acheinu Bnei Yisrael*.

I was privileged to have been selected to be the chair of several of these missions, which were extremely rewarding and truly unforgettable. Those meticulously planned missions achieved their goals, but for me and most of my OU colleagues, there is one such trip that we'll always remember: the mission that left New York on Thursday, August 9, 2001.

Unfortunately, at that point in time, like so many Jews the world over, my associates and I had become somewhat desensitized when hearing of yet another bus, car, or roadside suicide bombing that claimed the lives of civilians and soldiers, young and old, citizens and tourists. This did not diminish the seriousness of our interactions with our suffering brothers and sisters, but rather strengthened our resolve to meet them so that we could personally demonstrate our empathy and support.

And then we began hearing details of the latest suicide bombing, which caused all of those on our mission to shed bitter tears and wonder if it was wise to actually board a plane and fly into the genuine danger posed by Palestinian madmen.

As we bid our families goodbye and headed to the airport, we were still trying to understand how, exactly, we would conduct our mission once we arrived. The news we had just heard was devastating: Fifteen people had been killed, including seven children, and about a hundred and thirty had been injured, some of them critically, in a suicide bombing at the Sbarro pizzeria in the heart of Jerusalem.

Concealing the explosives in a guitar case which he had carried with him into Jerusalem, the terrorist had entered the restaurant just before 2:00 PM and detonated an eleven- to twenty-two-pound bomb, which was packed with nails, screws, and bolts to ensure maximum devastation. It had completely gutted the restaurant, which was full of lunchtime diners.

The terrorist was killed in the blast. His controller was on the list of wanted terrorists submitted by Israel to the Palestinian Authority during that week. Hamas and Islamic Jihad each claimed responsibility for the attack, so proud were those terrorists of the innocent Jewish blood they had spilled.

And all of world Jewry mourned.

This happened before I began delving into the mitzvah of

shilu'ach ha-kan, and long before I began giving speeches about *kan tzipor* moments. But today, when I look back at how that mission played out, I realize that actually there were two significant *kan tzipor* moments associated with the trip to Israel we took that summer.

The first one happened at the airport. Picture the scene: All of us had just heard broadcasts about the carnage that had taken place as children and adults had been blown to pieces while innocently waiting in line at the Sbarro pizza shop on the corner of Rechov Yaffo and HaMelech George. All of us at the airport who were Jewish felt as if that bomb had obliterated family members.

JFK was its usual tumultuous self, but those in our mission, who had come a bit early, stood together near the El Al terminal entrance, waiting for the others, as we didn't want to go through security until everyone in our mission arrived.

As I waited, I noticed two other people, who looked like a religious husband and wife, enter the El Al terminal, and I wondered why they would be traveling to Israel at such a dangerous time. Was it the wedding of a close relative? The bar mitzvah of a grandson, which they simply could not miss no matter the danger? Otherwise, their intention to board our flight simply made no sense.

As if they had read the questions playing ping-pong in my mind, they walked over to me and, after introducing themselves, the wife said, "When we heard the news about what happened in Jerusalem today, at first we were paralyzed by the sheer horror of this latest tragedy. But then, each of us decided, separately, and then told the other, that we must immediately head to the airport and get on El Al's next flight out of New York. We felt that the only way we could absorb this terrible news and still live with ourselves was to fly to Israel to demonstrate our solidarity with our Jewish brothers and sisters. We read in our community newspaper about your mission. You are part of the OU group flying to Israel today, correct?"

When I nodded, the husband picked up where the wife had left off. "So, we'd like to join you. Is that possible? I really hope you say yes! Mind you, by nature Mindy and I are not globetrotters. In fact, the last time we boarded a plane was five years ago! But when we heard about the bombing at Sbarro, we dropped all of our plans for the rest of the day, and for as long as your mission will be in Eretz Yisrael. We had no time to shop for gifts for our relatives. We didn't even have time to say goodbye to our family, friends, and neighbors. In fact, we even forgot to call El Al and find out if there's room for us on your flight. We simply threw some clothing into duffle bags, grabbed our passports, and headed here. Can we join you? Would you go with us to the ticket agent and help us buy tickets?"

I was so impressed by this couple's genuine *ahavas Yisrael* that there was no way I could refuse them. So the three of us went to the ticket counter, where we were told that our flight was ninety percent empty. They didn't have much trouble using their credit card to purchase two seats in coach class, and I was happy to tell the ticket agent that they should be seated near our group, as they were our guests. Since we had made arrangements to wait for our departure in the King David Lounge, this couple, whom we'll call the Katzensteins, came along with us.

Since this took place long before I began seeking *kan tzipor* moments, I didn't think about what a truly *kan tzipor* moment the Katzensteins had experienced when they put their life on hold and flew with us to bring comfort and healing to Israel's reeling population. But as I write this book, I am convinced that this is exactly why they came to JFK, determined to get to Israel no matter the sacrifice, no matter the cost. Their heroic decision surely meets the four criteria that turn a simple story of *hash-gachah pratis* into a genuine *kan tzipor* moment.

When they heard the devastating news, they said to themselves, "What does Hashem want me to do that will be helpful?" With no previous planning or preparation, without consulting anyone, they did something way out of their comfort zone: they grabbed their passports, threw some clothes into a bag, and headed to the airport so as not to miss the opportunity to join our group, which they knew from an article they had read would be leaving that day. In order to truly make a difference in the lives of at least some Israelis, they simply showed up at the airport.

If that wasn't a *kan tzipor* moment whose reward would be *lema'an yitav lach*, I don't know what is.

When we landed in Israel, we immediately realized that the terrorist attack (as well as those preceding it), had dealt the entire country a major blow. Our first indication of that very sad fact was how empty Ben Gurion Airport was; it was practically deserted. Our second indication of the shock that bomb had created was how swiftly we traveled from the airport to Jerusalem; there were hardly any cars on the highways, and traffic on the capital's streets was a fraction of what any of us remembered.

But our biggest barometer of how badly that bomb had disturbed Israelis came after we had checked into the Plaza Hotel and settled into our rooms. I had arranged for us to meet with Jerusalem's mayor, Ehud Olmert, who eventually became prime minister, in a conference room at our hotel about two hours after we were scheduled to land, and...he simply didn't show up! When I called his secretary to ask if he was on the way or had been unexpectedly delayed, she said, "You really arrived? I'm shocked! Everyone's been canceling on us, so we didn't dream Americans would actually come after what happened yesterday afternoon!"

To Olmert's credit, he showed up a short time later and said, "I sincerely apologize. I noticed in my calendar that I was expected to meet with members of the Orthodox Union early this afternoon at the Plaza Hotel, but I'll be honest with you. Every other group canceled, so I assumed that you canceled, as well. I should have realized that no matter what happened, you'd keep your appointment, since Orthodox Jews come to Israel even when the level of security we can provide visitors is quite low. My mistake, ladies and gentlemen. I apologize."

We spent a glorious Shabbos in Jerusalem, going out of our way to converse with, and comfort, as many Jews as possible. And after Havdalah, we kept to our meticulously prearranged schedule that included meetings with political leaders, as well as heads of communities around the country.

One day, we went to visit a community in Yehudah and Shomron, which back then was the least secure area in Israel since the Palestinians, who called that section of the country "the West Bank," claimed that every Israeli who lived there was not a resident but an "illegal occupier." Many of the terrorist attacks during the Intifada took place on its roads. Israelis who lived there, and even those who came to the area to visit relatives, were afraid to drive their cars for fear of roadside bombings. Residents were afraid to leave their homes, and buses in that part of the country ran their regular routes only if they were specially fitted with bulletproof windows and other safety devices that would provide the drivers, as well as the passengers, some measure of protection.

But we had made the long, grueling trip to Israel to show our solidarity with all of its citizens, so we arrived as scheduled in the Shomron and drove to a small community whose name I've forgotten. We met with the mayor as well as with regular citizens, and whomever we spoke with shared with us what it was like for them to live in disputed territories during the Intifada; how fear stalked them each and every day; how from minute to minute, they never knew in what danger they would find themselves; how if you got into your car, you were never sure if you'd reach your destination alive, and if you did, you didn't know if you'd make it back home.

I clearly recall one woman, who was dressed in a nurse's uniform, telling us, "I'm a bit embarrassed to tell this to you, but when I leave my house in the morning — I work in Yerushalayim — I make sure every room in our apartment is spotless, that the beds are neatly made, and there are no dishes in the sink, because I don't know if I'll be coming back, and I don't want people to think badly about me as a housekeeper. I hug and kiss my children goodbye every time they go outside to play or to school, because I don't know if I'll ever see them again."

We met with people from different backgrounds who lived in that community, and each story we heard was more compelling than the last. When one of our local hosts spontaneously decided that it was time for our delegation to meet a group of teens, who would tell us what it was like for them to live under the constant threat of terror attacks, we readily agreed. Surely Israel's junior generation would be more hopeful, more upbeat.

When we were all settled in the local community center and had been introduced to the group of teenagers as people from America who had flown to Israel specifically to show their solidarity during the Intifada, one of the locals turned to the youngsters: "Which one of you will tell our guests what it's like going to school here?"

An obviously self-confident teen, who looked as if she'd be a stewardess one day, stood up and said, "Unfortunately, if you're a teenager living in our community, you can't go to school these days, and I'll tell you why. You see, elementary school kids have no problem with getting an education even now because our community has a great school for them right here in our *yishuv*. But there is no high school here. Each day we older kids have to commute for about half an hour to the closest one, which for us, given the level of Palestinian terror, is impossible."

When the motherly Mrs. Katzenstein asked the girl why it was impossible, the young lady smiled at her and replied, "Because our school buses are not bulletproof and their windows aren't shatterproof. And since our community has no funds to get the buses retrofitted, we haven't been able to attend school during the last few months, since the Intifada heated up way more than before."

This conversation took place long before Zoom was even on anyone's drawing board, so all of that small community's teens, who in the past traveled to their high school each day on two buses, were stuck at home with no possibility of continuing their education. A tall, lanky boy with a shock of red hair then stood up and addressed us. "In most of the families who live here, both parents work, so once they leave in the morning, and our younger siblings scamper off to the elementary school, we're really both bored and lonely. And since we never know when we might be attacked, we can't even meet outside to play sports or do other activities. There's no fun in the world worth being injured or killed."

All of us were watching the kids who had come to share their predicament with us, and seeing their forlorn faces and hopeless body language made a huge impression on us. Compared to kids their age living in our neighborhoods, these teenagers seemed almost depressed.

We expected other kids to speak up, but no one seemed to want to say anything more, so a heavy silence descended on the simple community social hall in which we were meeting, until one of the gentlemen in our group, I'll call him Jake Schmidt, quickly raised himself to his full height of six feet, three inches, pivoted to face the rest of us, and spontaneously said, "Listen here, ladies and gentlemen. Why did we come on this mission? What are we doing in this small town? It's not so we can go back home and tell the folks what a good time we had. We've just listened to representatives of these boys and girls telling us about their life, how they can't go to high school because their buses are not retrofitted so that they're safe enough to transport them to the nearest high school building.

"Now, we came on this mission with no clear idea of any little side trips we might make after meeting the movers and shakers, the politicians and the businessmen. But G-d arranged that we should come here, to this lovely small *yishuv*, and He arranged that we should listen to these teens' problems."

Jake didn't use the phrase *"kan tzipor* moment" because I hadn't invented it yet, but he did continue speaking as if he were prophesying what I would do a few years down the road:

"When I hear G-d calling out to all of us saying, 'Well, you OU *chevrah* from New York, what are you going to do about this really perplexing problem?', although I'm not the leader of our mission, if it were up to me, we wouldn't leave here until we'd raised enough money to retrofit those two buses so these kids can go back to school. I'll donate five thousand dollars. Who's going to match me, and is anybody ready to double my donation?"

Before I knew it, pledges of $5,000, $6,000, $1,000, $500, whatever each of us could give, flew past me at the speed of a hockey puck at a professional game. And in a very short while, our mission had raised enough money to retrofit the two buses. People wrote out checks on the spot and handed them to the town's mayor, who kept saying, "I can't believe this, I simply can't believe this!"

When I asked Mr. Mayor how long it would take to retrofit the buses, he answered, "Not that long, maybe even under two weeks." Then he turned to the teens who were ecstatic and jabbering like a gaggle of happy geese — the guys slapping each other on the back, the girls hugging each other — and when he had quieted them, he announced, "In two weeks from today, thanks to the generosity of these wonderful people from America's Orthodox Union, you'll finally be able to go to high school and catch up on all the learning you missed! Please, all together, tell these wonderful people thank you!"

And that's what those happy teens did.

Thinking back on that solidarity mission, I know that although we had been granted the opportunity to meet briefly with Prime Minister Ariel Sharon and had other encounters that had strengthened our connection to our People and our Land, what we did for those kids in those few minutes was the most uplifting part of our entire trip. Today, I know that I was left with that feeling because it was a true *kan tzipor* moment. When Jake Schmidt stood up and called upon us all to hear G-d's call, we stepped up to the plate and made a big difference in the lives of those teenagers. No committee was formed, no agenda was typed up, no meetings that featured endless debate were held, and certainly no board of directors took all the credit!

None of us had the slightest inkling, when we entered that small town in the Shomron, that we would be called upon to write checks for serious sums. But not one of us refused Jake's call, which was actually G-d's call. And in exchange, we all felt, even before our bus pulled out of that *yishuv*, the glow of *lema'an yitav lach*.

That wasn't simply a great *kan tzipor* moment, it was a great *group kan tzipor* moment. All of us, as a united group, heeded G-d's call and collectively seized the moment, that one moment in time when G-d put us in a place where we could make a difference in so many lives.

And we are forever grateful.

More than twenty years have passed since that day, and when I meet anyone who was on that mission to Israel with me, I invariably hear, "Hey, remember when we went to that small community and we retrofitted those buses? I still feel that glow, Steve, and I bet you do, too!"

A Strange Encounter at Burlington

ONE SATURDAY NIGHT IN the fall, when Shabbos is over early, our daughter Penina went to the Burlington department store in Lawrence, New York, with her teenaged son Josh to buy some clothing. Although they realized that the store might be crowded, they decided to go anyway. But the store was so jammed with shoppers flocking to an advertised sale, that the long lines at the cashiers' area predicted that it would take well over an hour and a half simply to check out.

This is how Penina told me what happened there.

My first thought when I realized that we most probably should have saved this outing for another time was to simply leave. But when Josh said, "Aw, Mom, I really need some of the things I put on that list you asked me to make!" I came up with what I thought was a brilliant plan.

"Listen carefully," I told Josh as we worked our way around a large group of boisterous teens shoving their way through the crowded aisles to the exit. "You have the list that you made of the items you need. Go to the check-out counters where you'll surely be able to grab a cart that's just been emptied by a shopper who is about to pay. I'll head to the very back of the store, where I'll get on a line to the cashiers. While I wait our turn, you can shop the teen department where I trust you to select whatever you need, in colors that please both of us, and work well with your other clothing. After you try on everything you pick out, come back down here to the main floor and find me. By the time you return, my place on line should be about halfway to the cashiers' area.

"Then we'll switch places; you'll stay with the wagon while I pick up a few important items I need, and by the time I rejoin you on the line, it shouldn't take us that long to finish our business here. This is the only way we'll get home at a decent hour. Can I count on you, Josh?"

We smiled sheepishly at each other as we noticed several others on that line who also didn't have carts or even items in their hands, happy that we were far from the only ones who had figured out a clever way to contend with the overflow of shoppers and too few clerks to check them out. Josh went toward the front of the high-ceilinged main floor to grab a shopping cart, and I made my way in the very narrow space between what might have once been an aisle but was now bordered on both sides by heavily laden racks touting sale merchandise, through which a long, snaking line of shoppers reached almost to the very back of the store. When I finally took my place in the back of the last shopper who was standing in that line, I realized that even with our ploy, I was in for a very long wait. *What moms don't do for their kids!* I thought.

Hoping that Josh would be back quite soon so we could switch places and I could look for the items I planned to buy, my mood was as upbeat as the popular music blaring from the sound system. And since there was nothing for me to do but wait until Josh returned, when the woman in front of me on that slow-moving line smiled and then struck up a conversation, frankly, I was delighted. Since I'm a mom to six kids, bless them, and I also invest lots of hours each day in my event-planning business, I'm kind of an expert at making casual conversation with teachers, the moms of my kids' friends, and people sitting near me during the long stretches of time I spend in doctors' waiting rooms, so there was no reason for me not to welcome the diversion.

Eyeing the bedlam in that store, the woman commented, "Now we know why increasing numbers of Americans prefer ordering what they need from department stores that home-deliver." I told her that when I returned home I was definitely going to sign up with Amazon, thinking that since we had been polite but distant, she'd turn to face the front of the store and our interaction would be over.

I discovered how wrong I was when she said, "My name is Flora Rainer, and when I'm not wasting my time in Burlington on a beautiful Saturday night, I'm enjoying every minute of the work I do as a divorce attorney."

After that more personal gambit, Flora asked me for my name and what I did, and since her sense of humor amused me, I introduced myself as Nina Wiener, the best event planner in Woodmere, swallowing the beginning of my Hebrew first name so that it shouldn't become a topic of inquiry, and possible confusion.

Flora took a step further toward our possible friendship when she added that she was a divorced mom living with two teenaged kids in the Forest Hills section of Queens, New York, so I shared that our house and my business were situated in Woodmere. And when I did not mention that we had been blessed with six children, a fact that in the past had garnered various unwelcome comments, she was mensch enough not to pursue that topic, which raised my opinion of this Flora person several notches.

After that, our conversation ping-ponged from one topic to another — from work schedules to the weather, from politics to the current most popular diet craze — constantly peppered by the penchant we both seemed to have for a mixture of wit and, I'm not ashamed to say, womanly wisdom. And as the line of shoppers inched forward, we passed the time we were forced to wait in a most enjoyable manner.

Before I realized how much time had passed since I had stepped onto that line, Josh returned to my side pushing a cart that contained what he hoped I would pay for without putting up too much of a fuss at some of his choices. Yes, I *do* know my son inside out, and I love him to pieces. And before he could utter even one word of the little speech I was sure he had prepared to prevent my objections to one or two items that he suspected I might not fully approve of, I noticed Flora's jaw drop and her eyebrows shoot up at the sight of his *kippah*.

"Wow!" she said. "I'm more than impressed with you and your son! I...I didn't realize that you were an Orthodox Jew, Nina! I'm also Jewish, although I bet you wouldn't have guessed, right? The truth is that I know very little about *being* Jewish, but lately I find myself increasingly interested in learning more. Meeting you here, enjoying our conversation, and now seeing your son has kind of perked my interest even more."

Having been raised in my parents' home, and having listened for years to the speeches Dad has given countless times about his favorite topic, namely the opportunities presented by *kan tzipor* moments, it suddenly dawned on me that G-d might have just tapped *me* on the shoulder, offering me the opportunity to help Flora draw closer to her roots. With lightning speed, the following thoughts flashed through my mind:

I've always loved to do chesed for people, and I know all about my dad's kan tzipor moment concept but I've never been presented with my very own kan tzipor moment. Here I am on a Saturday night in Burlington, where I've had the most interesting conversation with a woman who I was sure was a total stranger. And now, thanks to Josh's kippah, I discover that she's Jewish, too! And she just volunteered, unashamedly, that she's interested in learning more about the religion we share! As Dad would say, "Penina, this is your kan tzipor moment! It's now or never!"

So I silently signaled to my dear, slightly confused Josh to step aside so that I'd have a bit of privacy, which he immediately did. His unexpected, unquestioning agreement led me to believe that he'd use this favor he had just granted me as a bargaining chip if I put up a fuss about any of the flashy-colored weekday shirts he had selected. How I loved that boy, and how I wished that by now he'd have learned to hide his thoughts from me a bit more successfully! Anyway, when he was out of earshot, I asked Flora, "Do you have a specific aspect of Judaism that you're interested in learning about? If you ask me a few questions while we're schlepping forward in this line as if we were snails on vacation, I'll do my best to answer them."

"Great," she said with a smile. "I know that the Orthodox don't go to work on the Sabbath, and they don't shovel snow or wash their cars in their driveways then either, which I can understand, since they consider it their day of rest, and all of those chores *are* tiring. What I *don't* understand is why you also don't turn lights on or off, turn on your TVs, light up your grills so you can barbecue, or drive your cars. If you did, trust me, you'd enjoy your Sabbath even more. But as far as I've heard, the rabbis won't allow any of it, so I'm sure you're not about to change your lifestyle."

Ignoring her last remark, I did my best to explain how the

Torah defines the concept of "a day of rest," and I also made sure that Flora heard me say that it was G-d who had prohibited many tasks that to the uninitiated appeared to limit the enjoyment of Shabbos, not "the rabbis." And that's when I also mentioned that since G-d had created the universe in six days and had "rested" on the seventh, observing Shabbos as we Orthodox do by refraining from performing all tasks that involve even the slightest bit of creativity — as defined by the Talmud — we proclaim to all of humankind that G-d is the world's Creator and Master.

As both of us inched along, ever closer to a cashier, Flora challenged me with additional questions while Josh followed me with his shopping cart at a slight distance, puzzled by how seriously I was participating in Flora's spontaneous interrogation instead of leaving that slow-moving line and shopping for the items he knew I had planned to buy. But with an agenda of his own, which he thought I wasn't aware of, he wasn't about to interrupt my conversation with Flora by questioning me about this strange encounter at Burlington.

Little did my dear Josh know that a part of me — the part that was always so proud of how my dad mesmerized audiences with the life lessons he imparted, gleaned from his in-depth study of the puzzling mitzvah of *shilu'ach ha-kan* — was eager to fully embrace this long-hoped-for *kan tzipor* moment. But there was another part of me, a strong negative voice, that was urging me not to get involved in Flora's life, and to allow Flora and her hopes for herself and her kids to find someone with fewer responsibilities to deal with her yearnings. After all, where would I find the strength, the time and the stamina to also be the best mom, wife, and daughter that I longed to be, if I took Flora fully under my wing as I must do if I jumped at the opportunity to fulfill this *kan tzipor* moment? Allowing this mitzvah to become a priority in my life would leave little time or energy for me! And proof of that was that although when I had headed out to this store I had planned on treating myself to several items I really didn't need but simply wanted, thanks to Flora's interrogation, I would not be doing any such thing tonight!

But when I noticed that Flora was sorting the clothing in her cart so that when it was her turn to hand over her credit card, immediately after the couple standing in front of her, the transaction would be handled as quickly as possible, I reminded myself that if I didn't take the serious conversation we had been having to the next level, my very first *kan tzipor* moment, which very well might be *the only one* granted to me, might slip away, forever.

So pushing all other concerns from my mind, determined not to allow this moment to slip away, I said, "Flora, it looks like both of us will be checked out of this store in a very short while after which I guess you'll return to Forest Hills and I'll head back to Woodmere, and the friendship I felt blossoming between us tonight will simply wilt and die. I so don't want that to happen! I know you're a busy attorney, and I have two events that I'm in charge of pulling off with pizazz this week, so there's little chance of us having any time together given our whirlwind weekdays.

"Flora, please, please agree to come to our house in Woodmere this Friday afternoon and spend Shabbos with me and my family! Bring along your kids, and let's give ourselves a real chance to become the sisters-by-choice I felt we were this past hour here in Burlington!"

"You want me and my family to actually experience twenty-five hours of what you call Shabbos?"

"That's exactly what I want! You can't imagine the island of serenity that G-d gifted us when He commanded us to observe the laws of Shabbos! And trust me when I tell you that you and your kids have never tasted the very special foods I prepare to honor the day! Flora, I guarantee that after you accept my heartfelt invitation and spend the hours between sundown on Friday and nightfall on Saturday as our guests, you will understand that I'm not trying to brainwash you but rather to give you a gift no one has ever given you before."

The spontaneous hug Flora gave me was interrupted by the cashier shouting, "NEXT," so Flora quickly dropped her arms to her side and proceeded to place her merchandise on the counter. Not three minutes later, Josh heard another shout of "NEXT." I handed my credit card to a smiling Josh who, I knew, was thrilled that because Flora and I were involved in what teens like to call a DMC[1] he would now be able to pay for his clothing without having to justify some of the more trendy items that might have not met my instant approval.

When the three of us were finally finished with Burlington, I heaved a sigh of relief. And as Flora, Josh, and I walked out of that merchandising madness into the starry, crisp night, I handed Josh the keys to the car and instructed him to wait in the front seat for me to finish my conversation with Mrs. Rainer.

As Josh's back receded into the darkness, the two of us leaned against the store's façade. "So, Flora," I said, "can I count on you and your kids? Will the three of you be our Shabbos guests this coming weekend?"

Flora didn't have to tell me her answer; it was totally understood from her posture. So, eager to take my *kan tzipor* moment to the next level, I added, "Come on, say yes! Not only will you

---

1. Deep Meaningful Conversation.

have to diet for at least three days after you get treated to my culinary delights, but I know that you'll enjoy the prayer services at our synagogue, and we even have a teen service, so your kids will enjoy the services as well."

Flora placed the purchases she had been clutching onto the asphalt sidewalk, inhaled deeply, and declared, "Nina, I might take you up on your invitation, if not this week then sometime in the future. I'm not planning to disappear from your life. But whenever that happens, know that I will not go to services in your synagogue."

The pain in Flora's voice was so strong and so genuine that all I could say was what I whisper to any of my kids when they come home from school utterly distraught: "Do you want to talk about it?"

And to my utter surprise, she did.

Staring out into the dark night, she said, "About a month or so ago, during the High Holidays, I decided that it might be a good idea for me to go to a synagogue. As I told you, I live in Forest Hills, so I walked into that community's Young Israel just to look around and try to feel what one feels in the House of G-d. To their credit, people *did* notice me, and one of them even asked me what I was doing there, and if I was looking for someone. I answered honestly by telling her, 'I don't know.'

"Now, as I think back on that very painful experience, I realize that my answer must have raised their suspicions, because about three minutes later, as I was reading a bronze plaque that was hanging on the wall, a security guard walked over to me and said, 'Look, if you didn't reserve a seat in the sanctuary, and you really don't know what you're doing here, perhaps it's best that you leave.' So I left. In a very polite way, to me they practically threw me out of that synagogue! So please, Nina, don't for a minute think I'm going to relive that experience."

"They didn't throw you out," I protested. "Since you admitted that you didn't know anyone there, and didn't know *why* you were there, given the anti-Semitism so rampant these days, and that in Israel terrorists often use women as suicide bombers, what else could they do? Had you told them that you were seeking connection to your religion, and that you wanted to hear a bit of the High Holiday service so you could decide whether it touched your heart, I'm sure they would have welcomed you with open arms."

Flora turned to me, her brow wrinkled in deep thought, and said in a pain-filled voice, "Most probably you're right, but that one of them summoned the security guard was a...surprise that turned me off synagogues, of that you can be sure!"

Flora's pain hurt me beyond measure, but I can't deny that there was a lilt in my voice when I said, "Well, my dear new friend, not all surprises are sad ones, and the one I'm about to share with you is what I'd call 'heaven-sent': Believe it or not, one of my nephews, Ashie Schreier, a young, talented, and tremendously capable man, is the rabbi of the Young Israel of Forest Hills. He will be appalled that this is what happened while High Holiday services were taking place in his synagogue, and I'll prove it to you right now!" I whipped out my cell phone and punched in my nephew's cell number. It's difficult for me to describe how delighted I was when he picked up after only two rings.

"*Shavua tov*," I greeted him. And relying on caller ID to allow me not to have to introduce myself, I plunged right in, sharing the entire story of Flora Rainer's unfortunate encounter with his synagogue's security guard during the High Holidays.

Ashie was shocked and dismayed, and he asked to speak directly to Flora. Handing over my cell phone to her, I said, "My nephew, the rabbi, would like to speak to you."

I stepped back so as not to eavesdrop on their conversation, but I didn't take my eyes off of Flora the entire time she conversed with Rabbi Ashie. After she finished, as I replaced my cell phone in the pocket of my handbag, I asked Flora, "Well, my new friend, how did it go with the rabbi?"

"He apologized profusely, telling me that the guard most certainly didn't understand my reason for stepping into the synagogue, and that due to the stress of all the recent attacks on Jews in their places of worship, the man was being extra cautious, for which he, Rabbi Shreier, couldn't stop apologizing. And then he extended a personal invitation to me to return to his synagogue this coming Sabbath. He said to me, 'Mrs. Rainer, I'm not only inviting you, but I also insist that you come to morning services that begin at 8:45. We have a gala *kiddush* arranged for this Shabbos, and I want you to come to the synagogue so I can introduce you to some really special members.' When I told him that after my painful experience a few weeks ago I wasn't sure how I'd feel, he begged me with such genuine caring in his voice that I told him that I *would* try again, this coming Sabbath, to see what going to synagogue is all about."

A part of me kept congratulating myself for having fulfilled the opportunity offered by my *kan tzipor* moment, but I knew the truth. After Flora assured me that she would not disappoint my nephew by not showing up in shul, I asked her to take her kids along. She admitted that her two teenagers knew hardly anything about Judaism, and that she would really like them to learn more.

Since Flora had just given me a cue I could not ignore, I once again whipped out my phone and called someone I knew who was affiliated with NCSY. "*Shavua tov*, yes, it's me, Penina Wiener! Sorry to bother you on a Saturday night, but I need some information right now, because I'm standing with a mom of two kids who go to the Forest Hills high school, and—"

I didn't have to provide any more information, as the person I had called told me that she'd text the exact time and place of the next Queens NCSY meeting. "Text me their names and ages," she said, "and I'll see to it that they get treated royally when they arrive. Trust me, Mrs. Wiener, this is my specialty, and I won't disappoint you!"

I was sure she wouldn't, but I had one more step to take until I would feel that I had not only pleased G-d by how I had responded to my *kan tzipor* moment, but that I had achieved that goal in a way that would reflect well on my dad's criteria for such encounters. So after making sure that Flora and her children would both receive red-carpet treatment when they showed up as scheduled for their first genuine tastes of *Yiddishkeit*, on Shabbos no less, it was time for me to prove to myself that when called upon I had what was needed to reject Western civilization's mistaken principle that involvement in the lives of others diminishes one's pleasure in life.

So I punched in the number of Josh's cellphone and asked him to return to where I was standing. When he arrived, I asked him to escort the two of us to Flora's car, so we could see her off safely. When she was buckled up and about to drive off, I motioned to her to roll down the driver's side window and I said, "Before you go, Flora, you *must* accept my invitation to the three of you to join me and my family for our Shabbos dinner a week from this Friday night, if that works for all of you, and if not, for the first Shabbos after that when being our guests will enrich your life.

"And since I've already explained to you why we don't drive on Shabbos, it makes the most sense that the three of you should arrive before candle-lighting time — I'll text you our address, of course — enjoy the meal with us, sleep over, and then we'll all walk over to the synagogue where we pray for morning services. If any part of what I've offered, Flora, doesn't appeal to you, then simply enjoy attending services in the Young Israel near your home next week, and for many more. And please, dear friend, see to it that your kids join NCSY at the time and place I'll shortly text to you. No pressure, ever, just lots of good will. Deal?"

When Flora's eyes filled with tears, and she bit her bottom lip to stop it from quivering, I realized that I might have come on too strong, too soon. Or was it that she wasn't used to being showered with so much caring? I wasn't sure, so I turned to face the still-crowded parking lot and leaned against the outside of her car door. Then, out of the earshot of Josh, who was totally focused on texting someone, I removed my cell phone from my purse once again and punched in Dad's number.

"Dad," I whispered when he picked up, "you're not going to believe me, but I think I just had my very own *kan tzipor* moment. I've heard you speak about it a lot, and I never thought it would actually happen to me, even though I have wished for it for a long time. But…but I think I might have…ruined it.

"I'm standing outside of Burlington, Josh finished buying what he needed and is standing about ten feet away from me texting a friend, and I'm trying to convince an attorney I met while waiting on the checkout line, Mrs. Flora Rainer who lives in Forest Hills not far from Ashie's shul, to come to our house for Shabbos dinner a week from Friday night, but she seems totally…overwhelmed. She told me she wants to learn more about Judaism, and she asked me all kinds of questions about Shabbos. I thought I answered her well, but now I want to take it to the next level, give her and her two teenagers a chance to experience their first real Shabbos, but I think I didn't handle it in the best possible way."

Dad was his usual calm self. "I'm sure she appreciates every word you exchanged with her, Penina, as well as everything you did to make her wish to learn more about her roots become a reality. But since you're concerned enough to call me, ask her if she'd like to speak to your dad. I'll be glad to do so."

Now, with tears slipping out of *my* eyes, I turned around to Flora and asked her if she'd allow my father to speak to her for a minute or two. When she nodded, her wet cheeks shining in the lights that partially fought off the darkness that had enveloped the super-store's parking lot, I handed her my cell phone, thanking G-d for the wisdom and experience my father always shared.

That's where Penina's telling of her *kan tzipor* story ends, and my very minimum involvement with Mrs. Rainer began.

When Flora said, "Hello, rabbi," I gently corrected her by simply saying, "Steve Savisky, here, Mrs. Rainer. Thank you sincerely for befriending our daughter. She's looking forward to strengthening her relationship with you and your children. I understand that you are interested in learning more about your heritage. Make sure our daughter has your contact information, so I can text you the name and cell number of a woman who has been sharing her vast knowledge of Torah with professional women like yourself for several decades.

"As a volunteer for Partners-in-Torah, an organization I've been affiliated with since its inception, I know that she'll be delighted to arrange to be available to study Judaism with you over the phone for one hour a week, at your convenience and at your own pace, for as long as those sessions enrich your life. How does that sound?"

"Actually, rabbi — I mean, Mr. Savitsky — it sounds like just what the doctor ordered!"

And that's how Flora Rainer's journey back to her roots began. I made the "*shidduch*" between her and the Partners-in-Torah teacher I had mentioned to her, and to this day, many years since Penina reached out to me to help her succeed at her first *kan tzipor* moment, Flora is still studying with her original partner.

Flora was deeply impressed by Penina's caring; by the sincerity of my grandson, Rabbi Schreier; by the NCSY volunteers who welcomed and befriended her two teenagers; and by her Partner-in-Torah, who called the next day to set up their one-hour-a-week learning session that would ultimately fill in much of the knowledge of her religion that she had been denied for decades. It did take some months — after meeting Penina in Burlington, however — before she actually accepted an invitation to come, with her two teenagers, and spend a full Shabbos at the Wiener home.

Their friendship has endured, and today Flora awaits her very own *kan tzipor* moment, a moment for which she'll be ready, whenever it happens.

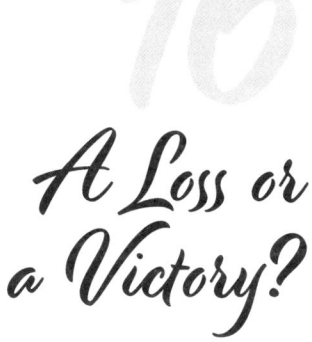

A Loss or a Victory?

THIS STORY WAS TOLD to me by a man whom I'll call Mr. Gary Jacobs, who was on a Kosherica cruise on which I was one of the invited speakers. After I had given my *kan tzipor* speech, he came over to me and shared this story.

After high school, in the 1980s, I attended UCLA.[1] I had been raised in a totally secular family, which meant that when I enrolled in college I knew little about my heritage. I had been given a bar mitzvah of sorts, but not much more than that. At UCLA, I was very active in extra-curricular programs, as well as in school politics, and in my senior year I decided to run for president of the Undergraduate Students Association Council (USAC), so I began the process and was gratified to become one of the designated candidates.

During that year, I also started to get more involved in our

---

1. The University of California, Los Angeles.

campus's Chabad House.[2] Many Friday nights found me there, enjoying a tasty Shabbos meal in the company of other Jewish students. And during the week I stopped in now and then to study with the rabbi. Over time, I developed a positive relationship with the rabbi and "the rebbetzin," as the rabbi's wife was called. Looking back, I now realize that her homemade Jewish food that filled the Chabad House with the enticing scents of freshly baked challah, golden chicken soup with fluffy matzah balls, and gefilte fish to die for — all new and enticing to someone who had been raised on take-out foods of every ethnicity but his own — had as much to do with the ending of this story as did the rabbi's vast Torah knowledge.

During my senior year's first semester, slowly but surely I became far more interested in religion than I had ever been. And what surprised me was that I genuinely enjoyed every minute I spent at that Chabad House, discussing religion with the black-hatted, bearded young rabbi, beating him at chess, and relishing his rebbetzin's soul-nourishing meals.

Of course, as election fever gripped our student body, I devoted most of my free hours connecting with recognized class leaders who could deliver large blocks of votes to me from their admirers. I was an involved, well-known member of my senior class, acknowledged as a left-wing, progressive activist who had volunteered to work for many popular student causes — from Black Rights to Free Speech; from Women's Rights to Homelessness — and could be counted on to deliver everything my campaign slogans promised. My chances of winning over the other candidates appeared to be quite good.

Confident in the viability of my campaign for president of the

---

2. The first Chabad House established at any American university.

student council, and also convinced that my newfound interest in my heritage would add a valuable dimension to my post-college life, I devoted all of the hours during which I was not obligated to study to my election campaign and to my search for spirituality.

One Friday night, while I was in the campus Chabad House talking to the rabbi and then learning one of his favorite holy books with him,[3] I heard myself say, "You know, Rabbi, I really enjoy this religion thing. I'm more than impressed with the Torah topics you've shared with me, and I think I want to begin observing one commandment. Keeping Shabbos and kosher are still much too drastic for me, so I was thinking that I might begin with something much less daunting, like wearing a small, discreet yarmulke.

The rabbi didn't look all that happy, but I attributed that to the fact that I had just beaten him at chess. His reply to my last comment was, "That's very gratifying to hear, Gary, and I applaud your desire to draw closer to G-d. Wearing a yarmulke will certainly be a constant reminder of your Jewish origins, and of your decision to become a more committed Jew. But I want you to contemplate whether your choice isn't a bit too radical at this time in your life. Each commandment we commit to observe must be something we will keep no matter the consequences, so when someone asks me which mitzvah they should embrace as they begin their journey to full Torah observance, I usually advise a commandment that is not as public as the one you just mentioned."

Being a young man of action, I could not fully understand the rabbi's advice, but I respected him enough to agree to wait

---

3. Translated into English, the only language in which I was fluent.

at least one full week before publicly donning a yarmulke. Then something interesting happened. With each passing day of that "week of waiting," as I had dubbed it, I began noticing hundreds of students sporting various symbols of their religion, items I had hardly noticed before I contemplated donning a yarmulke. And what an array they were! There were turbans worn by Sikhs, a wide variety of crosses worn by Christians of many denominations, *chai* and six-pointed stars worn by Jews, the eight-spoked Dharma Wheel worn by Buddhists, and many other such items. I also noticed some Jewish young men wearing yarmulkes, and since I had been raised by parents who genuinely respected all people so that at that point "I didn't have a discriminating bone in my body," as the saying goes, I became increasingly convinced that fellow students would surely respect any religious symbol I adopted, as much as I respected theirs.

Based on that conclusion, I purchased a small, black leather yarmulke that matched my hair color and became partially hidden in my head of unruly curls, and I began wearing it while in the Chabad House. The first time the rabbi noticed it, he complimented me privately, and then paid no further attention to it. From his low-key reaction, I understood that for me this was simply a trial run instead of a lifetime commitment. If not, why hadn't the rabbi congratulated me publicly, so that all the others at Chabad House would take note, congratulate me, and good-naturedly dare me to never take it off?

When I wasn't at Chabad House — for example, in class or campaigning around campus — my yarmulke was nowhere in sight. For a while, I lived two lives: the first one my private life, in which I had started to wear my yarmulke, and the second one my public life, in which my "religious symbol" was nowhere to be seen.

Until the night of the big debate.

That evening, around a thousand students were crammed into an auditorium on campus where the final pre-election debate was to take place. With no prior planning, I had run over to our Chabad House to ask the rabbi for a blessing that I win the debate and the election. Our discussion about the meaning of a rabbi's blessing and how it had the power to influence one's actual life lasted much longer than I had envisioned. When I realized that I was running extremely late, I dashed across campus at lightning speed, determined to arrive on time despite having been sidetracked with the rabbi.

And in my haste, I was still wearing my yarmulke when I sprinted up the steps leading to the doors to the auditorium. I was about to fling open those double doors and hurry onto the stage when I realized that if I didn't immediately unpin and remove my yarmulke, all the students gathered inside would immediately know that I identified as an Orthodox Jew.

The debate would begin in two minutes whether I was at my designated seat or not. If I was on stage, I had a good chance of participating in the debate and winning it, and subsequently also winning the election. So I had exactly one minute to decide: Do I wear my yarmulke or not? I could snatch it off, stash it into my pants pocket, and continue to live a double, dishonest life. But if I flung open the doors and ran down the aisle and up onto the stage wearing my yarmulke, no matter how brilliantly I performed, because yarmulke-wearing Jews were perceived as being in the Dark Ages when it came to social justice, I was at great risk of losing the debate and the upcoming election.

Looking back now, I realize how naïve I was back then. Along with thousands of other unobservant Jewish students at UCLA, I was strongly drawn to left-wing, liberal causes. But at the same time I also mistakenly believed that I could one day become a practicing Orthodox Jew while continuing to whole-heartedly espouse them.

As my moment of truth began to descend on me, I had to make a vital decision. Was I a proud Jew who recognized the Torah's truth and was ready to give up fame and self-gratification to prove it, or simply a dabbler in religion who would sell what he believed was true for the price of winning a student election?

This was the most difficult decision I had faced in all of my twenty-two years, and it almost paralyzed me. Yes, no; no, yes. How would I feel if I lost the election, and the power that winning would give me to promote my strongly held left-wing agenda? On the other hand, how would I be able to look myself in the mirror if I stuffed my yarmulke into my back pocket in order not to risk losing?

The rabbi hadn't asked me those two questions; they had risen from the depth of my pure Jewish soul. And yet, I was torn. So I pulled open the heavy double doors, sidled all the way to the right-hand wall in the now-darkened auditorium, and raced down the incline to the front, where the steps up to the stage were located. All of my maneuverings only gave me an extra thirty seconds to decide before anyone noticed my yarmulke. I was still safe and all options were still open to me.

Yet while I was still somewhat protected by the dark of the auditorium and I had not yet stepped into the part of the room illuminated by the stage lights, I found that I didn't have to make a conscious decision. Both of my hands simply refused to move up to the top of my head where, if they didn't immediately remove the bobby pins that held my yarmulke in place, it would stay exactly where it was.

That is how I reached my place at the debate table in time to be accepted as one of the official debaters, and that's how I appeared in front of about one thousand of my fellow students, looking like any other Orthodox Jew, with one exception: This now-openly proud Jew was also hoping to convince all those in attendance that he, and he alone, should be entrusted to lead the entire undergraduate student body that year.

By the time the debate was over, I was sure of two things: Firstly, that I had spoken masterfully, and secondly and even more important, that from that moment on I would never stop wearing my yarmulke.

Now I had to wait to learn whether I could win the election as an Orthodox Jew.

While my opponents were stating their views, I observed the audience. Many of my fellow students looked surprised at my appearance, as they had never before seen me wearing a yarmulke; others simply didn't notice anything different about me. From many discussions I'd had with my Chabad rabbi, I was certain that G-d would decide, based on what was good for my soul and my future, whether I would win or lose the election. As I walked out of that auditorium, my head was held high. I had been tested and felt that I had passed that test with flying colors.

But although my head was held high, I was puzzled that not one of those who had worked so hard with me on my election campaign rushed to my side to congratulate me on my exceptional speech. That was truly strange, but I suspected that the yarmulke was the reason for their defection, and I was saddened, rather than angry, by it. So I ended up walking out of that building and into the night all alone, as I struggled with being totally friendless only because I had chosen to wear a small, black leather head-covering that was barely visible on my head of the same color curls.

And then, out of nowhere, a young woman approached me and said, "Gary Jacobs, I've been observing you throughout your campaign, and I never guessed that you were a religious Jew.

That's really interesting to me, because obviously you seem as if this has been a challenging change for you. These past weeks I've seen you out and about on campus many times without a *kippah*, and tonight I saw you wearing it.

"The reason I noticed all of this is that I, too, am struggling with the issue of religion. I came to UCLA as a secular Jew, but I've gotten involved in some of the Jewish organizations on campus, including Hillel and Chabad. I'm determined to explore more about Judaism, so please tell me a little bit about your struggle — you know, what you went through, how difficult it has been, what made you decide in the final analysis that this is something you really want to do. I feel a need to learn more about you and what impelled you not to remove your *kippah* before going onto the stage tonight."

And I said, "That's fine with me. I don't even know your name yet, because you didn't introduce yourself, but I'd love to help you figure out how to call a halt to your struggle with your Jewish identity."

And I did just that.

And tonight, Mr. Savitsky, it's twenty-five years since our wedding. That's why we came on the cruise: to celebrate our twenty-fifth wedding anniversary, and to celebrate the beautiful Torah family that we have been granted the privilege to establish.

Gary concluded his *kan tzipor* moment story by telling me that the minute when he decided never again to remove his yarmulke in order to influence how others judged him was probably the most important decision he ever made. He said, "I had no idea what I was going to do about wearing the yarmulke until the very last moment. But now I realize that that was my *kan tzipor* moment, which hit me by surprise, exactly as you described it, Steve: *Ki yikarei!* I had to decide right then and there how I wanted to move forward with my life. Thank G-d, I made the right decision. And because I took full advantage of my personal *kan tzipor* moment, tonight I'm here with my dear wife and precious family after twenty-five years of a happy and Jewishly committed life.

"And if you want to tell others about *lema'an yitav lach*, I need to share with you that life has been exceptionally beautiful and good to me.

"But I also want you to tell others that my *kan tzipor* moment was a bit different than the other ones you've described, because not only did I have to make my decision in a split second, but when I made that decision all I knew was that wearing my *kippah* or not would only affect me and no one else. I had no idea that what I perceived as my life going totally downhill if I kept wearing my *kippah*, was totally wrong. Now I know that had I taken it off in order to win the debate and probably the election, I would have lost much more than the fleeting honor of being elected president. I would have lost the deep, abiding connection I have had since then with Hashem, and I would have lost the opportunity of meeting and then marrying my dear, devoted wife, and the best mom my kids could ever have! I can't stop thanking Hashem enough that I made that very difficult yet right decision!

"Another important point: All the other *kan tzipor* moments you describe when you give your speeches are about opportunities to be there for someone else. My *kan tzipor* moment was one of conflict between my public actions and my yearnings to enjoy the trappings of This World, and my private, soul-prompted desire to build a true Torah home.

"And in the end, what I thought was the meaning of *lema'an yitav lach* — which I interpreted to mean that I would win the debate and the election, and serve as president of the Student Body — was totally not what Hashem had in mind for me! I decided to wear my yarmulke, which led to losing the debate and the election, but I won something much more permanent and valuable: The chance live a full life openly and proudly connected to Hashem, and to raise a Torah-observant family.

"Even today, I shudder when I think that had I not made the correct choice about wearing my yarmulke, my wife would have never introduced herself to me, and we would never have met and married! Since our very first encounter, she was the one whose constant encouragement has enriched and strengthened my mitzvah observance.

"Thank You, Hashem," Gary ended, "for allowing me to fully experience my *kan tzipor* moment, to live to understand the true meaning of that concept, and to enjoy the true meaning of *lema'an yitav lach*."

Go Figure

BY NOW IT IS clear that in the last few years I have become known in certain circles as "Mr. *Kan Tzipor*" thanks to the many opportunities I've had to share with diverse audiences such stories that happened to me and to others. Although most of the stories in this book leave those who have been blessed with *kan tzipor* moments feeling that they have enjoyed something extremely pleasant and uplifting that has also been the catalyst to lasting life changes, it was from my most recent *kan tzipor* moment that I learned a somewhat different yet important life lesson.

I've been fortunate to be involved in various groups whose goal is to benefit *Klal Yisrael*. One of them is the Conference of Presidents of Major Jewish Organizations, which was founded in 1956. At that time, John Foster Dulles, Secretary of State under President Dwight D. Eisenhower, sought a unified voice of America's Jewish community on certain important foreign policy issues without having to poll the heads of each organization. This diverse group included the heads of the Anti-Defamation League, AIPAC,[1] the Women's Zionist Organization of America,[2] the

---

1. The American Israel Public Affairs Committee.
2. Colloquially known as Hadassah.

RCA,[3] B'nei B'rith, the Orthodox Union,[4] the National Council of Young Israel, Emunah Women, and Bnei Zion,[5] among others. This group of about fifty leaders, who represent a cross-section of Jewish America's Orthodox, Conservative, and Reform Jewish communities, is quite powerful, and since its inception, its voice has been sought not only on points of foreign policy but also on legislative issues that impact American Jews.

An annual highlight of the Conference's activities is a mission to a foreign country with a small Jewish community that is nonetheless important to the well-being of the State of Israel. Each year, many countries vie to host the Conference, during which the heads of state and other high-placed dignitaries meet for several days with mission participants, along with the Jewish leaders of the host country. In the past, when I joined trips to Azerbaijan, Georgia, Ukraine, Morocco, and other countries, I had been gratified to witness the tremendous elevation of the status of the local Jews in the minds of their government leaders that was engendered by our missions, as well as the appreciation of our co-religionists that no matter their relatively small numbers, their welfare was our priority.

This *kan tzipor* story took place in February 2020, less than a month before the world closed down due to the COVID-19 pandemic, and half a year before the Abraham Accords between Israel and the United Arab Emirates was signed during President Trump's administration. At that time, as I was the president

---

3. Rabbinical Council of America.

4. Of which I had been president for twelve years.

5. An American non-profit dedicated to accelerating Israel's growth and strengthening the Jewish People by building partnerships with our friends and allies across the globe.

of Bnai Zion,[6] my wife and I were invited to join the Conference's several-day mission to Saudi Arabia, where we were slated to meet with people at the highest level of government. This would not be our first foray into a country that had no diplomatic relations with the State of Israel. We had previously visited the United Arab Emirates, by invitation; I like to think that mission paved the way for the eventual signing of the Abraham Accords.

All of us who had been fortunate enough to be selected to participate in this mission understood that our trip to Saudi Arabia would be extremely different from past missions since, as an official policy, not one Jew resided in that Middle Eastern country. Saudi Arabia's king, then-eighty-six-year-old Salman bin Abdulaziz Al Saud, is its official ruler, but it is an open secret that one of his many sons, Mohammad bin Salman, colloquially known as MBS, the Crown Prince,[7] is its de facto head of state. Although all of his brothers were educated in the West, he had insisted on remaining at home, perhaps so that he could consolidate his power base and secure his future. However, wishing to build his reputation as more moderate than his father,[8] and also determined to curry favor with America in order to forestall possible plans of his many enemies both within his

---

6. An American nonprofit dedicated to accelerating Israel's growth and strengthening the Jewish People by building partnerships with our friends and allies across the globe.

7. He is also deputy prime minister, minister of defense, chairman of the Council of Economic and Development Affairs, and chairman of the Council of Political and Security Affairs.

8. He has put many of his brothers under house arrest so as to block their ability to usurp his power, and is believed to have been the mastermind behind the vicious, brutal murder of a Saudi journalist who opposed him.

country and without, MBS might have been behind his government's strongly-worded invitation that led to the Conference's visit, which was the first time in a quarter of a century that any Jew had stepped onto Saudi soil.[9]

When MBS saw fit to extend an invitation for a Conference mission to visit his country, we felt that it was a unique opportunity that we could not refuse; we must accept. But before accepting that invitation, the Conference's leadership made it clear that they would accept only if certain conditions would be meticulously adhered to. Although only a minority of participants who went on that mission observe the laws of *kashrus,* we insisted that they allow Israeli members of the Orthodox Union to be brought in from Israel to *kasher* one of the hotel's kitchens and prepare strictly kosher meals throughout our stay. In addition, one conference room was to be reserved as the dining room, as well as the venue for a daily *minyan* during the four days we would be there. We also insisted that our group would meet not only with MBS but also with others in the highest levels of government.

Since my wife and I had enjoyed a previous Conference mission to the United Arab Emirates, we looked forward to the Saudi Arabia mission for two reasons: firstly, for the good that we might be able to accomplish, and secondly, at the very least, for a replay of the absolute red-carpet, royal treatment that we had experienced during that previous trip to a decidedly Muslim country. To our delight, the Saudis imposed no traditional

9. The invitation might also have been extended at the behest of his good friend, Jared Kushner, President Trump's son-in-law, who at that time might have hoped that such a visit might encourage Saudi Arabia to also join the Abraham Accords.

Muslim dress code on the women among us, for which we were thankful. No one made Malcolm Hoenlein[10] and me feel uncomfortable for wearing our *kippah* (some preferred caps and, of course, the non-religious went bareheaded), and we all did our utmost to be respectful of their culture.

Under MBS's influence, certain Saudi women had been given permission to drive cars, which raised our hopes of additional concessions to our Western way of life. However, since Saudi Arabia was home to millions of Muslims who considered themselves the guardians not only of their two holiest religious sites, Mecca and Medina, but also of their most stringent interpretation of the Koran, MBS could not risk alienating such a large segment of his population by taking more than baby steps towards westernizing his country. Saudi Arabia permits no political parties or national elections, and as much as MBS is friendly and dynamic, he is, at the same time, politically astute. Although he wields absolute power, his biggest current challenge is walking the political tightrope, a fall from which he might, with one misstep, lose not only his kingship, but his life.

When we landed in Saudi Arabia, we were immediately extended royal treatment. We were promptly ushered into a separate lounge where, after welcoming us with broad smiles, officers collected our passports and whisked them away to be stamped while we relaxed in fine style. After all of the official entry formalities had been taken care of and our passports were returned, we were invited to board modern, fully air-conditioned chauffeured limousines that transported us in style to our hotel. And throughout that mission, "royal treatment" meant that we had only to express a wish and it was immediately fulfilled by

---

10. Executive vice chairman of the Conference since 1986.

members of the royal entourage whose main mission in life, it seemed, was to keep us happy.

Of course, we realized that this utmost personalized attention also kept us from making even the slightest one-on-one contact with any Saudis who had not been fully vetted and therefore could not be trusted to keep secret anything about the country or its leader that might reflect negatively upon it. We fully understood that their goal for our visit was that we Jewish Americans should bring back to our countrymen, but most importantly to America's Jews, the message that Saudi Arabia was not the monster country that the world believes it is.

Each day, after our morning minyan,[11] we were served a sumptuous breakfast under the eagle eye and very professional handling of our OU-Israel staff. The rest of each day consisted of a succession of meetings — attended by everyone who had flown with us to Riyadh — with the ministers of every one of the government's many departments, overseen by MBS, who did his utmost to conduct serious, open discussions far more wide-ranging than we had anticipated.

And ten of us men, as well as two women,[12] were even more impressed when that first night, Malcolm Hoenlein unobtrusively invited us to a private meeting with MBS that lasted from around 9:00 p.m. until 12:30 a.m., during which, without any reporters or others present, the Crown Prince, who speaks perfect English and knows how to charm an audience, discussed

---

11. Joined by those for whom daily minyan attendance is non-negotiable, and whose only lack was a Sefer Torah, which we didn't risk bringing into what was a somewhat hostile environment despite all of the surface cordiality and smiles.

12. To our great disappointment, MBS limited the number of our group with whom he would meet privately to twelve people.

with us the upcoming Abraham Accords and the always-elusive issue called "peace with the Palestinians." He conveyed his belief that each of us, myself among them, must take full responsibility for actions geared to fulfilling that goal, while he implored us to brainstorm until we find a way to break the impasse that seemed to exist between the supporters of the Palestinian people and the government of Israel.

While in that room with the Crown Prince, it became eminently clear to me that while MBS spends millions, and often tens of millions, on satisfying any one of his whims, it pained him that all of his wealth could not resolve the conflicting realities of being engaged in what is known as a proxy war with Iran. The so-called Iran–Saudi Arabia proxy conflict is the ongoing struggle between those two countries for dominance in the Middle East and other Muslim regions. The two countries have provided varying degrees of support to opposing sides in nearby conflicts, including the civil wars and disputes in Syria, Yemen, Bahrain, Lebanon, Qatar, and other regions with large Muslim populations such as Nigeria, Pakistan, and Afghanistan.

The conflict is waged on multiple levels over geopolitical, economic, and sectarian influence in pursuit of total, recognized regional control. American support for Saudi Arabia and its allies, as well as Russian and Chinese support for Iran and its allies, exists in large part because Iran is home to mostly Shia Muslims, while Saudi Arabia sees itself as the leading Sunni Muslim power.[13]

---

13. The main difference between Sunni and Shia Muslims is their belief surrounding who should have succeeded the Prophet Muhammad in 632 AD. Shia Muslims believe it should have been Ali ibn Abi Talib, while Sunni Muslims believe that Abu Bakr was the rightful successor.

I understood from MBS that to him it was frightening to think that the Chinese, with their astronomical number of soldiers and untold wealth, would increase their support of Iran.

To strengthen China's realization that an Iranian attack on his country would be considered an act of war by both Iran *and* China,[14] MBS very much wants to remain a strong American ally.[15] He believes that before any country dared to attack Saudi Arabia they would be deterred by realizing that its super-power American ally would immediately unleash the full force of its military on any country responsible for such aggression.

When we weren't attending meetings, we were taken to visit tourist attractions, and sometimes to shop. Although I was happy to observe that English is being taught in some Saudi schools, I was less happy to think that one day Chinese might become as popular as a foreign language to be studied, since I am aware that MBS is courting that country's favor as well as working to strengthen his ties to America, which is one of the reasons he invited our group to visit. And throughout our visit, to keep us happy and go home with only praises for this very autocratic Muslim kingdom, if any one of us expressed any need, the staff assigned to see to our comfort went out of its way to accommodate and please.

Even though some time had passed since our mission to the United Arab Emirates, what we still remembered from that trip, and missed on this one, was the great opportunity we had had back then to meet other Jews, something that simply didn't exist

---

14. With repercussions from America and its allies that China was not ready to risk.

15. This visit took place when Trump was still in the Oval Office. Today, with Biden in the White House, I am not sure what MBS is thinking.

in Saudi Arabia because no Jews reside there. Since each organization that is a member of the Conference holds elections at different times, on each mission Genie and I enjoy meeting new people, and this time, we were again not disappointed, which in some measure made up for the lack I just mentioned. One couple with whom we connected immediately on this mission was very prominent, wealthy, and well-known. They were intensely involved in the UJA-Federation,[16] and had strong positive feelings for Jews the world over. Since this *kan tzipor* moment involves one of them, I decided to keep them anonymous and will refer to the wife as Karen.

She and her husband, Jake, are traditional Jews with strong feelings towards Judaism and Israel. My wife and I immediately recognized their wonderful natures and their utmost devotion to our People, and therefore felt a strong affinity to them. And because, as I have already mentioned, I like to think of myself as an "Observant Jew," which means I have trained myself to observe those around me no matter how busy or distracted I might otherwise be, one morning while we were eating breakfast it didn't take me long to realize that Karen was suffering a more than usual level of discomfort, which I could not believe was simple jet lag.

I asked, "What's the matter, Karen? You look as if all is not right with your world right now." She replied, "To tell you the truth, I suffer from a very bad back. I've undergone several spinal surgeries, and I recently spent three weeks in the hospital. Although I thought I was well enough to make this trip, I...I guess I'm not. It just hit me that it's something I'll have to live

---

16. United Jewish Appeal-Federation funds hundreds of nonprofits, local and global, to tackle today's most pressing problems.

with for the rest of my life. In addition to that painful realization, I also have to deal with the actual excruciating pain in my
back, despite the painkillers I'm taking, and the strengthening
exercises I've been taught to do on my own."

After that revelation, every morning when we met at breakfast, I'd ask, "So, Karen, how's your back treating you today?"
And sometimes, I'd quip, "Just remember, Karen, that I've got
your back," which made us all laugh, although my wife and I
recognized that this was no laughing matter. We wished there
was something we could do to minimize Karen's pain, but since
there was nothing we knew of, the least we could do was to com-
miserate with her and let her know that we cared.

Our mission to Saudi Arabia went as planned, and the first
half of it was all-too-quickly coming to an end. As was the usual
itinerary, each of these focused trips ended with all participants
traveling to Israel, where we'd meet with government officials,
including the prime minister and foreign minister, among others,
who would debrief us about what we had learned and what prac-
tical steps could be taken to implement positive change. Having
just spent four days in Saudi Arabia, we were now headed to
Israel for Shabbos and this second, most important leg of our
trip.

There are no direct flights from Riyadh to Tel Aviv, so we
were scheduled to take a two-hour flight to Amman, Jordan, and
another much shorter flight from there to Ben Gurion Airport,
which was a much better choice than opting to cross into Israel
from Jordan via the Allenby Bridge.[17] Each of us had paid our

---

17. Anyone who has chosen the Allenby Bridge option will strongly agree
that flying could save anywhere from five to ten excruciating hours of discomfort and delays.

own way throughout this mission. We had all traveled together, but some of our travel agents had been more professional than others. That is why, once all of us had been dropped off at King Khalid International Airport and had been given a royal send-off by our hosts, our travel experiences differed greatly.

When we boarded our flight from Riyadh to Amman, we immediately realized that we were no longer enjoying the perks we had been receiving until then. Obviously, since the Crown Prince had achieved his goal, and his part of the mission was officially over, there was no further need to provide royal treatment for those of us Jewish men and women whom they knew were headed to the land of their sworn enemy, namely Israel. As we began the journey that would take us to Amman that Thursday, not only weren't the members of the Conference mission any longer treated royally at check-in,[18] but the airplane that would fly us to Jordan contained about 150 seats in what they called "coach," but was what we would call "beneath human ability to endure." About twenty seats in the front of the plane, which they had dubbed Business Class, could barely be compared to what we in the free world deem acceptable in Coach Class.

After a long and grueling check-in experience, and our great shock upon entering the airplane and realizing what awaited us, Genie and I were thankful that our travel agent, who did not rely on any perks or accommodations from a Middle East airline, had booked us on that airline's Business Class. We were also each saddled with a large box containing a long, voluminous ceremonial Arab robe, presented by the Crown Prince's brother, their minister of defense, who was forced to cancel his meeting

18. A nightmare that was beyond words to describe.

with our group when the Iran-backed Houthi tribe of Yemen attacked Saudi oil fields. Since we had no room for such a box in our suitcases our first order of business after boarding was trying to stuff those bulky items — that few of us would don even during the upcoming holiday of Purim — into the tiny overhead compartments, while the local passengers looked on enviously into our "upper class" section.

And it was only once we had snapped those inadequate overhead bins closed that to our utter dismay Genie and I noticed that while our "business class" compartment was filled only with eighteen other men and women of our group, thirty of our cohort were contending with the vociferous anger, in Arabic, of their seatmates who were incensed that Jews were hogging more than their share of the space in the overhead bins, totally not aware that we were as upset as they were.

Once every overhead bin door had finally been snapped into place, we watched helplessly as our coreligionists did their best to squish themselves into narrow seats with the least amount of leg room that we had ever envisioned. My first feeling was a mixture of embarrassment and guilt that our seats were so much better, but I managed to calm myself with the thought that, *Thank G-d the flight will be a bit less than two hours.* And then I busied myself in settling into my own not-too-comfortable seat so that the stewardess could rush by me to the rear compartment to try to soothe close to one hundred vocally unhappy passengers.

Looking about me, I realized that Malcolm and I were the only two participants in our mission wearing a *kippah*, and what was even more disconcerting was that for some unfathomable reason, Karen and Jake's travel agent had not thought to seat them up front with us! I was shocked, and then sorry, as I realized that this must be the very first (and hopefully the last) time they had been seated in anything less than true first class.

But determined to keep the lowest profile possible so as not to cause a *chillul Hashem*, after making sure that Genie was coping well — as she always does, G-d bless her — I buckled up, closed my eyes, and did my utmost to relax, as I urged myself to remember to call our travel agent as soon as we got to our hotel to thank her for our "business class" seats.

The plane took off, and about ten or maybe fifteen minutes into the flight Karen ambled by us. When the lower edge of her sweater poked my face and woke me from my reverie, I said, "Karen, it's good to see you again," and she answered, "Same here, Steve, Genie. My back just started acting up something awful, and since it was impossible for me to sit in my seat without writhing, I figured that maybe if I stood up and walked a bit my excruciating pain would minimize. But the truth is, I can't actually walk in this very narrow aisle, so it isn't doing me much good. If anything it's made it worse. I hope I'll survive until we get to Amman!" And without allowing another second to elapse, trying her best to apply pressure to her pain, she slowly inched her way back to her seat.

And that's when that proverbial light went on in my brain and I said to myself: *Thank you, Hashem, for giving me a relatively comfortable seat! But Karen is in a lot of pain, and this is a perfect example, an exact word-for-word instance of Ki yikarei...lefanecha ba-derech. It's happening exactly while I am* ba-derech, *while I am on my way, traveling. So I should really go back there and tell her,* "Karen, let's switch seats." *But...I really don't want to do it! I know what it's like back there!*

At least at that time I thought that I knew what it was like, which I didn't, not to that extent! And I especially didn't want to sit back there since I was one of the two Jews on board who was wearing a *kippah* — my cap was in my checked luggage — and those seated in that part of the plane would not welcome anyone among them who was so visibly religiously Jewish. In fact, I told myself that the mitzvah of *v'nishmartem me'od l'nafshoseichem*, the mitzvah of taking steps to protect my own life, surely took precedence in this instance! So for a moment or two, I sat immobilized.

But then I realized that two of the four criteria for designating an occurrence as a *kan tzipor* moment were staring me in the face: I had no Rav to ask which mitzvah took precedence at that moment, and I strongly wished to remain at Genie's side in our comfortable seats.[19] "So," I said to myself, "you have no choice. You have to do what is right; you have to seize the moment."

That's when I said to Genie, "Listen, I'm going to the back of the plane so that Karen can come and sit in my seat, near you."

Genie was shocked. "You mean you are actually going to choose to sit in the back of this plane where you'll not only have to twist yourself like a pretzel to fit into one of those baby-sized seats, but you'll also be putting your life in danger by placing yourself among people who have been indoctrinated their entire lives to kill Jews?"

"I don't *want* to do that, Genie, but I feel that it's the right thing to do, no matter how hard it is for me. I think this is a genuine *kan tzipor* moment, and I have to seize it or lose the special mitzvah that is being presented to me by Hashem! You know as well as I do that not every *kan tzipor* moment makes a person feel great, like when I was involved in influencing Martin to return to his roots or when I helped that bride get her wedding gown to Columbus in time for her wedding. As I tell everyone when I make my *kan tzipor* speeches, sometimes you just

---

19. The third reason was that it happened when I was actually "*ba-derech*," traveling, and the fourth was that it was way, way out of my comfort zone.

have to do what's right simply because it's the right thing to do.

"People coming across a nest with a mother bird and her young could think, *Why should I send the mother bird away? That would be utterly cruel!* But the Torah tells us not to think we are smarter or more compassionate than Hashem. That's the mitzvah, so we must do it even though we don't fully understand the reasoning. We do it because Hashem commanded us to do so, and also because it's one of only two mitzvos in the Torah that guarantee not only *lema'an yitav lach*, that we'll experience goodness in our lives, but also *v'ha'arachta yamim*, that our days will be lengthened."

The smile Genie gave me and the sheen in her eyes were all the validation I needed. So I got up, made my way to the very back of the plane with great difficulty, as the aisle was blocked with many passengers visiting with friends and relatives who were totally oblivious to my wish to reach Karen, or who had decided, despite my "Excuse me, please" over and over again, that they simply would not make it easy for me to get there. When I reached her row, I said, "Karen, I'm sorry it took me so long to get here, but what I came to tell you is that we're going to change seats now. I'm taking yours and you're taking mine, in business class."

She was in so much pain, she couldn't even answer me. All she could manage was to shake her head back and forth, back and forth, indicating that she would not do such a thing to me.

"You are in excruciating pain, and you can't hide it from me, Karen. No more arguing, even silently. Please get up and go sit near Genie."

My assessment of her level of pain was on target, because without another word that's exactly what she did. And it was when she was making her way down the aisle to the front of the plane, and I turned around to actually take her seat that I realized that what I had suggested was *way above* my comfort level.

Not only had she been seated in the very last row of the plane, but she had the middle seat between two of the most unsavory men I had ever laid my eyes on — "up close and personal," as the saying goes.

At that point we hit a bit of turbulence, so I had no choice. I simply lifted my legs, one by one, over the knees of the passenger sitting in the aisle seat, and wedged myself into her very narrow vacated space. And since I was much taller than Karen, and wearing a *kippah*, believe me when I say that at that moment I was not thankful to Hashem for having chosen me for this *kan tzipor* moment. Actually, what I was thinking was, *Hashem, please let me get off this plane in one piece, none the worse for having chosen to do what I just did.*

And then, to my great surprise, each of the Arabs sitting on either side of me, politely taking turns, began talking to me, and to my utter amazement, they both spoke English and were clearly educated. One worked for a large accounting firm, and the other was a business consultant who was employed by a large company that serviced the entire region. Even though they had struck me as sinister, once they began speaking to me I realized that they weren't exactly as they had appeared. Their opening gambit was not unexpected: "We see you are wearing a *kippah*, so we understand that you are Jewish and therefore, even if you don't actually live in Israel, you have a strong connection to the government that robbed us Palestinians of our homes in 1948, correct?"

Well, at least their "cards were on the table," as the saying goes. After they threw more than a few other accusations at me, taking turns to hammer me with their pent-up anger, they seemed to have run out of steam. I then said, "Truthfully, although over the years I've read about what you just accused me of, I never before had the opportunity to actually sit alongside Palestinians to hear their side of the story. But I've just done that. I've just done my best to listen to what is on your minds and in your hearts, without interrupting, until you finished speaking. Will you afford me the same courtesy?"

When they both nodded, I explained the Israeli/Jewish point of view of their perception that "we" had robbed them of their ancestral land. I began with the creation of the world by Hashem, continued on to His promise to Avraham that Yitzchak — not his other son Yishmael — would inherit the land of Canaan, and on down through thousands of years of our blood-soaked history. I only ended after mentioning the Holocaust, in which six million Jews had been starved, beaten to death, shot, gassed, and cremated, mostly because no country in the world would grant entry to fleeing Jews, and most non-Jews delighted in betraying the few who had managed to hide.

I also countered my seatmates' accusation that their hatred was fueled by the European Jewish survivors who had come to Palestine after the Holocaust and had "robbed the Palestinians of their ancestral homes," by pointing out to them that pogroms against Jews in the Holy Land had been carried out by Arabs way before World War II, and that the slaughter of over sixty-four men, women, and children in Chevron had taken place in 1929, way before the State of Israel had been proclaimed.

When I realized from their rapt attention that they had never heard our side of the story, I added, "And for your information, the Palestinian-led BDS movement,[20] whose goal is to

---

20. The worldwide movement in support of the Palestinian cause that urges its adherents to Boycott, Divest, and Sanction Israel as a means of destroying her economic viability.

destroy Israel by decimating her economy, in 2015 forced the SodaStream company to move out of Judea and Samaria, which they call 'the Occupied Territories.' When they relocated to the town of Lehavim in Israel proper, more than 500 Palestinian workers who had been employed by the company were laid off and lost their livelihoods. So you see that the actions of BDS, along with the current war of terror and all of the previous un-provoked acts of terror, are all unjustified."

I concluded by telling them that the only way to achieve peace between both sides — because both sides have claims — was compromise. "This," I said, "is something the Palestinian Authority, Hamas, and Hezbollah do not accept because their goal, their stated blood-thirsty mission, is to wipe Israel off the map and destroy every last Jew living there."

To my surprise, after each of our sides had been calmly artic-ulated, although we each continued to adhere to our perception, the level of suspicion and even animosity toward each other was much lower. And for the next approximately hour and a half, we sat together discussing, in a civilized manner, the differ-ences between our points of view, and what could possibly be done — people to people instead of waiting for innovation from the self-interested political leaders in each country — to find common ground, so that all peoples in the Middle East could live in peace and raise future generations in peace.

"Surely," I said, "war has been tried too many times, with too much loss of life on both sides, to believe that more war will be a blessing to either side, correct? Will you agree that sometimes in a conflict, both parties have justified points, and they simply have to find a way to resolve their differences in a civil manner?

"Now I have a better understanding of your position, and I hope you have a better understanding of ours. So going for-ward, maybe, thanks to our being thrown together on this plane, something that only G-d could have orchestrated, each of us will speak up, first to our families and friends, and then to those in power, and maybe, just maybe, something good will come of our meeting today. Remember, your government pays people — pays terrorists reward money — for every Jew that they kill. That this is the official policy of the Palestinian Authority tells you and tells us that their so-called quest for peace is a sham. No government yearning for peace does that.

"And no government yearning for peace hides caches of arms, and even missiles, in places such as schools and hospitals. It's quite apparent why this is done. These missiles attack Israeli civilians. The Israeli army then retaliates in an attempt to destroy the ammunition that just killed our people, and prevent them from continuing to kill additional Israeli civilians. But thanks to those who represent the Palestinian people condoning the stockpiling of armaments in civilian centers, the maximum number of Palestinian women and children are killed. Knowing that this is happening should arouse Palestinian civilians — the husbands and brothers and fathers of these women and children — to demand that both of these 'methods of madness' be halted immediately.

"Since both of you are nodding, which means that you agree, know that your job is to convince your leaders that Israel can't make peace with an enemy that wants to wipe us off the map, to totally destroy us, and that you can't support a government that does all in its power simply to enjoy the prerogatives of power, not to protect its citizens and help them achieve a peaceful, prosperous life. If you have relatives living in Israel, ask them if they would move to any Arab-ruled country after having enjoyed life in a democracy. I am certain they would laugh at you. Then ask them why, if Israel is such an evil country, they choose to live there and not under the Palestinian Authority.

"Go back and tell all the Palestinians who are as educated and aware as you are that in order to live in peace, both sides need to compromise. Tell them that Israelis don't want war. We don't want our sons to be soldiers. We want them to be doctors and architects and lawyers, pharmacists, businessmen, and scientists who find cures for the world's illnesses. And yes, we also want those who have the calling to be rabbis, scholars, advisors, and teachers. And we want all of our children in the Middle East, no matter in which families they have been placed by G-d Almighty, to grow up in peace and never again to have to contend with war. But your leaders force us to have a large standing army to protect our families, with the help of G-d. And for that alone, for turning our Jewish young men into soldiers, it's hard for us to forgive you."

That's the conversation we had during that flight when I sat squeezed between those two Arabs in Karen's seat in the back of that plane. If I had met those two men on the streets of Yerushalayim, I would have certainly hurried across the street, and possibly have run in the other direction. And had I met them on a dark night in New York, I would have done the same. But on that flight, thanks to that *kan tzipor* moment when I instructed Karen to take my seat up front, we had that incredible encounter.

That's when I understood that "*lema'an yitav lach*" can have many meanings, because when we landed and I got off that plane, I felt that my flight time had been spent in a very constructive, very good, way. Granted, for Karen it was surely *lema'an yitav lach*, because my wife later told me that once Karen settled into my seat, her back pains eased considerably, thank G-d. But for me as well, I am certain that I would never have gotten a chance to have that important conversation had I not seized the opportunity presented to me by that particular *kan tzipor* moment. In fact, looking back on the mission I had just participated in, not one such honest, important conversation had taken place during the entire time that our group was in Saudi Arabia.

As the title of this chapter proclaims, "Go figure…"

18

Second Chances

BERNIE (BERISH) FUCHS IS a great philanthropist, *askan*, and *talmid chacham*, and he is married to a wonderful woman named Hannah. They are fun-loving and seek ways of doing *chesed* every day of their lives. We've known Bernie and Hannah for many years, and right before the COVID-19 pandemic turned the entire world upside down, we had the great privilege of going with them on a Kosherica cruise to South America, during which I was a scholar-in-residence. When I finished telling the others on our tour my story about Martin Leibovich and the *kan tzipor* moment that completely changed his life, Bernie came over to me and said, "I have a wonderful *kan tzipor* story to tell you, and if you retell it to others, I'd be honored."

✻

I was eighteen years old when this story took place. At that time, I was a student of Yeshiva Torah Vodaath, which was located in the Williamsburg section of Brooklyn, New York, and truly loved learning Torah. I was so immersed in my Torah studies that I literally wanted to learn day and night. My parents were happy that I was such a dedicated Torah student, but as was the norm in those days, they were determined that I also earn a college diploma. They constantly told me that with my intellect I could train for any profession that caught my interest, and they let me know that they expected me to honor their wishes.

This age-old conflict between teenagers and their parents took its toll on both me and my parents. Intent on not allowing me to wake up one day when I was in my mid-thirties with a house full of children and little income, they applied maximum pressure on me to enroll in college and "make something of myself." They told me that I could pick any profession — medicine, law, engineering, journalism, whatever rang my chimes — but I must prepare myself to become a professional.

When the pressure became so great that I couldn't take it anymore, I decided to leave Torah Vodaath, from which I went home every night to my parents' constant criticism, and enroll in a yeshivah that offered dormitory accommodations. Before I made this big move, which, you can imagine, angered my parents very much, I went to discuss my plans with my Rosh Yeshivah.

"I don't think you're going to enjoy learning in that yeshivah, Beirish," he said. "They don't learn on your level. You won't find even one *bachur* there who is worthy of being your *chavrusa*. And when you will want to return here, it's going to be a problem because at the beginning of each *zeman* we assign every student a *chavrusa*, and I'm not sure that anyone of your caliber will be available if and when you want to return."

I thanked the Rosh Yeshivah for his caring advice and wished I could accept it, but the pressure at home was so great that I promptly enrolled in the other yeshivah, so determined was I to distance myself from the constant tension at home due to my refusal to enroll in college. I stuck it out in my new yeshivah for less than three months, after which I grudgingly admitted that my Rosh Yeshivah had been right; it was not for me. And, always one to put any of my decisions into immediate action, one morning I simply packed all of my belongings into my one suitcase and returned to Brooklyn where I planned to return to Torah Vodaath.

Upon entering the yeshivah building, which was redolent with the scents of old *sefarim*, freshly washed floors, and a good meal cooking in the basement kitchen, I felt as if I had come home. Intent on re-enrolling in the yeshivah in which I had succeeded beyond anyone's belief, I had left a message about my imminent arrival with the school's secretary, who we'll call Mr. Fischer, and now I waited in the main hallway for the Rosh Yeshivah to summon me into his office.

As I stood leaning against a wall, holding a pocket-sized *gemara* that I was currently learning, I closed my eyes for a moment and envisioned the Rosh Yeshivah's small, bare-bones office, in which his beloved *sefarim* stood like soldiers on the many bookshelves that lined the room from floor to ceiling, eager to be called to duty by the middle-aged rabbi who remained immersed in Torah studies in that room eighteen hours a day.

I only opened my eyes when an extremely bright *bachur* my own age, whom we'll call Chaim, whispered, "Bernie, I can't believe you're here. I heard that you had left us!"

I snapped out of my reverie and found myself gazing at the yeshivah's black sheep. Chaim, as usual, was dressed not only a drop differently than the yeshivah's other students, but also differently than most Orthodox Jews living in Williamsburg at that time. Even though I knew Chaim's reputation, I tried to figure out why he was in the main hallway when, at Torah Vodaath, once the *seder* began, nobody ever left his regular seat next to his steady *chavrusa* to stroll as if he had nothing better to do.

Forcing myself to remove my thoughts from how he was

dressed, I asked him, "Chaim, what are *you* doing in the hallway at this time of day?"

Chaim turned aside, hung his head, and whispered, "I know you won't believe it, but…but today I was asked to leave the yeshivah, never to return. The Rosh Yeshivah told me that, unfortunately, many parents complained to him about me, saying that I am a bad influence on their sons. He told me that he had no choice but to ask me to leave. As a matter of fact, he told me he had never, ever thrown out any other boy from the yeshivah. I am the first one, and it pained him, but an additional problem was that no one wanted to be my *chavrusa*, so he had no other option.

"I…I don't know what to do, Bernie! If I go home in shame today, my parents will be beyond grief. They won't forgive me for ruining our family's good name. For all I know, they will also throw me out of the house so that I won't destroy my sisters' chances at good *shidduchim*. I guess marching to the tune of my own drummer has ruined my own life *and* my sisters' lives, Bernie. And since I cannot go home and do that to them, it's either the Bowery or…maybe the East River for me."

Listening to this troubled young man's story launched a ninety-mile-an-hour train of thought to roar through my brain: *Hashem, you brought me here, to this very place at this very time, for a purpose. I thought it was to wait until the Rosh Yeshivah calls me into his office so I can apologize for not heeding his advice and beg him to allow me to rejoin my friends in the beis midrash. But since he still hasn't summoned me into his office, I realize that You, Hashem, might have arranged for me to be here, in the hallway of Yeshivah Torah Vodaath, for reasons of Your own. Why did I decide today, of all days, to pack my bags and return to my beloved yeshivah? Why did I walk into this hallway to wait for the Rosh Yeshivah precisely at this time? How can I allow Chaim who, from what he told me,*

*is beyond despondent, to leave this building when to him "the East
River" is an option?*

*It must be that You, Hashem, wanted me to hear Chaim's pain
so that I can help rescue this bachur from taking a most tragic step.
But what can I do? Actually, whatever I do for Chaim will surely
infuriate the yeshivah parent body…unless I get the Rosh Yeshivah
on my side!*

At that moment, Mr. Fischer motioned to me that the Rosh
Yeshivah was ready to see me. So I begged Chaim to wait for me
in a corner of that hallway no matter how long it would take for
me to return from the Rosh Yeshivah's office. Then I knocked
gently on the door, and when I heard a faint, *"Kum arein"* (come
in), I slipped into the Rosh Yeshivah's office and quietly closed
the door behind me. Could it be that the Rosh Yeshivah had
aged in the three months I had not seen him? Granted, a faint
smile lit up his face, but there were definitely additional, deep
lines radiating from his eyes. Dealing with Chaim's non-con-
forming ways, and ultimately being forced to ask him to leave,
seemed to have taken a toll.

The Rosh Yeshivah had heard my tentative knock on the
office door and had replied to it, but his mind still seemed thousands of miles away, immersed in the world of the Babylonian
scholars whose holy words filled the Talmud with a light and
power still felt thousands of years after they had first been uttered. Before the Rosh Yeshivah looked up from the page that he
was studying and could even motion to me to take the one chair
in front of his desk, my *yetzer ha-ra* began pummeling at me.

*Bernie, don't make a fool of yourself! Before you left Torah
Vodaath, the Rosh Yeshivah clearly told you, "When you can't ac-
climate to the lower level of learning in that other yeshivah do not
return here because we won't be able to take you back. Our yeshivah
works on a chavrusa system, and we won't have a chavrusa of your*

caliber to assign to you then!" Don't be a fool, Bernie! Turn around, run out of this building and earn for yourself the blessing of long life by honoring your parents' wishes that you enroll in college so that your brain won't be wasted studying ancient tomes that nobody in the modern world cares about! Grab Chaim's hand and run with him to Brooklyn College, or any other institute of higher secular learning! Today is a lucky day for both of you; don't waste it!

I could not refute even one of the words barreling through my beleaguered brain. In fact, I could add quite a few in the same vein. Chaim was not my best friend, not even a good friend. He was simply one of the *bachurim* in the *beis midrash*, and while I had been away he had obviously crossed one too many red lines. The plan that was slowly percolating in my mind about how to save Chaim while allowing me to return to the yeshivah might be totally unacceptable to the Rosh Yeshivah, and by proposing it, I might be making a total fool of myself.

But I felt Hashem's Presence with me in that cramped office, a Presence I could not ignore. Hashem had brought me to this place at this precise moment, where my heart had absorbed Chaim's anguished cry. Hashem had "tapped me on my shoulder" and had given me a once-in-a-lifetime opportunity! So when the Rosh Yeshivah finally embraced me with his ever-caring eyes and said, "*Nu*, Beirish, the last time we spoke your plan was to leave our yeshivah, and I warned you that the learning there was not on your level. I also told you that when you finally realize the truth of my words I would not be able to accept you back because there would not be one *chavrusa* of your caliber free to learn with you. So tell me, Beirish, what's your plan now?"

And that is when I, after stifling my doubts, seized the moment and presented a proposal to my Rosh Yeshivah that would rescue two floundering *talmidim*. "Could...could the Rosh Yeshivah find it in his heart to give two *talmidim*, who love Torah Vodaath more than anything in the world, a second chance? I very much want to rejoin the Rosh Yeshivah's *beis midrash*, and I'd appreciate it more than I can express if the Rosh Yeshivah would allow Chaim to be my *chavrusa*."

The Rosh Yeshivah's eyebrows shot up until they almost reached the large yarmulke that was more like a black, inverted bowl perched on his head. And, for a few moments, he sat still, deep in thought. "Beirish, did you mention this plan of yours to Chaim?"

I shook my head. "No, because I wasn't sure the Rosh Yeshivah would agree."

"What makes you sure *he* will agree? Being your *chavrusa* will chain him to his seat in the *beis midrash* for countless hours every day. It will give him no break in his learning, and no time to do anything else at all except to learn. This is not who Chaim is, Beirish. His mind is brilliant, but right now he is strongly pulled to…other activities, other interests."

I could not prevent myself from blurting out, "Could the Rosh Yeshivah at least give me a chance to convince Chaim to help me return to Torah Vodaath by agreeing to my plan? I fully understand that if I fail to turn Chaim into a regular yeshivah fellow, both of us must leave, so please, please give me permission to try."

"It will be no easy task for you to keep Chaim focused on his *gemara* hour after hour after hour. The reason he was asked to leave and not return was a serious one. What makes you feel you can change this *bachur* so radically?"

"All I ask is for the chance to do so."

When I left the Rosh Yeshivah's office, I understood that I had exactly one hour to convince Chaim to agree to all of the Rosh Yeshivah's rules. In one hour, I was to report back to the Rosh Yeshivah, either way.

I walked out into the hallway, gently closed the door behind me, and headed directly to where Chaim was still waiting for me. From behind the closed double-doors down the entrance hall that led into the *beis midrash*, faint sounds of dozens of *bachurim* learning loudly and vigorously as they engaged in the age-old *milchemta shel Torah* was the backdrop to the conversation that I had with Chaim.

"Chaim," I began, "I just got permission from the Rosh Yeshivah for both of us to rejoin the *beis midrash* under one condition."

"And that is?" asked Chaim, the position of his eyebrows halfway up to his *tchup* (forelock), signaling the height of his suspicion of any plan I might propose.

"That you and I become serious *chevrusos*."

"Me learn with you? You are the most brilliant *bachur* in your *shiur*. And I am no longer a *talmid* here. In case you forgot, I was thrown out because I am a bad influence on the *bachurim*. Their parents complained about me. I'm history. Toast!"

"That was an hour ago. From this minute onward, you are my *chavrusa* and I am yours. We'll be learning, *fest* (strongly), together behind those double doors, with all the other *bachurim*, without breaks for anything except davening, meals, and to use the facilities. Both of us are going to prove to the Rosh Yeshivah that his confidence in us has not been misplaced. Can I go back into his office and tell him we're both on board with this plan?"

"I'm totally not on your level, Bernie. Not in learning and not in anything else."

"But you have a great mind, Chaim. At first, it will be difficult, no doubt about that. But I promise you that as time goes on the sweetness of Torah will change you. The power of Torah will turn you into a top *bachur*."

I gave Chaim a few minutes to absorb my pleas. When I realized that I hadn't fully convinced him, I figuratively smashed my *yetzer ha-ra* in the nose, banished him, accepted Hashem's tap on my shoulder, and said, "Chaim, please, for my sake, agree! If you don't agree to be my *chavrusa*, I too will be banned from this building. Please have *rachmanus* on me and say you'll give it a try!"

The genuine pleading in my voice broke through Chaim's last defenses, and he was so overcome by conflicting emotions that he could do nothing more than nod. I allowed myself a sigh of relief, and with a silent prayer of thanks to Hashem, I led the still somewhat hesitant Chaim into the Rosh Yeshivah's office.

The Rosh Yeshivah smiled at both of us and then he said, "I want you to know, Chaim, that even though you're the same age as Beirish, from today forward he will be your *rebbi*. He'll also be your *menahel*, and your Rosh Yeshivah. Whatever he tells you, you have to do. If he tells me it's not working out, then both of you will have to leave. For good, no more chances. Understood?"

It was apparent that Chaim was fighting with himself not to cry in front of both of us, and it was only when I begged him in a whisper to agree, for my sake, did he nod and manage a whispered, "Yes."

The Rosh Yeshivah continued: "These are the rules, Chaim. You've got to be here by seven in the morning for Shacharis. No matter what, you may not come late. You have to dress the way everyone else dresses, you have to take a *yeshivish* haircut, and act the way everyone else acts. And you have to obey every additional rule that Beirish sets for you. Agreed?"

Again, Chaim nodded, but with much less hesitation.

And with that, we both left the Rosh Yeshivah's office.

Chaim understood that if he slipped up even once, both he and I would have to leave, so he worked very hard on himself to change. It wasn't easy, and it took several weeks, but change he did. Both of us had an excellent *zeman* in the yeshivah, at the end of which we were summoned into the Rosh Yeshivah's office, where he praised us both and said, "Your trial period is over, so both of you are free to choose other *chevrusos* for the next *zeman.*"

I looked at Chaim, and Chaim looked at me. Then we thanked the Rosh Yeshivah for giving each of us a second chance, and rejoined our friends.

That's how Bernie ended the story he offered me about his long-ago *kan tzipor* moment, a moment when he felt Hashem was tapping him on the shoulder and giving him a once-in-a-lifetime opportunity.

His story needs no elucidation or comment from me. Even before Bernie and I met, even before I had begun collecting and telling *kan tzipor* moment stories, Bernie had lived through one that he never forgot.

Ten years later, at a dinner held to benefit Yeshiva Torah Vodaath, at which the now very elderly Rosh Yeshivah was an honored guest, Bernie went over to his Rosh Yeshivah and offered him a hearty "*Shalom aleichem.*"

The Rosh Yeshivah said to him, "Beirish, I am *mekaneh* the *zechuyos* you have, and the *s'char* you will be awarded for having saved that young man whom you learned with ten years ago. I want you to know that he's now a *marbitz Torah* and constantly *shteiging* in his learning and *yiras Shamayim.* The *zechuyos* that you have for his learning, and the Torah learning of his children, his grandchildren, and great-grandchildren, are your ticket to *Olam HaBa.*"

When Bernie ended his tale, he added, "And Steve, what you tell everyone about *kan tzipor* moments is so true. So many decades after that incident with Chaim, whenever I think of how

I seized that moment to save him from totally leaving the Torah world, or even *chas v'shalom* ending his own life, I feel a very special glow. Thanks to your teaching me that it was a *kan tzipor* moment, I know what *lema'an yitav lach* feels like! Thank you, Steve, for giving me that gift of understanding."

The Gift That Got Away

AS ALWAYS WHEN I speak publicly, I get very animated by the message I deliver, and I also make a point of making eye contact with those in the audience. This brings them into my world, and helps them better absorb the significance and relevance of my message. I had been invited to a Shabbaton in Riverdale, New York, and between Shacharis and Musaf, I was giving my *kan tzipor* speech.

As I spoke, my attention was caught by a woman who was sitting in the first row of the balcony of that beautiful shul. I noticed that she was listening intently to my *kan tzipor* story, as if she were fearful of missing even one word. When I concluded speaking, I knew that I had made a great impact on that woman, and I wondered whether she would come over to me when davening was over.

I wasn't wrong. But instead of trying to outdo the *kan tzipor* moment I had vividly described, Mrs. Kessler, the name I'll use for her, presented me with a story that I want to share with every one of you before you close this book. This is what she said:

233

I'm a busy executive who does most of my food shopping for Shabbos on Friday. Several Fridays ago, as usual, I went to the supermarket on my way home from work, and after filling my cart with many Shabbos necessities, and even some extras with which to enhance my family's enjoyment of the day, I got on line at the checkout counter.

The person in front of me was a well-dressed, profession-al-looking, sophisticated, African-American woman. When I noticed that this woman's cart contained only five or six items — a loaf of bread, milk, eggs, a few pieces of chicken, and some vegetables — I was thrilled to know that I'd be out of the store in the least amount of time possible, since I still had many tasks to complete at home before candle-lighting time. After we both waited a bit for the customer in front of the woman to pay, she began placing her items on the conveyor belt, which she did quickly and efficiently. I was expecting to be back in my car in under five minutes.

Not to waste even a minute of the time during which I was forced to wait for my turn, I concentrated on deciding what I should do first once I reached home: pop the salmon into the oven, place the container of compote I had frozen the past week into the microwave to defrost, or switch the load of towels from the washer to the dryer. I was slightly annoyed at being distracted from my thoughts by a conversation, or maybe it was a heated argument, that I half-heard between the cashier and the woman.

I quickly brought myself into the present and was discom-fited to see that by then the cashier had actually summoned the store manager to her station. So much for getting home with lots of time to spare!

Before I was fully aware of what was happening, the well-dressed shopper fled the store, leaving all of her items on the counter, and as the cashier shoved them into a large plastic bin for another employee to return to their proper places, she motioned to me to start unloading the items in my cart onto the conveyer belt. By then my curiosity was piqued, and I asked the cashier what had happened.

"You won't believe what I go through with some customers," she said, and then sighed. "Today's the thirtieth of the month. I know that shopper; she comes in often. She's had a lot of hard luck in her life, and she's on the Food Stamp program." As she spoke, she deftly scanned each of my items, which the packer who stood at the end of the counter nimbly bagged. I switched my attention back to the cashier, who hadn't stopped talking. "So as I was sayin', she handed me her card, which was declined. She knows that the Food Stamp card is refilled on the first of each month, but she must have thought today was the first, cuz yesterday was the thirtieth. But this month has thirty-one days, got it?"

I nodded.

"But that woman, she didn't get it. She begged me to let her have the food anyway, and when I told her I couldn't, she looked like she was gonna cry. She pointed out that she was only taking milk and bread and a few other basics, but there was nothing I could do. I felt so bad for her that I called my manager, thinking he might be able to help, cuz truth is, she needs that food for her kids. But our hands were tied. What could we do?"

"The reason I am telling you this story, Mr. Savitsky, is that you cannot imagine how bad I felt while you were speaking to us about being alert to *kan tzipor* moments. How I wished I had heard your speech two weeks ago! Then, I would have been an 'Observant Jew,' alert to those around me! I would have heard Hashem calling out to me to pay for that woman's groceries so that her children wouldn't have had to go to bed hungry that night! I would have instantly recognized my very own *kan tzipor* moment, and would have earned for myself a huge mitzvah, in addition to making a *kiddush Hashem*!

"Imagine, Mr. Savitsky, I could have bought a piece of *Olam HaBa* for about twenty dollars! But I wasn't alert to such opportunities then, so I missed out, and I simply can't forgive myself. That woman looked like such a decent person. I'm sure she would have thanked me profusely. She would have jotted down my phone number and told me she'd repay me when she got her next paycheck. But…but I didn't know to look for such opportunities, to be constantly alert to hear Hashem calling out to me. I was simply too wrapped up in my own world.

"What a wonderful moment that would have been for me, and what a great lesson I could have taught my children when I got home. The reason I waited to speak to you after davening was so that I could thank you for making me aware of this mitzvah today, and also to give you permission to tell my story so that others shouldn't ever feel like I felt that Friday as I unpacked what I had bought and made my final preparations for Shabbos. What a great *kan tzipor* moment that would have been for me, but I missed it because I hadn't yet heard your speech. But now, I've learned my lesson, and I'll always remember it."

When I heard Mrs. Kessler's story, I realized that when people internalize my message, what they will be doing, in essence, is training themselves to be prepared for the "unpreparable;"[1] so that

---

1. A word I invented to describe all the moments in their lives for which no one could have prepared them.

when they are faced with such inevitable moments, no matter what they are, they will instinctively react as loyal Torah Jews.

When I heard Mrs. Kessler's story, I *also* promised myself that if and when I ever wrote a book about *kan tzipor* moments, I'd end my book with the story she had told me.

And now I've kept that promise.

About the Author

STEPHEN J. SAVITSKY, known to his friends as Steve, earned a BA from Yeshiva University and an MBA from the Baruch School of Business, and has been an active leader in the Jewish world for several decades. From 2002 until 2014, he served as president and chairman of the board of the Orthodox Union (OU). Additionally, he was the founder and president of the Kew Gardens Hills *Eruv*, chairman of Partners in Torah, president of Congregation Anshei Chesed in Hewlett, NY, and a member of the executive committee of the Conference of Presidents of Major Jewish Organizations. Mr. Savitsky has also served on the board of the Mesorah Heritage Foundation, the Jewish Agency, and HIAS (Hebrew Immigrant Aid Society). He has spoken extensively throughout North America, has served as scholar-in-residence at many synagogues as well as at kosher hotel programs and on Kosherica cruises, and serves various Jewish organizations in an advisory capacity.

Currently, Mr. Savitsky is a member of the board of Hatzalah of the Five Towns and Far Rockaway, is president of the Bnai Zion Foundation, and president of the Vaad Hakashrus of the Five Towns and Far Rockaway. Mr. Savitsky is also founder and president of ATC Healthcare, a nationwide provider of medical staffing.

Steve resides in Woodmere, New York, with his wife, Genie. They have been blessed with four children, grandchildren, and great-grandchildren.